D1570412

# THE LOST ROMANOV ICON AND THE ENIGMA OF ANASTASIA

12-13-12

Jim,
   A little reading for the holidays, most of which is true.
         Enjoy
         Bob Trouch

# THE LOST ROMANOV ICON AND THE ENIGMA OF ANASTASIA

Carlos Mundy and Marie Stravlo

THAMES RIVER PRESS

The Lost Romanov Icon and the Enigma of Anastasia

THAMES RIVER PRESS
An imprint of Wimbledon Publishing Company Limited (WPC)
Another imprint of WPC is Anthem Press (www.anthempress.com)

First published in the United Kingdom in 2012 by
THAMES RIVER PRESS
75-76 Blackfriars Road
London SE1 8HA

www.thamesriverpress.com

A CIP record for this book is available from the British Library.

ISBN 978-0-85728-201-9

Cover design by Jose Carmona Chavez

In fond memory of Prince Sergei Nazarewicz

# ABOUT THE BOOK

Although most of the events in this book are founded on accepted historical facts or controversial theories already published in several books, some fresh evidence presented here is based on new documents related to the Anastasia saga, as well as other information that had been suppressed from the public for over ninety years, which contradicts the official version of the events in Ekaterinburg. Some of the characters mentioned in the plot were real, and played an active role in the Anna Anderson/Anastasia Romanov–Manahan story; others are fictitious and purely the product of the authors' imagination.

The authors also want to state that most of the documents mentioned here are real; the originals are kept in different archives and they have copies that will be published in the future. The "pearls letter" is fictitious, and was elaborated by Carlos Mundy as part of the plot of this novel. Anastasia's confession is believed to have existed, and she had given instructions to very close friends to publish it only after her death. Further information, pictures and documents related to the story can be found at: www.thelostromanovicon.com

Facebook page: The Lost Romanov Icon and the Enigma of Anastasia.

# DEDICATION

This book is dedicated to the memory of H.I.H. Grand Duchess Anastasia Nikolaevna of Russia, better known as Anna Anderson or Anastasia Manahan. She never wanted to prove who she was, as she always knew. We also dedicate this book to some of the people that believed in her, and to all her self-sacrificing supporters: Ambassador Herluf Zahle of Denmark, H.H. Prince Frederick Ernst of Saxe-Altenburg, H.I.H. Prince Sigismund of Prussia, H.R.H. Princess Charlotte Agnes of Saxe-Altenburg, H.I.H. Crown Princess Cecilie of Prussia, H.H. Princess Xenia Georgevna of Russia, H.I.H. Grand Duke Andrei Vladimirovich of Russia and his wife Mathilde Kschenssinska, H.I.H. Empress Hermine Reuss of Greiz (second wife of Kaiser William of Germany), Grand Duke Carl August of Saxe-Weimar-Eisenach and his wife Grand Duchess Elisabeth of Saxe-Weimar-Eisenach, Princess Vera Constantinova of Russia, Prince Alexander Nikitich Romanov, the Duke and Duchess George of Leuchtenberg, Gleb and Nadine Botkin, Tatiana Botkin-Melnik, Edward Fallows, Adele von Heydebrandt, Gertrud Lamerdin, Carl August Wollmann, Prince William of Hesse Philippsthal, Princess Marianne of Hesse-Philippsthal, H.R.H. Princess Louise of Saxe-Meiningen, Princess Margaretha of Sweden, Princess Feodora of Reuss, Countess Olga of Pourtalès, Harriet Rathlef-Keilman, Dominique Aucléres, Lili Dehn, Ian Lilburn, Baron Curt von Stackelberg, Baroness Monica von Milititz, Frau Luise Mayhoff, Frau Berta Klotz, Paul and Gertrude Madsack, Baron and Baroness Ulrich von Gienanth, Felix Dassel, H.H. Prince Dimitri Golitzin, Sergei Rachmaninov, John E. Manahan (Jack), James Blair Lovell, Peter Kurth, Alexis Miliukoff, Isaac Don Levine, Jaap Bottema, Richard and Marina Schweitzer, Rey Barry, Greg Rittenhouse, Andrew Hartsook, Robert Crouch, and many, many others.

To H.M. King Alfonso XIII of Spain, whose actions saved thousands of lives during World War I. Together with his prime minister Eduardo Dato, he actively negotiated with the Bolsheviks to take the Tsarina and her children out of Russia and offered them asylum in Spain.

To Popes Benedict XV and Pius XII, as well as Cardinal Secretary of State Pietro Gasparri and Metropolitan Andrey Sheptytsky who worked diligently to obtain the liberation of the Tsarina Alexandra Feodorovna and her daughters. They offered to cover their living expenses outside Russia, and protected them while in exile.

# NOTES BY CARLOS MUNDY

We have mostly based the storyline of this historical novel on very well-documented published works. From the fascinating *Rescuing the Tsar*, published anonymously in the '20s, to the magnificent detective work of Guy Richards in *The Rescue of the Romanovs* and *The Hunt for the Tsar*, Summers and Mangold's *The File on the Tsar*, the well-researched *The Secret Plot to Save the Tsar* by Shay McNeal, *I Am Anastasia* by Roland Krug von Nidda, *The Romanovs: the Last Chapter* by Robert Massie, *Nicholas II* by Marc Ferro, and of course also the bibles on the matter: *Anastasia, The Riddle of Anna Anderson,* by Peter Kurth and *Anastasia, The Lost Princess,* by James Blair Lovell.

I also had the opportunity to meet Marie Stravlo, a prestigious TV producer/hostess, dedicated researcher and Romanov scholar who has examined this case for fourteen years, devoting the last four to a full-time investigation with astonishing results. The story about the lost Romanov icon was told to her and is supported by documents and testimonies.

Remains believed to belong to the Tsar and his family were exhumed in 1991 and reburied in 1998 in the imperial crypt of Peter and Paul's Cathedral in Saint Petersburg.

Some members of the Russian Imperial family support the theory of the Russian Orthodox Church and doubt that the remains belong to Tsar Nicholas II and his family. Other members of the family support the official version.

Professor Alec Jeffries of Leicester University, the founding father of DNA testing in Britain, said on record that if the bones had been switched with those of close relatives, it would be very difficult to tell them apart. A recent publication in Russia raises serious concerns about the mass grave excavated in 1991 and the authenticity of the bones, as well as the scientific tests used to identify the remains.

All the above leaves the door wide open to discuss again all the unclear facts and explore many new possibilities. I have had the privilege of seeing many of the thousands of documents that belonged to another of the surviving grand duchesses: Grand Duchess Olga Nikolaevna, better known as her alias Marga Boodts; as well as documents that belonged to Prince Alexis D'Anjou-Durassow, who claimed to be the grandson of

Grand Duchess Maria Nikolaevna, the third daughter of Nicholas II and Alexandra Feodorovna.

This novel, I trust, will not only entertain but will also cast a bit of light on the truth.

# PROLOGUE BY MARIE STRAVLO

Mystery has surrounded the story of the last Imperial family of Russia since they disappeared during the night of 16–17 July 1918, and words like "secrecy," "conspiracy" and "deceit" are frequently used to narrate the events that followed their obscure fate.

Historians, Romanov scholars, members of royal families and intrigued laypersons have followed the developments of this case and discussed the facts in lectures, royal forums, blogs, family meetings, etc. Movies have been produced, books and plays have been written in all languages, and the topic still attracts the attention of hundreds of thousands of people all over the world. The controversy re-emerged after the exhumation of the alleged bones of the Romanovs in 1991, and their subsequent interment seven years later, at the Cathedral of Peter and Paul in Saint Petersburg, Russia, in July of 1998.

Keeping the debate alive about the true fate of Nicholas II and his family is a very significant fact: the Orthodox Church inside Russia totally refuses to accept those bones exhumed at Ekaterinburg, Siberia, as authentic, and, together with other private organizations inside and outside Russia, is still waiting for the answers to ten questions posted many years ago to the Russian Committee investigating the "alleged" murder and the identifications of the remains. In 2012, no satisfactory answers have yet been provided.

The story of Anna Anderson, the woman who surfaced in Berlin in 1920 and claimed to be Anastasia, the youngest daughter of the Tsar, has been a huge enigma closely related to the Romanov mystery. She had the same eye and hair colour, the same birthmarks and scars, as well as a bilateral congenital foot defect called "hallux valgus," which she had suffered from childhood, and is popularly known as "bunions." Her smile and demeanour were just like the real Anastasia's. She spoke other languages the way the historical Anastasia did, but refused to speak Russian because of the psychological trauma from the last days in her beloved motherland. Her refined mannerisms, tone of voice, delicate hands and impressive knowledge of facts and things related to the Imperial family is something even her opponents cannot explain. Both women were of the same height and wore the same shoe size. She was recognized by several people as the authentic Grand Duchess Anastasia of Russia.

In 1938 a tedious battle started in different courts in Germany, where the claimant, using the assumed name of Anna Anderson, attempted to gain recognition as the real Grand Duchess Anastasia of Russia. The lengthy and costly process is recorded as the longest legal case in history.

During the court trials, several expert opinions were submitted to the Court. Dr Otto Reche, German anthropologist and professor at Glatz (Klodzko) in the Prussian Silesia was requested by the Court to make a study of her ears and facial features. He concluded that she was Grand Duchess Anastasia, or her identical twin. Dr Minna Becker, a renowned graphologist who had assisted in the identification of Anne Frank's diaries, also determined that the two women's handwriting was exactly the same and declared: "There can be no mistake. After thirty four years as a sworn expert for the German Courts, I am ready to state on my oath and on my honour that Mrs Anderson and Grand Duchess Anastasia are identical."

After countless court hearings where hundreds of witnesses gave their testimonies in her favour, the Hamburg Court gave its last negative verdict in 1967. An appeal was presented later to the Supreme Court in Karlsruhe.

In July 1968 Anna Anderson moved to the United States, and settled in Charlottesville, Virginia. She married Prof. John E. Manahan (Jack) on December 23rd, that same year, and her legal name became Anastasia Manahan, although many people continued calling her Anna Anderson.

Finally, on February 17, 1970, exactly fifty years after the day that the undocumented young woman was rescued from the freezing waters of the Landwehr Canal in Berlin, and was named *"Fraulein Unbekannt,"*[1] her real identity was still a mystery. The Supreme Court rejected the appeal, which did not necessarily mean that the case was closed. The judgment held that Anastasia's claim must be regarded as *"non-liquet,"*[2] and so remained. The option of starting a new legal battle still existed, but Anastasia wanted to live peacefully in her new home in USA, away from all the controversy.

---

[1] Miss Unknown.

[2] *"Non liquet"* translates from Latin as "It is not clear." It is used in court when the situation engaged in a case has no answer from the governing system of law.

She was living quietly in the US in 1974 when Anthony Summers and Tom Mangold, two journalists from the BBC of London, went to her house and interviewed her about the events at Ekaterinburg in 1918. She was not very cooperative, but suddenly she told them: "There was no massacre, but I cannot tell the rest." The British journalists produced a documentary that was broadcast by the BBC and in 1976 published the book *The File on the Tsar,* which includes a comprehensive chapter on Anna Anderson. It also reveals a series of facts and testimonies of witnesses that contradict the "official" version of the massacre. The book immediately became an international bestseller.

In October 1976, Anastasia Manahan, then seventy-five years old, sat in front of the cameras of ABC Television to be interviewed by a renowned journalist of the programme *Good Morning America.* The reason for this interview was to get her opinion about Summers and Mangold's book, which had just arrived in the United States, creating a lot of controversy.

Distant, thoughtful and almost reluctant to speak, it was a challenge for the experienced reporter to get some recollections or statements from her, but when questioned directly about what exactly the book *The File on the Tsar* meant to reveal regarding the true fate of her sisters, she looked at her husband, Professor Jack Manahan, and said in German: "I cannot answer to these things. I cannot tell it. I cannot. I will be killed at once."[3] Then she went silent. She died eight years later without revealing the truth.

Another significant event supporting her claim to be the real Anastasia Romanov happened in 1977. Professor Moritz Furtmayr, one of West Germany's most prominent forensic experts, made an extremely comprehensive analysis of the pictures of Anna Anderson's ears taken at different angles and with different lighting, and compared them with photos of the historical Anastasia's ears. Furtmayr found 17 points of anatomical similarities, five more than the 12 points that the Court considered sufficient to identify and confirm a person's identity.

Her lawyers and friends in Germany considered it to be a great opportunity to start a new legal battle for her recognition. But it was already too late. The strange woman did not want to get involved in any other legal process. She wished to be let alone with her memories,

---

[3] Interview with ABC TV, 27 October 1976. Published in Peter Kurth, *Anastasia: the Riddle of Anna Anderson*. Little, Brown & Company, Boston. p. 383.

and live peacefully the rest of her life. However, the legend around her was impossible to end, and she continued to attract the attention of writers, journalists and curious people from all over the world. She kept receiving the support of a group of people, some of them royals, who believed she was the real Anastasia, and they continued trying to reveal the truth.

Time passed and she became more and more eccentric, ill and difficult to deal with. In 1979 she went into surgery at Martha Jefferson Hospital to remove a gangrenous part of her intestine. Although she survived the operation, she did not recover completely and never walked again. On 12 February 1984 she died, and the same day she was cremated, following her instructions, due to her belief in the principles of the Anthroposophical Society. The mystery around her remained.

But her loyal supporters never forgot her, and never altered their belief that she was who she said she was.

When the "alleged" bones of the Romanovs were unearthed from the mass grave in 1991, there were two skeletons missing. A team of anthropologists from the United States, headed by Professor William Maples, was invited to participate in the identification. The Russian forensic team believed they were those of Maria and her brother Tsarevitch Alexei; Professor Maples however maintained that they were the ones of Alexis and Anastasia. That fact immediately encouraged the supporters of Anna Anderson, mostly in the United States, to prove her identity as the historical Anastasia scientifically, through DNA. A piece of her intestine that was removed in 1979 had been kept at Martha Jefferson Hospital in Charlottesville. But the hospital released the sample only after the court decided who had the right to have it tested. Since Anastasia Manahan did not have any legal descendant and her husband, John Eacott Manahan, had also died in 1990, the court appointed Mr Ed Deets as administrator of Anastasia Manahan's state. Several people wanted to have access to the sample, including the Russian Nobility Association. The whole situation revived the hostilities between former loyal supporters and furious opponents. Finally, after an intense legal battle, the Court granted the right to the samples to Mr and Mrs Richard Schweitzer, who turned them over to Dr Peter Gill for testing. Some hair strands, which appeared inside an envelope in a bookstore in North Carolina, were also tested in a separate lab, as well as a blood sample from the claimant kept by Dr Stephan Sandkuhler since the fifties.

Dr Gill's results were revealed on 5th October 1994, during a press conference in London: the mitochondrial DNA extracted from the putative tissue sample of Anastasia Manahan did not match that of the Duke of Edinburgh, who is supposed to carry the same maternal blood line as Queen Victoria and therefore the same mtDNA as the Tsarina Alexandra, but matched the mtDNA of Karl Maucher, allegedly a grandnephew of Franziska Schanzkowska, a Polish peasant. This announcement shocked thousands of Anna Anderson's supporters, who immediately claimed that the tests were fraudulent and engaged in ardent discussions around the globe.

Julian Nott, a TV producer in England, had been keeping visual records of all that was happening during the process, from the legal battle in Charlottesville, Virginia, to gaining access to the putative sample, to the analysis made by Dr Peter Gill in London. On the same day Gill's results were revealed, and despite the DNA results which linked the claimant to a relative of the Polish peasant, Nott broadcast his documentary. Dr Peter Vanesis, anthropologist and professor of forensic medicine at Glasgow University, had been hired by the producers to perform, once again, a comparative analysis between Anna Anderson's ears and those of the historical Grand Duchess Anastasia Nikolaevna of Russia. The disclosure of his findings did not surprise the world: Dr Vanesis, who was also a frequent consultant to the police, based his analysis on a careful study of photos of the face and ears of the two women and concluded that they were probably one and the same person. That was exactly what Dr Otto Reche and Professor Furtmayr had stated many years before in Germany.

To this day, believers in the authenticity of Anna Anderson's claim hold strong opinions about the hidden and obscure facts in this entire saga. Based on their own experiences, those who knew the claimant personally or have studied her case deeply refuse to accept that she was an impostor or an insane woman with great acting skills, capable of maintaining her charade for over sixty years. It is absurd to think that she fooled a wide range of people, from doctors and illustrious people like Ambassador Herluf Zahle and Duke George of Leuchtenberg to friends from childhood like Gleb and Tatiana Botkin, as well as family members like Prince Sigismund of Prussia or Grand Duke Andrei Vladimirovich of Russia. That is why, despite the efforts of opponents and detractors of Anna Anderson to close the case and gain control of any information still unexamined, her supporters keep a strong alliance that will never give up maintaining the truth of their version of events. This legend is very much alive and probably will outlive all of us.

My personal involvement in this case comes from a unique experience. I had heard about the enigma of Anastasia when I was a child. Years later, in July 1998, the international media announced with great fanfare the official burial of the alleged remains of Nicholas II and his family in the Fortress of Saints Peter and Paul in Saint Petersburg. That year I met Prince Alfred of Prussia, the only son of Prince Sigismund of Prussia, in Costa Rica. He explained to me his uncommon genealogy, dating back several hundred years. Because I had at hand a close relative of the illustrious characters that were going to be buried in Saint Petersburg, among them Anastasia, I asked his opinion.

Prince Alfred told me that everything in this case was too complex and that what really happened in Ekaterinburg was known only by a few people, his father being one of them. That is why he was sure that Anna Anderson was Anastasia. In the early thirties Prince Sigismud had sent to Anna Anderson fourteen questions that only the real Anastasia could answer and she responded to all of them correctly. He also told me that his father reconfirmed his certainty about her true identity when they met in 1957 in Unterlengenhardt. She knew details that were known only by people who had lived through the real events, and it was impossible for even the best of impostors to have knowledge of them. According to Prince Alfred, another person who knew the truth was his uncle, Prince Frederick Ernst of Saxe-Altenburg. Both always gave him absolute certainty of her authenticity.

Spanish historian and author Ricardo Mateos y Sainz de Medrano corresponded with several members of Prince Sigismund's family. Prince Alfred also made the same statements in writing to Ricardo; and in the late sixties he narrated the same story to some of his closest friends in Costa Rica, as it was told to me by several people I interviewed, including the distinguished researcher and laureate author Alfonso Chase.

The stories recounted to me by "Don Alfredo," as I called him, about his father's memories of family reunions and childhood plays with his imperial cousins, showed a very close relationship between them. Regarding the issue of the fourteen questions of 1932, Prince Sigismund himself told Summers and Mangold during their visit to Costa Rica in 1974: "The replies were perfectly correct and could only have been given by the Grand Duchess herself. This has convinced me that [she] is without any doubt Anastasia of Russia."[4] To his astonishment, she even offered extra details that Sigismund

---

[4] Summers and Mangold, *The File on the Tsar*, Harper & Row, New York, 1976, p. 225.

had forgotten. The prince confirmed this to Baron Ulrich von Gienanth and her daughter Baroness Marion von Gienanth during his visit to Germany in 1957.[5]

Knowing all that unpublished information really aroused my interest, and in 1998 I started reading all that was available at that time on the Romanov affair and Anna Anderson's case, both in books and on the internet, including the two "bibles," as Carlos Mundy calls them: Peter Kurth's *Anastasia: The Riddle of Anna Anderson* and James Blair Lovell's *Anastasia: The Lost Princess*. I also read the books recommended by Prince Sigismund to his friends: *I am Anastasia* by Roland Krug von Nidda, *The File on the Tsar* by Anthony Summers and Tom Mangold, and many more. I have to admit that the more I read, the more I was convinced that there was another side of this story that had never been told.

In July 2007, another amazing discovery of bones was made by members of a Russian military club in Ekaterinburg. Looking in the southern part of the site known as "The Pig's Meadow" they found the remains of a campfire that contained 44 scorched bone fragments and 7 teeth, which they said possibly belonged to Tsarevitch Alexis and his missing sister, Grand Duchess Maria Nikolaevna. Some scientists in Ekaterinburg, like Dr Nevolin, disputed that possibility from the very beginning, arguing that "44 bone fragments were not sufficient to identify a person, much less two!" After DNA tests were performed on those putative remains, the Russian government made the official announcement in December 2008 that the bones indeed belonged to the bodies of the missing children and therefore the case was closed.

These remains have not been buried yet, and the Russian Orthodox Church inside Russia urges no rush in confirming their identification. The Moscow Patriarchate believes it is necessary to compare "results of the investigation held under Kolchak to the current investigation..."[6] To this day, those 44 bone fragments are kept inside a plastic bag somewhere in Moscow, and probably will end in a common grave in a Russian cemetery.[7]

---

[5] It was given to the author in a written statement by Baroness Marion von Gienanth.

[6] "Russian Church urges not to hurry confirming...," Interfax Religion, 16th June 2010, http://www.interfax-religion.com/?act=news&div=7367

[7] "Royal remains return to Moscow," Ria Novosti, 21st February 2011, http://en.rian.ru/papers/20110221/162700243.html

After that announcement of December 2008 my interest greatly increased, and I decided to take a break from my busy professional life in order to start my own research. I travelled to visit libraries and private archives, and contacted people I knew who had lots of information and documents. For four years I was completely devoted to studying in depth the mystery that has captivated many generations throughout the world since 1918.

In August 2010, at the request of the self-proclaimed Head of the Russian Imperial family, Maria Vladimirovna Romanova, the Basmanny Court ordered the government of Russia to reopen the investigation into the case of the death of Tsar Nicholas II and his family, given the controversy that has existed since they disappeared in 1918, and also because during all these years of mystery, there have been strong rumours that support the theory of the survival of other members of the Romanov family.

But on January 17 2011 Russia's investigative committee announced that it was closing the case on the murder of the Imperial family. Immediately, the members of the House of Romanov involved in the legal battle protested. "Until now the church has found no grounds to accept the Prosecutor General's conclusion that the remains belong to members of the Tsar's family, canonized by the church," said Alexander Zakatov, director of the office of the House of Romanov, to Komsomolskaya Pravda. "If these are the true remains, they automatically become holy relics to the orthodox people, but while questions remain and there is no complete clarity, neither the Church nor the Imperial family can make such a statement."[8]

About the living descendants of the Romanov family I can only say what everybody knows: they are divided with respect to the identification of the remains. Some grouped in the "Romanov Family Association" believe and accept what the Russian government proclaims. Others around Maria Vladimirovna and her son George, heir presumptive to the throne of Russia, take the side of the Orthodox Church inside Russia and demand new investigations.

In late 2011 a group of former members of the Russian government commission investigating the fate of Nicholas II and his family, as well

---

[8] Andy Potts, "Anger as Russia closes the case of the murdered Tsar," The Moscow News, 18th January 2011 http://www.themoscownews.com/russia/20110118/188342580.html

as the remains found and their dubious origins, decided to make public a series of facts which reveal serious problems with respect to the mass grave "discovered" in Ekaterinburg. In a book written in Russian titled **кому же верить?**,[9] Andrei K. Golitsyn, former member of the Government's commission, exposes the terrible mistakes made from the very moment that the bones were exhumed until the DNA tests were performed. It suggests that everything was planned and perpetrated to hide the true facts and close the controversial case. However, regarding the alleged massacre, Golitsyn and his group adhere to the report of Nicholas A. Sokolov published in 1924.

Anastasia's case has been one of the most complex and compelling mysteries of the twentieth century, and one that still captures the attention of thousands of people around the world in this new century. Rumours of family and state secrets, intrigues, political and diplomatic implications of catastrophic proportions, and claims of extraordinary amounts of money and jewels supposedly deposited by Tsar Nicholas II in different foreign banks before World War I have circulated since 1918, at a time when nearly all the crowned heads of Europe had lost their thrones.

Coming now to agitate the waters of history, another fact supporting the claim in favour of Anna Anderson adds to this endless saga: the whereabouts of a lost icon, a holy relic from the fifteenth century given to Anna Anderson/Anastasia Manahan in 1946 when she became the godmother of a baby boy – heir to one of the most ancient and respected royal houses of Europe – as a lifetime loan intended to be returned to Germany upon her death.

This historical novel is set in the year 1994, when scientists from different countries were still examining the alleged remains of Nicholas and his family, and were preparing to present the results of the DNA tests in an attempt to clarify the events of the summer of 1918. That same year a legal battle took place in Charlottesville, Virginia, USA, to seek control of the tissue sample from Anastasia Manahan in order to extract her DNA.

I met Carlos Mundy three years ago. Our paths crossed one day on the road, at an imaginary street corner named "Anna Anderson/Anastasia Manahan." From that very moment, in him I saw an excellent writer, whose imagination and creativity were nourished by all the experiences

---

[9] *Whom to Believe?*

of a fascinating, glamorous and cosmopolitan life. I also discovered an exceptional human being, very concerned about social issues, devoted to noble causes and willing to fight against the injustices of the world. So we decided to work together on this project, in order to present our findings to the world in a literary form that would attract the attention of readers of diverse ages, educational and cultural backgrounds; and in a narrative that would captivate historians, Romanov scholars or aficionados, as well as avid readers of historical fiction.

We present here what we believe is an interesting plot that is very easy to read and understand, despite the complexity of the case. As the main character we choose Rodney Mundy, who was Carlos' father and also a former MI6 agent in real life. The previous adventures of Rodney were narrated by Carlos Mundy in *Gestapo Lodge*. Rodney introduces the readers to a new dimension of knowledge and secrets never before revealed about the true fate of the Russian Imperial family. Anastasia was caught up in this vortex, making her a slave of a "pact of silence" that had to be protected at all costs, and a victim of the dramatic circumstances that she created when she mistakenly surfaced in Berlin and revealed details about the secret dealings of her family.

The new version of events that this novel subtly reveals is surprising and even at times incredible. The complicity of the Vatican and the documents found in the secret archives were not invented to emulate any other thriller; they are absolutely true and their existence fully supported by documents, newspaper articles, letters, books, and testimonials from nobility, historians and priests – some still alive – who knew the real actors and the hidden facts.

The lost icon did indeed exist. It was a valuable and sacred object, which belonged to Grand Duke Carl August of Saxe-Weimar-Eisenach and his wife Grand Duchess Elizabeth of Saxe-Weimar-Eisenach (born Baroness Elisabeth of Wangenheim-Winterstein). After World War II, Anna/Anastasia took shelter in the castle of Winterstein, property of Princess Louisa of Saxe-Meiningen, together with the Grand Dukes of Saxe-Weimar-Eisenach and other members of royal houses and the nobility who escaped from the areas occupied by the Soviets. The Dukes gave the religious relic to Anna Anderson/Anastasia Manahan on a lifetime loan in 1946, when she became the godmother of their only male heir, Prince Michael Benedict of Saxe-Weimar-Eisenach, current head of the Grand Ducal House of Saxe-Weimar-Eisenach. During the baptismal ceremony she shared the honour with Queen Juliana of the Netherlands.

The story behind the icon takes us back to 3rd August 1804, when Grand Duchess Maria Pavlovna of Russia (1786–1859) married the Grand Duke Charles Frederick of Saxe-Weimar-Eisenach (1783–1853). After moving to Germany, she carried the precious icon with her, and for 142 years her descendants, who considered it a very dear and valuable treasure, guarded it. It was similarly highly appreciated by Anna Anderson/Anastasia, since it represented her family and spiritual roots. She always believed that the icon protected her, and kept it beside her bed in Unterlengenhardt, Germany. After she moved to Charlottesville, Virginia, USA, she had it displayed inside a vaulted shelf in the living room of her house at University Circle.

The disappearance of this marvellous relic after the death of Anastasia Manahan in 1984 remains a mystery. The investigations never could determine what happened to it. Readers may now decide to start a new search, when modern technology and amazing electronic resources might help to locate it and return it to its rightful owners: the Saxe-Weimar-Eisenach family.

The historical moment in which this work is presented to the public could not be more timely. The year 2013 is the four hundredth anniversary of the Romanov dynasty, and the celebration is about to start, not only with ceremonies, musicals, plays, art exhibitions and new publications inside Russia, but also with a parade of festivities around the globe.

Now, ninety-four years after the disappearance of the last Imperial family, and twenty-eight years after the death of Anastasia Manahan, new voices rise, demanding answers: demanding empirically sound and legally irrefutable.

The emblem of the double-headed eagle emerges from the waters of history to stir them. Those waters that seem to be stagnant pools will move to bring to the surface new information and evidence for people to see, analyse and judge it. And then history will reveal itself.

Marie Stravlo
Paris, France
June 2012

# INTERESTING QUOTES ABOUT
## ANASTASIA MANAHAN

"Anastasia is no adventuress, nor, in my opinion, is she merely the victim of delusion that she is the daughter of the Tsar. After living with her for a number of months, I have become firmly convinced that she is a lady accustomed to intercourse with the highest circles of Russian society and that it is likely she was born to a regal rank. Each of her words and movements reveals such a lofty dignity and commands a bearing that it is impossible to claim that she learned these characteristics later in life."

*Inspector Franz Grunberg, 19th June 1925.*

"That is Anastasia!"

*H.R.H. Princess Martha of Sweden (later Queen of Norway),*
*after meeting the claimant in Berlin.*

"My intelligence will not allow me to accept her as Anastasia, but my heart tells me that it is she. And since I have grown up in a religion that taught me to follow the dictates of the heart rather than those of the mind, I am unable to leave this unfortunate child."

*H.I.H. Grand Duchess Olga Alexandrovna (sister of the Tsar),*
*after meeting and spending a few days with the*
*claimant in Berlin.*

"She does not want and is not striving for recognition."

*Baron Osten-Sacken, 1926.*

"All I want is that my Royal House of Denmark be blameless in the eyes of history in this affair. If the Imperial House of Russia wants to let one of its own die in the gutter, then we can do nothing."

*Herluf Zahle, Danish Ambassador in Germany.*

"The claimant has no signs of mental deficiency, nor any evidence of suggestions or influence. It seems to me impossible that the numerous and apparently trivial details she recalls cannot be attributed to anything other than her own experiences. Also from a psychological point of view, it seems unlikely that anyone engaged for whatever purposes in acting the part of another would behave as the patient does in displaying so little initiative in achieving her aims."

*Dr Lothar Nobel, at Mommsen Clinic, March, 1926.*

"To view Frau Tchaikovsky as an intentional fraud is, to my mind, quite out of the question. It is impossible that this woman originated from the lower ranks of society. Her entire character is so distinctive, so completely cultivated, that even if nothing be known with certainty about her origins, she must be viewed as the descendant of an old, cultured, and, I feel, extremely decadent, family."

*Professor Saathof, Stillachhaus Sanatorium,*
*7th December 1927.*

"When I first saw her face close up, and especially her eyes, so blue and so full of light, I immediately recognized Grand Duchess Anastasia Nikolaevna. Her unforgettable blue-grey eyes had exactly the same look in them as when she was a child."

*Tatiana Botkin, after meeting the claimant in 1926.*

"At all times she was herself and never gave the impression of acting a role. She never, no matter what the pressure, ever made an error that would have shaken my growing conviction and final complete embrace in her identity. She speaks perfectly acceptable Russian from the point of view of Saint Petersburg society. She never gave the slightest impression of acting a part."

*Princess Xenia Georgievna of Russia.*

"I had the opportunity to observe and judge the invalid closely over two days, and I can categorically state that there is no doubt in my mind that she is Grand Duchess Anastasia. It is out of the question not to recognize her."

*H.I.H. Grand Duke Andrei Vladimirovich.*

"I am convinced she is the Emperor's youngest daughter. Now that she is a mature woman, I can occasionally detect in her the features of her mother. But more pointedly, her behaviour and cordial manner suggest to me an intimate familiarity and past association that bonds those of common origin together."

*H.I.H. Crown Princess Cecilie of Prussia.*

"I am still convinced it is she. You understand when she looked at me with those eyes, well, that was it. They are the Emperor's eyes, the same exact look that the Emperor had."

*Mathilde Kschessinska, Paris, 1967 (Widow of H.I.H. Grand Duke Andrei Vladimirovich and former mistress of the Tsar).*

"I think there's something we don't know about DNA."

*Ian Lilburn, supporter of Anna Anderson who attended all the trials.*

"Rational experience of those who knew her far outweighs scientific evidence. It's like saying she was a man."

*Richard Schweitzer, after Dr Gill's press conference in 1994.*

"To be able to impersonate another would require a surpassing intelligence, an extraordinary degree of self-control and an ever-alert discipline – all qualities Mrs Tschaikowsky in no way possesses."

*Dr Willige at the Ilten Sanatorium, 1931.*

"Mrs Tchaikovsky is without any doubt Anastasia of Russia."

*H.I.H. Prince Sigismund of Prussia, in sworn affidavit, 1938.*

"I know perfectly well who I am. I do not need to prove it in any court of law."

*Anna Anderson (H.I.H. Grand Duchess Anastasia Nikolaevna).*

# 1. MADRID, 12TH FEBRUARY 1995

Today was a day that would shake the world, as one of the most enigmatic cases in history was about to be resolved.

For years the world had been made to accept that on the night of 16–17 July 1918, a squad of Bolshevik secret police murdered Russia's last emperor, Tsar Nicholas II, along with his wife, Tsarina Alexandra, their fourteen-year-old son, Tsarevitch Alexis, and their four beautiful daughters: Olga, Tatiana, Maria and Anastasia. History books have told us that they were cut down in a hail of gunfire in a half-cellar room of the Ipatiev house in Ekaterinburg, a city in the Ural mountain region where they were being held prisoner by the Bolsheviks. The Grand Duchesses were finished off with bayonets. The bodies were supposedly carted away to the countryside, dismembered, burned and hastily buried in a secret grave. Since that day the murder of the Imperial family had been surrounded by controversy and the debates had continued for decades.

I have to admit that I had not been too interested in the fate of the Romanovs and had accepted what we were told happened to them as absolute fact.

I had not been able to sleep too well the night before, and had woken up early. My wife Rosa was abroad and I had invited my son Carlos for breakfast. He would be responsible in many ways for my involvement in the news that would be revealed to the world this day, and which would make historians rewrite what had been believed as the truth for decades. Through the windows I could see the dense snow covering everything. Carlos called me on the phone and told me that the traffic was heavy, and it would take him a few more minutes to arrive at my house. He begged me to wait for him before reading the newspapers. I knew he was very happy, but I also knew that this revelation would make many people in high places very angry, and I was not sure what the consequences would be – but it was too late for regrets.

My eyes rested on the white landscape outside, which looked like a blank screen. Suddenly that screen appeared in my mind magically, and I started to remember through vivid images the first day I had heard my mother discuss the Romanovs. We were having breakfast at our home, set in a lovely terraced land overlooking the bay of Cap Ferrat.

It was early July 1938. I was at that time completely cured from an injury that I had suffered at Mill Creek in England, which had badly damaged the muscles and ligaments in my left arm and leg, so I had spent the winter recovering in the Côte d'Azur.

My father had died over a year earlier and we lived with a friend of the family whom I called Uncle Jack, whom my mother adored, and with Princess Jane Magaloff, the English widow of an impoverished Russian aristocrat.

"How can they do that to her?" I heard my mother exclaim as I entered the dining room where she was having breakfast with Princess Jane and Uncle Jack.

"Good morning, mummy! How could they do what to whom?" I asked.

"Rodney, you have heard me talk of Frau Anderson, the woman in Germany who claims to be Grand Duchess Anastasia," she replied.

"Yes mummy. So what have they done to her now?" I asked, not really interested in my mother's breakfast ramblings.

"I've just read in the paper that those Nazis have forced her to meet the family of that peasant woman named Franziska Schanzkowska!" she protested.

"There is nothing wrong with that, darling!" Uncle Jack said. "It will probably help clarify the whole matter once and for all."

"It is absolutely disgraceful! Ernst Ludwig von Hessen was the mastermind of this absurd scheme to make us believe that this fragile woman is a Polish factory worker. After all that she has gone through, the poor creature, this is the ultimate indignity!"

"Dot, how can you be so sure she is who she says?" asked Princess Jane, trying to calm her down.

"No factory worker can have so much inside knowledge of the Imperial family; no factory worker can behave like a lady, and have the same hair and eye colour of the real Anastasia; and let's not forget that she has been recognized by some members of her family!"

"Darling, but some have also said that she's an impostor, including Grand Duchess Olga. She is her aunt, after all, and she would surely know. They would not be so cruel if she is really Anastasia," Uncle Jack said.

"She never said she was an impostor. Actually Olga treated her very well and after several visits she said: 'My reason cannot grasp it, but my heart tells me that the little one is Anastasia, and because I have been raised in a faith which teaches me to follow my heart before my reason, I must believe that she is.' But I also know that she changed her mind later and said that the sad girl was not whom she thought she was. This is disgraceful." Mama said.

I recall how surprised I was then that this matter upset her so much, but she had always been an opponent of any type of injustice.

"It's all about grabbing the Tsar's money." Princess Jane added in her usual coarse tone of voice.

"A total and utter disgrace! Poor child. She has suffered so much!"

My mother was beyond herself in indignation and it all made me smile inwardly. She saw herself as some sort of Don Quixote. She was such a character, and I loved her dearly.

In those glorious days, my best friends were Prince Igor Trubetskoy,[1] Prince Alexander Chavchavadze and Prince Basil Nakashidze. They were older than me, I was only sixteen; but we were so inseparable that we were known as the Four Musketeers! My friends were adamant about not discussing the tragic events that had occurred in Russia and forced them and their families into penniless exile. I suppose it was all too close in time, and the pain of losing many loved ones, their fortunes and comfortable lifestyles was too painful to endure. So they took refuge from their distress in partying hard and enjoying life on the edge in those carefree pre-war years.

We were handsome and fun, and many of our very wealthy friends were happy to pay the bills. But that morning, after having listened to my mother's conversation the day before, I decided that I would ask Igor what he thought about the Anastasia claimant living in Germany. To my surprise, he was quite prepared to share his thoughts on the matter.

"Mother believes her story. She says she has His Majesty the Tsar's very same eyes!" he confided in reverence.

"My mother is furious that the Nazis have threatened to send her to jail if she is recognized by the peasant's family as their lost sister!" I said.

"That is not going to happen, Rodney, because no peasant can pretend to be our Grand Duchess and get away with it. She might not be Anastasia, but she is definitely no peasant. I think this is just Hitler's manoeuvre to assure himself that he has a Grand Duchess living in Germany, and eventually to use her as a pawn to gain support for his plans in Russia. Those Bolsheviks are cold-blooded murderers! I hope he gets rid of them and we can return home. I hope Hitler does the job!"

---

[1] He later became the fourth husband of Barbara Hutton (1912–1979), an American socialite and one of the wealthiest women of the twentieth century.

The thought of what his country had become always made Igor angry.

"This is no life for us, Rodney! Look at what we've become: hotel porters, waiters, taxi drivers. What ever has happened to our world, to our marvellous way of life? If the Führer kicks those murderous bastards out, I will support his efforts!"

I could very well understand how he felt. So many wonderful people had not only lost their loved ones but their world had ceased to exist, and it was very painful to see them trying to survive the best they could without losing their dignity.

"Don't let yourself be tricked by Hitler, my friend!" I said, as I patted him on the back. "He is evil!"

"I'm going to share a secret with you but you must promise not to repeat it…" Igor suddenly said.

"You know you can trust me with your life, Igor."

"Mother says that the Tsarevitch also survived. In fact, she has met him here!" he confided.

"What? Here in France? But that is sensational. Why doesn't he tell the world?" I asked in bewilderment.

"According to mother, a pact of silence was made in exchange for their freedom."

"But who is he?" I asked, fascinated.

"He has an alias and no one must know or his life would be in danger. The Bolsheviks have a long arm and have murdered many prominent émigrés, especially White Russians,[2] who strongly supported the monarchy. Most of them belonged to the Tsar's army and were close to him. You've made a promise!"

✦ ✦ ✦

I smiled inwardly about how clear my memory of those days was now, probably due to the fact that the whole truth was about to be revealed. My mind then drifted back to Christmas in London in 1957, when I once again heard my mother discuss the Anastasia claimant, Frau Anna Anderson. It was to be the last Christmas lunch that the family would spend together, as mummy died of a stroke while she was taking her nap, and sweet Princess Jane died shortly after. Maybe that is the reason that last lunch is so clear and vivid in my mind.

---

[2] The army loyal to the Empire, which fought against the Red Army (Communists).

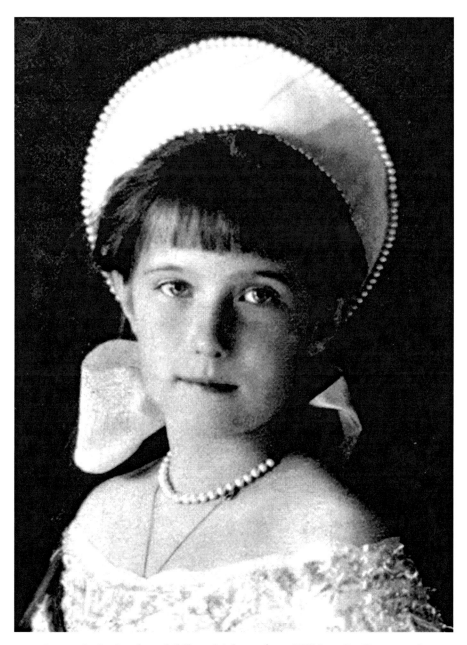

Anastasia during her childhood (photo from Wikimedia Commons).

My second wife Pepita was four months pregnant with our first son and the doctor had recommended she take it easy, so we decided to spend Christmas in London with my mother and not go to Bilbao to see her family. Stubborn as she was, she had already decided to travel to Bilbao in March, two months before she was due, to have our baby delivered there. Of course, I had agreed.

That lunch in the company of my loved ones was a delight. Princess Jane Magaloff and Uncle Jack were with us too.

After we opened the gifts, we sat down for the sumptuous turkey lunch that Mummy had prepared with much attention to following family tradition: homemade stuffing and cranberry sauce for the turkey, and a wonderful Christmas pudding with brandy butter. The conversation flowed easily and the sounds of joy and laughter filled the room. As I was about to serve the pudding, my mother raised her glass of champagne and made a toast.

"To my family! And to the recognition of Frau Anderson as the Grand Duchess Anastasia!"

We all looked at each other in bewilderment.

"Dot!" Uncle Jack exclaimed, laughing.

"Rodney, you know how your mother feels about this matter, or have you forgotten?" Princess Jane smiled, recalling many previous conversations on the topic.

My mother giggled at my surprised face and, ignoring me, she proceeded to explain the story of Anna Anderson to my wife as I served the pudding in silence, not daring to interrupt her.

"I have read in today's paper that Anna Anderson is not going to fight any more against her relatives for the money that they inherited in 1933 from a certificate deposited by Nicholas II at the Mendelssohn Bank. Instead, her lawyers decided to sue directly for her recognition as Grand Duchess Anastasia. The case was moved for convenience from Berlin to Hamburg, and now she is preparing to sue a member of the family that wrongfully received and spent her money."

"Fascinating! Surely no one can fake an identity for so long." Pepita finally said with a sudden genuine interest, which made me remember one of the many reasons why I loved her so much.

✦ ✦ ✦

The maid entering the dining room brought me back to the present day. She brought me a cup of hot tea. Winter had been brutally cold, and that day in February of 1995 seemed to be even worse. It was snowing heavily outside, and while I was waiting for Carlos to arrive, I kept reflecting on all the reasons I had involved myself in the story of the fate of the Romanovs.

Flashes of my own life popped up once again: how I had become involved in MI6 when as a teenager I escaped from the internment camp in Foix and had, after many dangerous adventures, ended up in Madrid working for the British Embassy; my training with the firm and my life in London during the terrible final years of the war; my first marriage, and then meeting Pepita. Was this part of getting old? I asked myself. And while I was pondering these memories the swinging sixties came to my mind. Life in London in those days had been great fun, at the centre of the social revolution. We had entered the decade in black and white and came out in colour. Mary Quant had invented the mini-skirt, and the Beatles and the Rolling Stones had taken the music world by storm. The British establishment reeled with shock, having been quite unprepared for such radical changes, changes that were visible everywhere. This had amused me greatly as everything was then geared to the tastes of the younger generation.

I was then enjoying life to the fullest in the company of my adored second wife, Pepita, and my four younger children. Simon, my eldest, was attending King's College in Canterbury and I saw him on weekends and occasional holidays when he joined us at home. We lived in a lovely house on 9 Westleigh Avenue, in Putney. Life could not be better. Business was good and my life in MI6 was a thing of the past. I lived in a state of bliss.

Memories of Pepita came vividly to my mind. I recalled her as she entered my study one day in February 1967 with a copy of the *Times* and the conversation we had. "Darling, have you read the verdict of the Hamburg Court on the Anastasia case?" she asked softly.

"Have you been following it?" I asked with surprise, as she had never discussed it with me before.

"Yes, of course I have. Since your mother so passionately explained the case to me that Christmas lunch, several years ago now, I have been fascinated by the plight of this poor woman," she answered.

"You are always championing lost causes!" I teased. "So has she won?"

"She has in a sort of way, as the Court says that although she has been unable to prove her case, her opponents have also been unable to do so. She also has the right to appeal."

"That's not much of a victory, darling. This case has been dragging on for decades!"

"Precisely, Rodney. They claimed that she was not able to provide sufficient proof for her recognition and that the death of Grand Duchess Anastasia at Ekaterinburg cannot be accepted as a conclusively proven fact. And another thing which is striking is that the court has not taken into account the deposition of their expert witnesses," she said seriously.

"What do you mean, my love? You seem to have become an expert on the matter," I teased her.

"Well, the anthropological expert appointed by the court, Professor Otto Reche, testified under oath that, after studying hundreds of photographs of Frau Anderson and the historical Anastasia, they were the same person, or identical twins! It is unbelievable! In a sixty-page report he said that Mrs Anna Anderson was Grand Duchess Anastasia. I don't know what is wrong here. I definitely don't understand."

"That should have done it then!" I said her with interest.

"Not only that, but the expert graphologist Dr Minna Becker, who has been an expert for the German courts for over thirty-four years, concluded that her handwriting and that of Grand Duchess Anastasia were identical. The sad thing is that her opponents have won a battle, in some way, but I have faith that in the end justice will prevail and she will be victorious."

"I am very impressed, Pepita, by your knowledge," I said, smiling lovingly at my wife.

"I owe the interest on the case to your mother. She was passionate about it. Rodney…" she added as an afterthought, "why don't you use your contacts in MI6 to investigate the matter? Maybe you can discover some new facts that will help the appeal. You owe it to your mother's memory."

"I haven't been in touch with them for years now and I don't think it's a very good idea. I'm sure I wouldn't be useful to the case, anyway," I said, trying to get the idea out of her mind, as I very well knew how persuasive she could be.

"Please…" she pleaded, as she kissed me tenderly on the lips.

It's quite amazing that life's surprises arrive at the most unexpected moments. Soon after that conversation, and much to my surprise, I was asked to return to MI6 and move to Spain. Pepita had been most understanding and happy to be closer to her family, so we closed the house on Westleigh Avenue. Our furniture and belongings were shipped to Madrid and we travelled to Playa de Berria, not far from Santander, to spend the three month in summer with Pepita's mother, sister and family. In mid–September, we travelled to Madrid to our new home in Calle Cinca 16, in El Viso, an elegant residential area of Madrid. Pepita had chosen a nice, large house with a garden so that the children would not feel too unsettled by the move.

As a cover, MI6 had arranged for me to work for a company called Hierros y Aceros Europeos, a subsidiary of Harlow & Jones. Our job was to advise the Spanish steelworks on the purchase of scrap metal from the US, the UK and other European countries, chiefly Belgium and the Netherlands. Initially, I knew absolutely nothing about scrap metal nor did I have the slightest interest, but I soon learnt to enjoy my job, and eventually became very good at it. To cap it all, I had a generous salary and a wonderful assistant, Count Peter Potocki, whose family had given Poland several kings and who now lived in exile in Madrid.

My work in Spain, as it had been in the early forties, was to infiltrate Madrid's high society. I was to find out who was going to support the restoration of the monarchy and democracy after the death of General Franco, or who would back the impossible survival of the dictatorship under another general. Madrid had changed a lot since my last visit after the war.

Pepita, as usual, had been a great asset to my work. After only a month in Madrid, she had started giving her extravagant and elegant dinner parties that were so amusing and always the talk of town. She had a gift of mixing people and she knew how to charm the birds off the trees.

My contact with MI6 was a man I knew as Miles who was based in Madrid, to whom I passed the information I gathered. One morning, during one of our regular briefings at my office in Rafael Salgado, I caught him off guard.

"Miles, what do you know about the Anna Anderson case?" I inquired.

"Why do you want to know?" he asked, slightly surprised.

"It interests my wife, who has been following the case for years. In fact, it interested my mother very much since Anna appeared in Berlin in the twenties," I answered.

"It has been a very sensitive case from the start, and definitely something that the royal family prefer not to be discussed. You are aware that Lord Mountbatten headed the opposition to her after the death of Grand Duke Ernest of Hesse?"

"I'm not familiar with the case at all, Miles. I was just wondering if I could help my wife clarify some points. She tells me that Mrs Anderson's lawyer is going to submit an appeal against the court's verdict."

"That is correct, Rodney, but my advice is that you let the matter rest. It is still a very sensitive matter and I can assure you it won't help your career."

That was not the answer I expected. It sounded as if Miles suspected that Anna Anderson was the Grand Duchess.

"Miles, you know better than anyone that I accepted this post very much against my will, so my future in the firm does not worry me whatsoever. I do agree with you though, that we have more pressing matters than to concern ourselves with Mrs. Anderson... but if the royal family have known of her true identity and they've helped in the cover-up, I would be totally disgusted."

✦ ✦ ✦

Once again, I was amazed at the clarity of my memories. I thoroughly enjoyed those first two years in Madrid, trying to adapt to a new life. Time flew. We travelled extensively, entertained and were entertained by an array of new friends, played golf and of course spent as much time with our children as we could. Before we knew it, the summer of 1969 had arrived, and then, in early September, a terrible tragedy occurred. My beloved Pepita died in a car accident.

✦ ✦ ✦

"*Señor,* would you like more tea?" Esperanza asked, taking me out of my musings.

"No thank you," I replied, realized that I had become involved in this entire story mainly for Pepita. Today, finally, the 12th of February, he thick wall of secrecy and lies that buried a terrible truth would at last be broken. Today the long silence was going to end. Yes, I was doing that mostly for Pepita, which is how I'd become lost in recollection. Finally Carlos arrived, hugged me and apologized for the delay, again blaming the snow and the traffic. We sat down at the table to enjoy our breakfast, along with the great news...

## 2. MADRID, SPAIN, FEBRUARY 1984

In 1976 I had finally left MI6, as my work in Madrid was successfully carried out. The monarchy had been restored and King Juan Carlos had skilfully managed, in spite of all the odds, to make a peaceful transition from the dictatorship of general Franco to a fully-fledged vibrant and modern democracy.

The crown was now the supreme guarantor of this democracy. I was very proud of the young king's excellent work, and of the team of men that had helped him accomplish what in those early days seemed nearly impossible.

I was sixty-one years old and enjoying life. I was again happily married. All my children, who were my best friends, were healthy and independent and I looked forward to a peaceful and active old age. I had finally closed down my company when I felt that the steel business in Spain had passed its prime. I did not want to be inactive after retiring, and though I had an antique shop called "Brunswick" in Calle del Prado with my friend Jesus Rodriguez-Navia, I knew it would not keep me busy enough. I seldom went to the shop, and only made buying trips to England once in a while. So I had asked my son Carlos if I could work for him, supervising the accounts of his model agency, International Bookings, which was one of the most successful in Spain.

He hesitated at first, probably not wanting to have his old man around at all times, but he finally agreed, as we did have a close and friendly relationship.

One morning, just before leaving on my skiing holiday to Cloisters with my wife Rosa, I went to the agency to say goodbye. Carlos was with his close friend Sergei Nazarewicz, an extremely handsome blond ex-model of Ukrainian-French parentage who had become a talented photographer. He was my son's closest friend and by then a loved member of the family.

Sergei not only had class, he was also hard-working and a good influence on my son.

"Good morning, Rodney!" he said as he got up to greet me.

"*Hola* Papa! It's a sad day!" my son said.

"Why?" I asked.

"Grand Duchess Anastasia Nicolaievna died yesterday of pneumonia!" Sergei replied theatrically, being Russian.

"What's going to happen now?" Carlos inquired.

"Well, I suppose it will be one of history's unsolved enigmas," I said, amused that once again Anastasia Romanov was somehow reappearing in my life.

"So much has been said and written about her, and finally the poor woman has died without being officially recognized," Sergei said sadly.

"It is definitely a tragic story. Have you also been following the case, Carlos?" I asked my son.

"I'm passionate about it, Papa! To me it's a conspiracy. In 1977, Professor Furtmayr, one of Germany's most prominent forensic experts, who had already testified at the Hamburg trial in her favour, had by then improved his identification method, known as PIK. He compared the historical Anastasia's right ear with Anna Anderson's. And do you know what his conclusion was?"

The mention of Professor Furtmayr brought back a wave of memories, as he had been one of the expert witnesses at the trial of Baron von Jellenbach in Israel, some years ago. "So what were his conclusions, Carlos?" I asked.

"That both women's ears were identical in seventeen anatomical points and tissue formations, five more than the dozen points accepted by German courts to prove a person's identity. He concluded that without any doubt whatsoever they were one and the same person. In fact, the German Supreme Court offered to reopen the case, but by then, the Grand Duchess had moved to the United States, and I suppose she was tired of it all. She knew who she was, and that was probably enough for her. But I think her name should be legally restored after this scientific conclusion. I am disgusted by this injustice!"

"It's all very depressing," Sergei sighed.

"Did you know Sergei's grandfather was a Ukrainian prince? He met the Grand Duchess when they were children in Tsarskoe Selo, and he told Sergei and me when we were last in Biarritz that he was certain she was who she proclaimed," Carlos added.

"But why was he so certain, Sergei? Did he meet her?" I asked.

"He insisted that she had Tsar Nicholas' eyes, and after Grand Duke Andrei Vladimirovich recognized her he had no doubt whatsoever," Sergei answered, showing his excitement.

Where had I heard that her eyes and the Tsar's were the same? It was years ago. As I tried to remember, I asked Sergei, now genuinely interested in the matter, "Tell me more about your family, if you don't mind."

"My grandpa, who belonged to the titled landowners of the Empire, escaped from Ukraine in 1921 when it finally fell to the Soviets. He met my grandma, a Polish peasant, on the train that brought them to France. They fell in love and married. His life was very difficult. He studied to be a physician in Ukraine and ended up working in a car factory in France to make ends meet. Never practiced medicine. They had two sons," Sergei explained.

"You know papa, it was only because of my incessant questioning that I finally got him to confide in me. Sergei's grandfather had never revealed to him or his family who he really was or where he came from. It just happens that Sergei is a prince now!" Carlos interrupted, beaming with pride. "I persevered and finally took him out for a glass of red wine and bought him a Playboy and he opened up to me," he said jokingly.

"*Cest vrai!*" Sergei confirmed as he laughed at the memory.

"For the first time since he had taken the train into exile from Kiev, he candidly spoke about the details of his ordeal, how he fell in love with my grandma and the very difficult times in France in the twenties. He had tears in his eyes. He looked into mine, took my hand and asked me to take the baton, and that is why I have started using the title of Prince. Of course Carlos was more than insistent! And that is probably why I landed a job in Vogue as social editor. In some way, it was thanks to Grand Duchess Anastasia," he added.

"You have to see where they lived in the Ukraine. A fantastic palace that even had a swimming pool. Sergei has the pictures. You must see them, Papa," Carlos said with enthusiasm.

"Grandpa Nikolai's home was Châeau Belokrinica Wolyhnic, in a small town called Kremienic. He told us his mother was a Princess Voronin. He was an extraordinary man who always lived a very simple life in France. What a surprise all this was for my family and especially for me. I always thought my grandpa came from humble origins," Sergei said, as he hugged Carlos.

I will always remember that day, since it was fraught with by mixed emotions: sadness at the death of that enigmatic woman who had been in the minds and hearts of some of my dear ones. Happiness, because Sergei had found an unexpected truth about his life.

# 3. SAN JOSÉ, COSTA RICA, LATE JANUARY 1994

Rita Stern had become a friend after I met her in San José during a fateful Christmas holiday in 1992, when I had gone with Carlos to visit Costa Rica for the first time, and the ghosts of the past had come back to haunt me.

She was the daughter of Simon Stern, a banker and art collector in Hungary prior to the Nazi invasion. I had investigated the theft of his collection while I was working for MI6 after the war.

The day we met will be forever in my memory, as we both nearly died when the deranged son of a Nazi I helped arrest after WWII hunted me down and nearly shot us both. I suppose such a shared experience made us friends for life, and so I was not surprised to receive an invitation to celebrate Rita's sixtieth birthday in San José, and I accepted immediately. I asked my wife Rosa to join me, but she chose to stay at home, so I flew alone for a holiday which I was very much looking forward to.

I had a soft spot for Costa Rica, a country full of natural wonders. The *ticos*[1] were very friendly and welcoming, and the country had something special about it: such a stable democracy that it didn't even have an army.

Ringed by lush green mountains and valleys, San José is on a plateau in the Central Valley, at an altitude of about 1,200 metres. The weather was always very pleasant and I looked forward to my stay.

My flight arrived early that morning. I had booked a room at the turn-of-the-century Gran Hotel Costa Rica, where I had stayed two years earlier. It is the only hotel that had been declared a historical landmark by the government, and is conveniently located between national monuments, museums and pedestrian streets. It had been here, in fact, where I had met Rita, who had called me out of the blue to reveal that she was the daughter of my old friend Simon Stern, and whom I had not seen since she was a young girl in London in the years following the war. Rita and her husband Antonio, a Costa Rican, had

---

[1] Local inhabitants.

insisted I stay at their home, but being very independent, I preferred the hotel.

"*Pura Vida!* Señor Mundy, welcome back!" A beaming receptionist welcomed me with an open and charming smile.

"It's nice to be back!" I replied.

I was escorted to a beautiful, quaint suite and called Rita to let her know that I had arrived. I was a bit jet-lagged and, being a great sleeper, planned to take a nap, so I accepted her invitation for dinner that evening. The big birthday party, a black-tie affair, was scheduled for the following day.

At nine o'clock sharp I was standing in front of Rita and Antonio's front door in the area of town known as Pavas. Their home was not far from the US Embassy, a lovely cubic construction with amazing light and shadow effects. Rita's antique shop was just next door. The memory of our near-death experience came to my mind as the door opened and young Rodney Blanco, Rita's handsome twenty-two-year-old son, welcomed me with a broad smile. He had matured over the two years that had passed since I had met him. He was over six feet tall and well built, with long, wavy blond hair and the warm blue eyes of his grandfather, Simon.

"Welcome, Uncle Rodney!" he said as he hugged me. "Mum is waiting for you."

As I walked into the house with my namesake, I felt a hint of bemusement at the thought that I barely knew this family but felt at home with them. I followed Rodney into the spacious living room full of marvellous antique objects from his mother's collection, where she was waiting. Rita looked delightful. She was wearing her beautiful string of pearls around her long, lovely neck and she approached me and kissed me on the cheeks.

"We are so happy that you came, dear Rodney!" she said, looking through her deep-set, dark eyes into mine. "Let's celebrate! Son, ask Consuelo to bring a bottle of champagne, please."

"Of course, Mama! I'll see you tomorrow for the party, Uncle Rodney. Now I'm going out with my girl, who you will meet tomorrow. She can't wait to meet you!" he said as he kissed his mother goodbye, and gave me another hug.

"She is a lucky lady, Rodney!" The three of us laughed as he left the room.

As we were chatting about what had happened in our lives since we saw each other two years earlier, Consuelo entered the room with the chilled bottle of champagne. I uncorked it and filled two glasses.

"To us!" I toasted.

"What happened to Martin von Jellenbach is such a tragedy! That family was doomed," I said, recalling the death of our assailant.

"Yes, but he was totally unstable. He nearly killed us, Rodney!" Rita said, perturbed at the thought.

"And how did his wife take it?" I asked.

"They had been separated for quite a while and fortunately they had no children. I see her often and she has remarried since then. She is a fine and nice woman."

"I'm glad to hear that," I said, as I drank my second glass of the delicious chilled French champagne.

"I have something special for you, Rodney," Rita suddenly said, as she gave me a small, burgundy velvet box.

"It's your birthday and I'm the one that gets a present!" I exclaimed in surprise, as I opened the box, which contained a beautiful pre-Columbian jade pendant.

"This was given to me by my father, who received it as a gift from Prince Frederick Ernst of Saxe-Altenburg, a German prince."

"What a beautiful piece!" I cried out as I took the pendant out of the box. "I can't accept it! It's way too precious!"

"Of course you can and you will. I absolutely insist!" Rita said forcefully.

"Ok! If you must have your way, my dear! I never say no to a beautiful woman!" We both laughed as I examined the exquisite pendant.

"Prince Frederick Ernst used to come to Costa Rica very often. His sister Princess Charlotte Agnes of Saxe-Altenburg was married to Prince Sigismund of Prussia, the nephew of Kaiser Wilhelm II. The Prince, as we called him, was an avid archaeologist. He found the pendant in 1935, when he was excavating some indigenous tombs with a friend of my father, Jose Maria Alba, and gave it to father in one of his visits; he knew how well my father appreciated art and antique things," she said, "As a matter of fact, I met him, too. He came regularly to Puntarenas to visit his family, where they had lived since the late twenties."

"This is incredible, Rita," I said in disbelief.

"Why?"

"My mother and then my late wife were fascinated by the case of Anna Anderson, who they believed was Grand Duchess Anastasia of Russia. And now my son Carlos is also deep into it. What a coincidence! You know that Prince Frederick Ernst was one of Anna Anderson's most loyal and staunch supporters?"

"Sure I know. I am also familiar with the case, and my father always said that Prince Frederick Ernst, Prince Sigismund and his wife had no doubt that Mrs Anderson was the legitimate Grand Duchess Anastasia."

"Tell me more about them, Rita, please," I begged, thrilled at the possibility of having some interesting information to take with me to Spain, and give to Carlos on the case.

"They lived in a beautiful, big and simple wooden house surrounded by large trees in Barranca. On the *finca*,[2] called San Miguel, they had several hundred beehives, cattle, pigs and planted *teka* and fruit trees. They were wonderful people and everybody loved them. Prince Sigismund died in Puntarenas in November 1978; his wife, Princess Charlotte got very sick and eventually returned to Germany, where she passed away in 1989."

"Did they have children?"

"Yes, two. The eldest is a daughter named Barbara, Duchess of Mecklenburg. She lives in Germany. Their son, Prince Alfred, lives here in Costa Rica with his wife, a charming Hungarian lady, in a house in Escazú, not far from here. They don't have children. They own an apartment in New York. Unfortunately Prince Alfred had his parents' house in San Miguel torn down after they died. Very sad! The most striking thing for me is his resemblance to King George VI," Rita told me, while serving herself another glass of champagne.

"Well, they do have very close family links to my royal family. Both Sigismund's parents were grandchildren of Queen Victoria. In fact, they were first cousins and therefore cousins of George VI and the current Queen Elizabeth II. Do you think you can arrange for me to meet him?" I asked excitedly.

"Let me call them now. Maritza is lovely. You will like her. When are you leaving?" She asked, as she picked up the phone.

"In five days. I would have liked to stay longer but we're very busy at the agency," I responded.

A couple of minutes later Rita put down the phone. They were not at home.

"They have just left for New York and won't be back for two weeks so it won't be possible. Well, this means you have a good excuse to return and see us again, Rodney!" Rita said teasingly, surprised at my curiosity, while acknowledging the obvious disappointment on my face.

"But why such a sudden interest?" she asked.

---

[2] Country estate.

"I don't know. I suppose the spy in me is still alive. Gut feeling!" I answered jokingly.

"I myself have always been fascinated with that story. I recently read in the newspaper that a hospital in Charlottesville, United States, where Anastasia moved to in 1968, kept a piece of intestine that had been extracted from her during a surgical procedure. Now a group of supporters of her cause want it to be tested to obtain her DNA. It seems that the mystery will be finally solved through science," Rita said with confidence.

"I had no idea of all that, Rita. It's my son who is interested in this affair. As far as I know, science has already spoken. The forensic experts at the Hamburg trials had no doubts that Anna Anderson and the historical Anastasia were one and the same person. Anyway, it seems that now we will have to wait until the analyses of the tissue sample are finished and the results made public. But I think that somebody has being trying to cover up the truth, since the very beginning of this affair in 1918."

"But who would want to cover up the truth, Rodney, and why? So much time has passed!"

"Precisely, my dear Rita. Precisely. How could they ever accept that they had made such a mistake then, and sacrificed one of their own – and mostly, why did they do it?"

# 4. MADRID, SPAIN, FEBRUARY 1994

My short stay in Costa Rica was very pleasant. I got back to Madrid and once again put the Anastasia affair in the back of my mind, as I had done since the first time I heard my mother speak about it in the late thirties.

Knowing how much Carlos loved history, carved stones and very old pieces, I thought he would love to have the beautiful jade pendant that Rita gave me. I passed it on for him to wear or collect, and told him the tremendous coincidence that it was Prince Frederick Ernst who had found it in Costa Rica, and all what I learned about his close relatives living there.

"Papa, I think this is like an omen!" he exclaimed. "Green represents the most powerful energies of nature, hope, rebirth. Green jade is a sacred stone. I can't believe I am getting this treasure, found by the strongest supporter of Anastasia! I love it, thanks!"

He was amazed; truly excited. I could see it in his eyes, which were sparkling and looked as green as the jade.

✦ ✦ ✦

It was collection time and we were very busy at the agency, with many foreign models coming over for the fashion shows.

When the Soviet Union collapsed and the countries of the Eastern Bloc overthrew their communist regimes, Carlos had foreseen that it would be a great opportunity to expand our business by opening our own offices over there to scout models for our main agency in Spain and launch their international careers.

He thought that if we were located at the source, we would be able to supply beautiful models to New York, Paris and Milan and not depend only on the local market. So, a few months earlier he had travelled to Prague, Warsaw and Budapest and organized offices in these cities with local partners. It was a brilliant idea, but unfortunately the timing was bad, as the models we found spoke no English and were penniless. It all ended up being a very costly affair that nearly took our Spanish business down. Having said that, a couple of years later it all took off when we had already left these countries, which proved he did not have such bad business sense after all!

"Papa, could you go to Warsaw next week, please?" Carlos asked me one morning. "The shows are starting and I'm much too busy to make the trip."

"What would I have to do there?" I asked, not being too knowledgeable about the business.

"Stanislaw will meet you. He wants to show us some new faces that he has scouted. It will only be a couple of days."

"I'll be happy to go, but you know that my taste in women is not that of the ideal model. They are all skin and bones and unsexy in my eyes," I joked. Carlos and I never agreed on which models were beautiful, though of course it was he who had the knowledge of what the market required.

"Great, Papa. I will make all the travel arrangements for you then."

# 5. WARSAW, POLAND, FEBRUARY 1994

The morning of the 23rd of February in Madrid was dark and bitter start to only start to imagine what freezing conditions I could expect in Warsaw. The LOT flight from Barajas airport departed on time and the trip was uneventful and seemed very short, as I dozed most of the time. I had decided to leave a day earlier as I wanted to discover Warsaw on my own, unhindered and undisturbed. I had wanted to visit the city for many years, having heard so much about it from my dear friends the Zawidskis in London, and of course from Count Peter Potocki, my friend and ex-business associate in Madrid. I felt a twinge of excitement as I drove off from the airport in a taxi to the Polonia Palace Hotel, where Carlos had booked me a room. He knew I loved staying at historical hotels and the Polonia was just that. Established in 1912, it has always been an integral part of the city's history. The building seemed to me, as I approached it, as though it had been transferred from the centre of Paris with its mansard roofs. It had been one of the few buildings that survived the bombing of the city, which was nearly destroyed during the closing stages of World War II.

After checking into a beautiful, cosy room I called Stanislaw to tell him I had arrived. He would come to pick me up the following morning at ten, so I had the whole afternoon to myself.

Though the skies were clear blue the temperature was well below zero. It was bitterly cold. I took a taxi to Starówka, Warsaw's old town, built in the thirteenth century and now a UNESCO World Heritage site. I was amazed by the incredible restoration work: the Zawidskis told me the Nazis had obliterated it after the 1944 uprising. Starówka had been meticulously rebuilt, with many original bricks salvaged from the rubble, and adorned with paintings by Canaletto to try to recapture its essence. I was enchanted. It was pure magic and I understood why Carlos had insisted that Stanislaw set up our office in this part of town, close to all the restaurants, cafés, antique shops and art galleries that had sprung up after the fall of communism.

✦ ✦ ✦

I was waiting in the hotel lobby when Stanislaw, whom I had never met before, came in looking for me at ten o'clock. He was a handsome young man in his late thirties. His Slavic features were enhanced by wavy, longish blond hair and penetrating blue eyes. He had a generous smile and a friendly manner to him.

"Ready to see the girls, Mr Mundy?"

"Yes, but please call me Rodney."

We drove in an old blue Volga towards the office, located in a charming old building on Pieharaska Street. Though Poland had made great leaps forward towards a market economy, it had been less than five years since the fall of the last communist regime of Wojciech Jaruzelski in May 1989, and the population was still adapting to the change. The middle class was still in the making.

The small office had just two rooms. In one of them about twenty girls were waiting. Painted white, it had simple furniture but was quite luminous as the sun shone through its large windows. Photographs of Linda, Naomi, Claudia, Christy and other supermodels decorated the walls. Stanisalw's sister Dorota, an attractive, fashionably dressed blonde, greeted us and led me to the empty room where I was to hold the casting.

"Ready?" She asked, as she handed me a sheet of paper and a pen.

"Do they have photographs?" I asked.

"I'm afraid they don't. They are totally new faces. Stanislaw has been scouting around the country. We have just brought them to Warsaw for you to meet, and they all go back home today," she said in a perfect English with a charming Polish accent. "But don't worry, we have a Polaroid and you can take some snaps!" She added, handing me the camera.

"OK! Lovely, let's get started."

The girls came in one by one and they spoke not one word of English. Using Dorota as an interpreter, I noted down their names and ages on the Polaroids, all between sixteen and eighteen. To my utter frustration, as I knew Carlos would be very disappointed, they were shabbily dressed, had very little grace and some of them badly needed dental work. Yes, some of them were tall, had long legs and, if you used your imagination, might look the part after much work; but being in charge of the agency's finances, I could see how costly the transformation would be.

"They need to be polished!" I said to Dorota when I thought the last girl had left.

"Yes Rodney, I know, but you see, Poland is still a poor country. We have a long way to go yet. These girls are uncut diamonds."

"I agree, but they need to speak at least a little English, as not only will they feel homesick, but they won't be able to work if they don't understand the photographers' directions. Unfortunately, they are just not ready yet to travel anywhere. You have a lot of work to do, I'm afraid!" I said to Dorota, trying to hide my disappointment.

"There is one more girl, and she speaks English. She is slightly older though, maybe too old!" She said hesitantly.

"How old?" I asked, expecting the worst.

"Twenty."

"Send her in. She might not do the editorials but if she's beautiful, she can work catalogues and commercials," I said, trying to sound very knowledgeable.

Dorota walked out of the room and came back seconds later with a ravishing, tall, lovely creature. Simply but elegantly dressed, I could immediately see she had a stunning figure. Her legs were long and well formed. She carried herself with elegance and grace. Dorota introduced me to her and to my surprise the girl lifted her hand and gave it to me to be kissed. As the girl spoke English, Dorota left the room.

"Please sit down. I am so happy to finally meet someone who speaks English. You are very beautiful, too. So what is your name?"

"Thank you, sir. My name is Tatiana," she replied, not a trace of an accent in her voice.

"Tatiana? That's a beautiful name. Did you know that one of Tsar Nicholas II's daughters was called Tatiana?" I said, to liven up the conversation.

"Yes, I know. That is the reason I am called Tatiana," she replied to my surprise. The girl was definitely beautiful but she had yet not smiled once. She seemed aloof and distant. I tried to get her to relax by asking her to stand up as I took some Polaroid shots and assured her that we would definitely invite her to Madrid to work if she was interested.

"I would love to," she said as she sat down.

"So tell me, why did you say that you were called Tatiana?"

"I didn't say," she replied with a straight face. She then suddenly laughed, her face becoming even more delightful. "My father is called Nicholas. He was the godson of the Tsar," she said.

"But my dear, that is absolutely impossible, as the Tsar was murdered along with his family in 1918 by the Bolsheviks! Well, with maybe the exception of Anastasia, whom many believe was Anna Anderson."

"The Tsar lived undercover in Poland and died in 1952. He is buried in the parish cemetery of Wolsztyn under the name Michael

Goloeniewski. He was my father's godfather," Tatiana said without any hesitation.

I was totally stunned by this revelation. I just did not know how to register the information and I must have looked lost, unable to utter a word.

"Are you OK, Mr Mundy? Have I said anything I should not have?" She asked.

"No. It's fine. I'm just a bit surprised. You see, my son, who you will meet soon, has followed the Anastasia case for years, and she seems to haunt me everywhere I go. I suppose the time has come for me to fully investigate and try to shed some light on this whole mystery." "Would you like to have dinner with me tonight?" I asked.

"Yes, it would be a pleasure. Would you like me to invite my father, too? He will be able to tell you many things about our family."

"Please do. It would be an honour! Let us say at 8 o'clock at the Polonia Palace for a drink." I just could not believe the coincidence. The magic of the universe at work!

✦ ✦ ✦

I rushed out of the office after thanking Stanislaw and Dorota, telling them that we loved Tatiana and encouraging them to keep up the good work. I did not accept their invitation for lunch as I needed to be alone and think over what Tatiana had just revealed to me. It was freezing outside and I walked through a few streets lined by medieval buildings such as the Barbican and the beautiful Saint John's Cathedral, towards the Starówka Market Place. Under different circumstances, I would have visited these landmarks, but I wanted to get into a warm coffee shop and order a glass of wine. Was it possible that there had been no massacre at the Ipatiev House in Ekaterinburg, as Summers and Mangold suggested in their book, *The File on the Tsar*? I had heard Carlos mention that Anna Anderson, towards the end of her life, had said the exact same thing. So, if that was the case, what had happened to the other Grand Duchesses and to the Tsarina? If they had all survived, who was behind the hoax of the murder and for what reason? And to whom did the bones, discovered in 1979 in a pit to near where the assassination had allegedly taken place, really belong? Too many questions to answer, and it seemed an uphill struggle to try to separate the facts from the myths.

✦ ✦ ✦

As I sat at the bar in the Polonia Palace, I nervously looked at my watch several times. It was just before eight and I ordered a glass of Cytrynowka vodka, a full-bodied spirit with a very pleasant and gentle lemon flavour. I was supposedly meeting the last godson of the Tsar of Russia. If it was true, it was an extraordinary moment, even for a seasoned spy like myself. I was about to order my second vodka when in walked Tatiana with her father, a man about my age and shorter than her. He had grey hair, and the same blue eyes as his ravishing daughter.

"Thank you for your invitation!" he said as we shook hands. "My name is Nikolai Przedziecki."

"I have booked a table at the restaurant. Shall we go and have a drink and order the meal? We will be more comfortable," I suggested.

"That's perfect," Tatiana said.

Once we had ordered dinner and after pleasantries and small talk about Tatiana's modelling career, I finally toasted to her brilliant future. The atmosphere then seemed friendly and relaxed, which is just what I wanted it to be.

"*Tatuś*,[1] as I told you, Rodney is very interested in the story of the Imperial family," Tatiana said in the impeccable English they both spoke.

"May I ask where you both learnt such lovely English? There's no trace of any accent whatsoever," I inquired in astonishment.

"My godfather, the Tsar, taught me to speak the language," Nikolai replied matter-of-factly. "And I taught my daughter."

"I'm sorry to be so bewildered by this. It just goes against all accepted historical facts. So what you're saying is that the Tsar lived incognito in Poland?"

"Yes, until his death in 1952 at the age of eighty-four," Nikolai replied firmly.

"But it seems so far-fetched. How can you be so certain?" I asked, still unable to believe his story. "And if they survived, why come to Poland?"

"My father told me that the Tsar had chosen Poland because it was easy for the family to blend in without raising any suspicion or attracting attention. There were a large number of Russians living both in the cities and on the farms at that time. He shaved his head and beard and no one recognized him. Being here would have also allowed him to return to Russia quickly if the political situation changed."

---

[1] Daddy.

"But where did they live?" I asked in astonishment.

"First in Wolsztyn and then in Karpicko, close to the German border."

"And the Empress?"

"She died earlier," he replied without flinching.

"What you are telling me is extraordinary. And the Grand Duchesses?"

"Grand Duchess Maria remained in Poland and died twenty years ago. I heard that Olga and Tatiana went to Germany, but but and I really don't know what happened to them. And of course, Grand Duchess Anastasia, you know her story.

"Yes. She was Anna Anderson!" I affirmed with conviction.

"No, no, no. Anna Anderson was a Soviet impostor. The real Anastasia was Eugenia Smith who lived in Illinois!"

I kept silent for a moment and observed him attentively.

"That, my friend, is even harder to believe. Mrs Anderson passed forensic tests with flying colours and was also recognized by different members of Europe's royal families. No impostor could do that, and this Mrs Smith, I have never even heard of her until now."

I could sense that Nikolai was not too happy that I was questioning his version of the story. He stiffened.

"Look! Mr Mundy, I have some photographs to show you," he said, as he passed me an envelope with some old black and white pictures. I looked at them with disbelief as he and his daughter stared at me in silence. There was a picture of the four Grand Duchesses, identically dressed in white bonnets, dated 1921 and supposedly taken in Poland. Here was a photo of Grand Duchess Maria in 1968, and an extraordinary photo of a younger Maria with her arms around Tsarevich Alexis and a shaved and bald Tsar in 1942. It was all just a bit too perfect and far-fetched for my taste.

"I don't see much of a resemblance to the Tsar here," I said provocatively, as I pointed to the photograph.

"He was the Tsar. I know. He was my godfather. Anyway, it doesn't matter what you think," Nikolai said, by now irritated by my incredulity. "If you don't believe me it is not our problem. I don't care," he continued bluntly.

"There was a pact of silence, Mr Mundy! That is why this is all a secret. My *tatuś* knows! He is very protective of his godfather's memory," Tatiana said, trying to excuse her father's irritation.

"I am open to any possibilities in this story, Tatiana, but please don't ask me to accept any other Anastasia than the late Mrs Manahan. There is no doubt about that. The forensic evidence is incontestable.

"I tell you, Mr Mundy, Mrs Anderson was a KGB spy. They manipulated all the evidence to sow discord. Eugenia was the Grand Duchess and Colonel Michael Goleniewski, the Tsarevich," Nikolai insisted with renewed calm, trying to convince me.

Michael Goleniewski! The name rang a bell. This man had been a Polish secret agent; he defected in the sixties, worked for the CIA and eventually moved to the United States, where he suddenly claimed to be the Tsarevich. Years ago I had discussed this case with Miles and he had confirmed that the CIA thought he had lost the plot. He also was much younger than the historical Alexis and did not suffer from haemophilia. I felt certain that the story these people were telling me was a fantasy and impossible to believe. Did they believe it themselves? I wondered. Obviously, Tatiana must have heard it as a child, and she had no reason to doubt her father. What were his motives? Why would he share this story with me, a stranger, if it was supposed to be a secret? Again, too many questions and very few answers! It was there and then that I decided to devote my free time and efforts to finding the truth, whatever it would take. I owed it to my mother, I owed it to Pepita and now I owed it to my son and myself.

# 6. LONDON, UNITED KINGDOM, MARCH 1994

I had flown from Warsaw to London to meet my friend Miles, now retired from MI6 and lived a placid life in a cottage in the charming village of Bridge in Kent with his wife and two golden retrievers. He had been very surprised at my sudden urge to see him after so many years. Though we had kept in touch with one another every Christmas since he had left Madrid, we had not seen each other. Being younger than myself, Miles looked great and was in good shape, but obviously bored in his retirement. He laughed when I recounted my trip to Warsaw and he explained that he knew for certain it was KGB policy to sow discord among the Russian monarchist movement with such stories, and that they had murdered many monarchists in exile over the years.

He also informed me that during the last two years, various newspapers in London had been publishing articles about the fate of the Romanovs and the discovery of some bones in Siberia.

"Last year," he told me, "on the tenth of July 1993, the Forensic Science Service in London announced the DNA results of the bones unearthed from a mass grave in Ekaterinburg in 1991."

"What else?" I asked, seeing that my old associate had the precise information I happened to require.

"One of our scientists, Dr Peter Gill, and Dr Pavel Ivanov of Russia announced that they had identified all the bodies. They said they were 98.5 per cent certain they were the Romanovs. But after eight months people are still talking and the controversy is growing. Apparently the Russian government insisted they were those of the last Imperial family. Others are not so sure, including the Orthodox Church inside Russia. Another team, lead by Professor William Maples, is working in the United States, trying to get DNA from some bones and teeth of the alleged Romanovs to find out the truth. Professor Maples believes that the bones of Anastasia were not found in that grave."

"Miles, I have not been following this case, so I know little about all these stories," I said to my friend. "Can you help me get more information and let me know whatever you think is relevant?

"Deal," said Miles, with his characteristic smile. He probably missed the action of working in the field for the firm.

So, after a couple of glasses of sherry, he also promised that he would contact some former KGB friends and ask what they knew about the whole issue. I took the train back to London and from there straight to Gatwick Airport to return to Madrid. I was amused at how much the game had changed since I had been a player.

# 7. MADRID, SPAIN, MARCH 1994

"Beautiful girl!" exclaimed Carlos, looking at the Polaroids of Tatiana. "When is she coming, Papa?"

"Next week! She really is lovely. Do you think you can get her booked for the shows?" I asked, trying to get her a quick booking to help pay the travel expenses we'd advanced for her.

"Too late, but don't worry, she will work because she is gorgeous and has a great body. Pity she's not younger, as she has star potential!" Carlos added.

"And you won't believe this. She was given her name in honour of the Grand Duchess Tatiana, as her dad claims to be the Tsar's godson. He is called Nicholas. All rather peculiar."

"What?" Carlos was startled.

"According to their story the Tsar lived and died in Poland! I even saw photographs. It's clearly a lie or he has been deceived, because they said someone called Eugenia Smith was the real Anastasia."

"Oh I see, that was a real impostor," Carlos said. "That woman appeared in the United States during the sixties claiming to be Grand Duchess Anastasia, but she didn't look like the real one and kept changing her story. Apparently she was a eccentric Polish Countess.

I read somewhere that her real name was Eugenia Drabek Smetisko, according to her naturalization papers. So how am I going to handle this Tatiana? If she knows we don't believe what she says…"

"I wouldn't worry too much," I answered. "I'd say she is only interested in working and making money."

"I hope so, Papa, because we are investing a lot of money and training on her. She needs to be focused on her career."

"I have a confession to make, Carlos: I am so intrigued by this affair now that I'm going to look into it more thoroughly. After all, I was a pretty good spy in my day! I'd like to organize some more model scouting trips with your permission. One never knows what one might find. I think my first stop is going to be the Black Forest," I said teasingly.

"Great. Please! That is just so cool! I don't think you will find many model agencies there though!" he exclaimed, as he laughed and embraced me, clearly excited at the turn of events.

## 8. BAD LIEBENZELL, GERMANY, LATE MARCH 1994

I took the Lufthansa morning flight to Stuttgart and from there I drove down the autobahn to Bad Liebenzell. I had booked a room at the Hotel Liebenzeller Adler, only a few miles from Unterlengenhardt, where Anna Anderson had lived from 1946 to 1968. I decided that this should be the starting point of my investigation, where surely I might be able to meet some people who had known her and could share some memories of her with me.

I had spent a few days prior to the trip devouring *The File on the Tsar* as well as *Anastasia: The Riddle of Anna Anderson* by Peter Kurth and *Anastasia: The Lost Princess* by James Blair Lovell. Since my return from Warsaw, Anastasia had been ever-present in my life, much to the annoyance of my wife, who could not comprehend my newfound obsession. I was suddenly taken by the plight of this poor, unfortunate lady, as I suppose my mother and Pepita had been before me. So, without realizing it, and to Rosa's annoyance, it was all I spoke about, even during our hands of bridge.

It was bitterly cold and there were signs of recent snowing. Bad Liebenzell with its original red-roof houses was about 25 miles from Stuttgart airport, so forty-five minutes later I was standing in front of a beaming Frau Schmidt, a friendly matron in her seventies who owned the hotel and spoke very little English. I settled into my cosy room and immediately afterwards left the hotel to explore the area. Frau Schmidt explained how to get to the house that had belonged to Her Imperial Highness. I just had to drive up towards the mountains, following the signs on the road.

The village of Unterlengenhardt is on the western edge of the Black Forest, a wooded mountain range bordered by the Rhine Valley. It is a charming romantic little place out of a Grimm brothers' tale, consisting practically of only one main street. Its most famous resident, along with Anna Anderson, had been Rudolf Steiner, the Christian visionary who founded the spiritual movement known as Anthroposophy. It felt as if the clock of history had stopped right there, and I was immediately charmed. There were very few people out, probably due to the cold, so

I parked my car and walked into a small coffee shop to ask for directions to the wooden house where Grand Duchess Anastasia had lived for twenty years of her sad life. A log fire was burning in a rustic fireplace and I could hear the hushed voices of about five elderly people sitting around a couple of tables. As I walked in, everyone stopped talking and turned round to look at me. The owner, a stocky man in his late fifties, greeted me warmly.

"*Guten Abend!*"

"Good evening. May I have a beer, *bitte*?"

"Certainly! You are English?" He asked, as he served me.

"Yes. Could you please tell me how to get to the house that used to belong to Anna Anderson?"

"Yes of course. It was sold to a family whose last name is Prömm, after she left for America in 1968. They are very nice and welcome researchers interested in the story, but they don't like to receive tourists in search of Anastasia relics."

"I understand. I would just like to look at it from the outside."

"Oh, Herr…"

"Sorry. Herr Mundy."

"Herr Mundy, the house has been restored and bears very little resemblance to the one the Grand Duchess lived in," he explained, as I noticed a younger man listening to our conversation get up and walk towards us.

"May I introduce myself?" he asked in a heavy German accent, without giving me time to reply. "My name is Fritz Fleischer. I just heard you speaking about Anna Anderson. Are you a journalist or an investigator, Herr Mundy?"

"Neither. Just an amateur historian," I lied.

"Would you like me to take you there?" He offered. "I know the Prömms and they might just invite you in."

I paid for the beer and followed my guide out of the coffee shop. We walked towards the house that had been for years the home of Her Imperial Highness Grand Duchess Anastasia. I felt a twinge of excitement run through me.

"Do you know anyone who knew the Grand Duchess well, or Prince Frederick Ernst of Saxe-Altenburg?" I asked nonchalantly.

"Frau Prömm never met the Grand Duchess but she was acquainted with Prince Frederick Ernst, Herr Mundy, and there might be some other people still alive. I did see her a few times when I was a teenager. In those days she was a tourist attraction and many people came to town just to catch a glimpse of her. I remember she had some big dogs and too many cats. The place was a sad mess in the end. She became a very eccentric woman!"

"You must all be tired of this affair I imagine, with so many of us coming and poking around?"

"Well, we all feel a deep respect and love for her. We like to refer to her as Anastasia, her real name. When she lived here it was madness. Busloads of tourists often came and pestered everyone with questions and stood in front of the poor woman's home for hours trying to take a photo. I remember my mother saying that the poor lady was terrified of those unwanted visitors who were mostly so terribly rude, and showed no respect for her privacy," Fritz replied.

"That, I imagine, was after the release of the film with Ingrid Bergman!" I said.

"I would not be able to say, Herr Mundy, as I was very young then, but I can tell you that the people of this town were not happy with that state of things and were very protective of the lady, as we are now of her memory."

"May I ask you where you would suggest I have lunch tomorrow?"

"I strongly recommend the Schwarzivaldhof," Fritz said.

As we arrived at the property, I could see the house from the pavement. Comparing it to old photographs, it looked completely different to the dilapidated house that had become Anastasia's headquarters before she left. Fritz opened the small metal gate into the front yard, walked to the front door and rang the bell. There was no answer and he tried again.

"Frau Prömm must have gone out. I'll call her later and maybe you can meet her tomorrow. Where are you staying, Herr Mundy?" He asked.

I felt quite disappointed. "At the Adler. Down in Bad Liebenzell," I replied.

"Very well. I will get in touch with you as soon as I have some news."

✦ ✦ ✦

The following morning, after a good night's sleep, I decided to return to the village, walk around and ask the locals if they remembered Anna Anderson. I felt quite frustrated, as most of the people I spoke to did not speak English or they were just not interested in talking. It seemed as if the memory of their famous resident had almost vanished – or maybe they were just protective.

I had lunch at the only restaurant in town, following Fritz's recommendation. The Schwarzivaldhof was a charming little place that served delicious German staples.

A red-cheeked, young and plump woman took my order, which included half a bottle of chilled Riesling. She seemed to speak fairly good English. As she uncorked the bottle I asked, "Would you know anyone who was close to Anna Anderson, or should I say, Grand Duchess Anastasia?"

She looked at me without answering, poured some wine into my glass and waited for me to taste it.

"Good!" I said.

She half filled my glass.

"Yes, I do. My grandmother was quite close to her. She was admitted to the house regularly. She always speaks with fondness about those days."

I could not believe my luck.

"Would it be possible for me to meet her?" I asked eagerly.

"Perhaps. She is ninety-two years old, in good health and has a clear head. I will ask her this afternoon. Maybe you can come over for tea. The company would do her good," she offered.

"Thank you. That is very kind. What is your name?" I asked as I handed her the hotel's phone number.

"My name is Astrid."

As I was leaving the restaurant, I saw that Fritz Fleischer was outside. He saw me, but pretended not to. He knew I would be here for lunch, but his behaviour seemed odd. Why did he not come up to me and tell me if we were going to meet Frau Prömm? Somehow it felt like he was keeping an eye on me and I didn't like that. Was it just the old professional habit of not trusting anyone? I drove back to the hotel to wait for the invitation to tea.

✦ ✦ ✦

Astrid lived in a gingerbread-style little house not far from the restaurant with her mother and grandmother. She kindly came to pick me up at the hotel and drove me to her fairytale home.

A small and fragile elderly lady welcomed me. She had a sparkle in her eyes and youthful charm that made her seem younger than her age. We looked into each other's eyes and without exchanging a word liked each other immediately.

"Please sit, Herr Mundy," she invited me in the friendliest of manners. "My granddaughter tells me you are interested in speaking about Grand Duchess Anastasia?"

Astrid came into the room with a tea tray and some biscuits and did the honours.

"These were baked by Grandma!" She said.

"So Astrid tells me you knew her well, Frau....?"

"My name is Frau Rosenthal, Herr Mundy, but please call me Augusta."

"Lovely name! Call me Rodney, then."

"It was our late Empress' name," she said with pride, pointing at an aged picture on the wall of Empress Augusta, first wife of Kaiser Wilhelm II.

I took a biscuit and waited for her to gather her memories.

"Yes, I knew Her Imperial Highness. We were a small group of ladies that helped her settle in when she first arrived here. I was and still am an Anthroposophist. Most of us were: Frau Heydebrandt, her sister Frau Mutius, Frau Thomasius, Frau Mayhoff and of course darling Baroness Monica von Miltitz. Anastasia left for America without saying goodbye to any of us. We were upset then, but in hindsight I understood her reasons," she said, lost in memory.

"What was Anastasia like?"

"She was charming, she was aloof, she was demanding, she was loving. She had suffered a lot and was a very fragile being. Very difficult and uncooperative, but we loved her. We did things for her, wrote her letters and helped with the cleaning and cooking; we tried to make her daily life easier. Two world wars combined with all the tragedy of her family was too much for a human being. We felt sad for all she had gone through. I think she was also heartbroken."

"Why?" I asked.

"As if what she had endured had not been enough, she also longed for her lost love." Augusta whispered.

"Had she been in love?" I asked, surprised at the unexpected revelation.

"Prince Heinrich XLV of Reuss was the only man she loved, but no one ever talked about him. Some of her German royal friends and relatives had made secret arrangements during the late thirties to marry them, so she could be protected, well cared for, and get a legal name and title. She told us that her cousin Princess Feodora of Saxe-Meiningen, had planned the wedding, together with Empress Hermine, the second wife of Kaiser Wilhelm II, from their exile in Holland. Prince Frederick agreed. They were excited about the idea, but then the war started in 1939 and the prince went to fight. At the end of the conflict Prince Heinrich disappeared or was held prisoner. Nobody knew for sure. I heard the Soviets murdered him." She sighed, and I didn't dare to interrupt her.

"Oh, what a sad story!" I said suddenly, as Frau Rosenthal's eyes filled with tears. "I never heard that." Then, trying to switch the conversation to something less dramatic, I asked her:

"Tell me, Augusta. Where you here when Anna Anderson first arrived in Unterlengenhardt?

"Sure I was. I remember everything like it happened yesterday. It was Prince Frederick Ernst who brought her here. It was strange! How childlike this already forty-five-year-old woman appeared! And laden with such a fate! At that time she was very ill. Under the scarf she wore to cover her bald head you could see an extremely pale, delicate face witha pronounced forehead, on which there was the suggestion of strong will, even obstinacy. Her nose gave the expression of a strong personality. And she always strove to hide her toothless mouth with her hand or handkerchief, understandably so! But what stood out most about her face were the eyes! They were of such a power, intensity, and clarity, like two mountain lakes reflecting a deep blue sky. There was something in them of purity and directness, and a depth of experience."

Listening to Augusta I felt like I was flying back in time. I was absolutely delighted with her memories.

"And you know, Herr Mundy, how evil people can be. And this woman, who was particularly incapable of any pretence, people labelled as a swindler! What insanity! After the war the country was devastated and things were extremely difficult for all of us. In those days, there was nothing to buy; one could only trade for things. Any project was a costly and arduous undertaking in 1946 to '47 when she arrived here. The Prince managed to buy an old barracks and we all helped to make it habitable. There were almost no building materials. The craftsmen were also difficult to find and wanted to be paid handsomely for their labour. Much of it we did ourselves, like painting the walls, installing windows and doors, the picket fence and the small building, the garden gate, etc. At the end, with a few inspired strokes, a young painter friend sketched the three Holy kings, or wise men. Their picture decorated the interior of the front door, while above it Prince Frederick Ernst festively painted the three holy runes: K+M+B, which were supposed to keep all evil away from the threshold. To furnish the interior of the house, everyone brought as much as possible in the way of used furniture, beds, curtains, and whatever else one needs.

The housewarming and the move into the "Three Kings Hut" became a big party. The street at the village entrance was blocked off by a children's round dance and the new tenants were greeted with flowers and a folksong. Herr Keck – a flower in his buttonhole – handed over the house and courtyard keys to the Prince. And as Anastasia stepped into the living room, the armoire opened and the dwarf-king Laurin appeared in order to give a heartfelt welcome to the queen of the household and scatter roses on her new life's work."

Augusta became pensive.

"So many cheerful memories," she said with a big smile. "Dr Marquart, her close friend, had found a big, homey floor lamp as well as the heat stove for the common room, and the pots and dishes for the small kitchen. The Grand Duchess handled these things her dear friends gave her with such caution and gratitude!"

I interrupted her just to let her know that yesterday I had visited the house where Anastasia lived years later, and hoped to have the chance to go again and speak with the new owners.

"Oh yes," Augusta recalled. "The barrack was too old and cold, so in the late fifties Prince Frederick Ernst again raised the money to build the new one, larger and more comfortable, but still humble."

"But Augusta, please explain me how you were all so certain that she was who she said she was?" I was thrilled, as Augusta's mind was sharp and her memories clear. She was so happy to speak to me of days long gone.

"We never had any doubt. Her mannerisms, education and bearing were so distinctive, so regal, that we could have no doubt she was who she said she was. Her voice was soft but commanding. She could be strong and delicate. Her hands were beautiful and always wore gloves when going out, even to sit at the garden table. And she was not acting, she was always herself; even when she was very ill, on the verge of death, you could see that she was uncommon, a gracious and special creature. The extraordinary thing is that she was never too interested in proving who she was. She just knew, and she behaved most naturally. She was at ease, as only a Grand Duchess would be. It was we, led by Prince Frederick Ernst of Saxe-Altenburg, who wanted the world to know who she really was. We felt it was so unjust that her closest relatives denied her true identity. It was a monstrous thing to do to her. I think being robbed of one's identity and forced to be someone else is more frightening than death. It's the ultimate torture!"

"I have to agree," I responded, pondering her words.

"Prince Frederick Ernst told me how well he remembered an incident that happened while his family was at Hemmelmark for his sister Charlotte's wedding in 1919. He said that a former German prisoner-of-war, who had been able to escape from Russia, showed up and informed the family that Grand Duchess Anastasia had survived and was living in Romania. The Prince was very young at that time, but he remembered that there was a lot of talk about Anastasia and the senior members of the family managed the situation. So you see, all the pieces of the puzzle fit together. And then, of course, another sign was that some other, more compassionate relatives sent many precious gifts to her house: paintings, family photographs, silver plates and furniture. She even had a bed that had belonged to her great grandmother, Queen Victoria! They would not have been so generous with an impostor, would they?"

"Definitely not. I must agree with that too. Did they visit her here?" I asked, fascinated.

"They did, and she was also invited to their homes. Some came here openly, others came covertly in luxurious cars with dark curtains, but all were very kind and generous. So you see, she had to be the Grand Duchess, or they would not have treated her in such a caring way."

"Maybe some relatives had their doubts and wanted to see her just to reassure themselves and their consciences," I reflected.

"Maybe! But there were some who were extremely supportive and came very often, like the Grand Duke and Grand Duchess of Saxe-Weimar-Eisenach, as well as Baron and Baroness von Gienanth, or Princess Margaretha with Miss Minzenmay. Their visits were also always like holidays.

But the greatest such holiday was the one on which Crown Princess Cecilie arrived. I remember that Princess Margaret brought her unannounced, and that day the house was a mess. I was helping with the cleaning and we had clothing boiling on the stove. Oh, it was such a surprise!" she said with a broad smile.

"Our Crown Princess came several times after that day and immediately gave her support. That, for me, was all the evidence I needed. Crown Princess Cecilie was a wonderful, warm-hearted woman! Very motherly, as Anastasia used to say. I wish we had a Kaiser again," she sighed nostalgically.

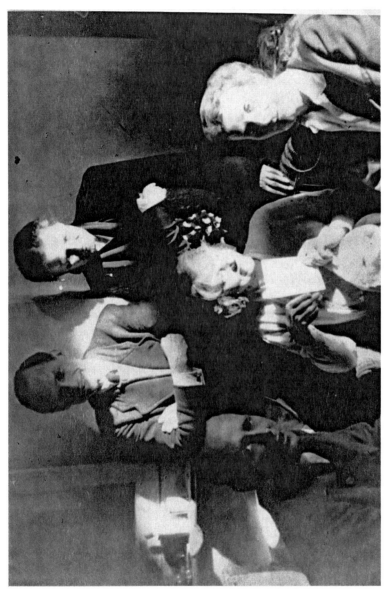

Anastasia surrounded by a group of friends: Hereditary Grand Duke Charles Augustus of Saxe Weimar-Eisenach, Grand Duchess Elisabeth of Saxe Weimar-Eisenach, who gave her the Romanov icon in 1946. Behind are Prince Frederick Ernst of Saxe Altenburg and Baroness Monica von Miltitz, around 1949–1950 (Anastasia's archives, Germany).

"How was their first meeting?" I inquired, fascinated.

"It was September of 1951; Princess Margaretha came inside the barracks unexpectedly and took Anastasia outside, and we followed them. She put her in front of this other visitor, a beautiful and elegant lady in her mid sixties, but Anastasia didn't recognize her at first glance. Then the woman with soft manners and a delicate voice told her: 'Darling, only look at me, I am your dear aunt, Cecilie!' Anastasia became pale, shaking, because the guest was out of place in the surroundings, but with great appreciation invited her inside the modest house. I remember the Crown Princess saying that her beautiful blue eyes were in colour, shape and expression exactly like those of the Tsar!"

"Grandma, are you tired?" Astrid interrupted her lovingly.

"Yes darling, I think I am. I'm very happy to have the opportunity to speak to you, Rodney, but I probably have said enough."

"May I come back at another time please?" I said, realizing that my luck for the day had finished.

"I am sorry, Herr Mundy, but I don't think it's a good idea. And now if you please, Astrid will escort you to the door," she said with a sudden and unexpected coldness.

As I left the house, I walked down the street, having no car to get back to my hotel. I could not stop wondering what had made Augusta's attitude towards me change so suddenly. And then I noticed him again. It was Fritz tracking my footsteps. The situation was nearly comic. There I was in the smallest of towns with barely one street, being followed by someone who was supposed to be calling me at the hotel. It was impossible for me not to notice him with so few people around, so I just went straight to him.

"Good afternoon, Fritz!"

The poor chap was startled. "I saw you walk in to visit Frau Rosenthal and I was just waiting for you to come out," He mumbled clumsily. "I have good news. Frau Prömm will be happy to meet you tomorrow for breakfast. May I drive you to the Adler?" he offered.

✦ ✦ ✦

The next day at half past eight in the morning, Fritz was waiting outside the hotel to drive me to visit the house where Anastasia had once lived and meet the current owner. I hoped she would remember some anecdotes from her encounters with Prince Frederick Ernst.

Twenty minutes later we were sitting in the living room of Frau Adrianne Prömm's cosy home. She was a delightful lady in her late seventies, full of energy and willing to explore new things around her. She invited us to move to the dining area and served us some hot coffee, dark German bread with honey, a delicious cheese and homemade strudel. She joined us at the table to start the conversation.

"That table is the only thing in the house that belonged to Anastasia." She pointed at a round wooden table in the middle of the living room. "The house was a ruin when we purchased it in 1970, so it has very little resemblance to the original, but I do love living here. It's the house where the youngest daughter of the last Tsar once lived." She spoke in English with a heavy German accent, and she beamed with satisfaction.

"So, Fritz tells me you are an amateur historian. Are you studying Anastasia's case?" she asked.

"I am in Stuttgart for business and as I was close, I decided to come here for a couple of days. Anastasia's story is definitely fascinating. Fritz tells me you met Prince Frederick Ernst of Saxe-Altenburg. Do you remember anything of your chats that would be worth mentioning?" I asked.

"Actually I first met Luise Mayhoff, the lady took care of Anastasia after Adele von Heydebrandt died. As you probably know, the poor sick woman left in a rush to America, taking very few things with her. I was told she was terribly angry with Prince Frederick Ernst and Baroness von Miltitz. They hoped that she would soon forgive them and come back to Unterlengenhardt, so they didn't want to rent or sell the house; but after six months, when they heard that she had married an American, they started planning what to do with the house and its contents. Frau Mayhoff told me it took several months to pack and clean everything, and prepare the house for sale."

"But why was she angry with them? They had always been her most loyal supporters," I enquired.

"The house was overrun with cats and dogs that were a health hazard for the village. Frau Mayhoff told me that in August 1967 Anastasia took a trip to Paris with Prince Frederick Ernst, Ian Lilburn and Countess Elizabeth von Oppersdorf. They were supposed to visit with Mathilde Kschessinska, a ballerina and former mistress of the Tsar who married Grand Duke Andrei Vladimirovich of Russia. Mathilde was ninety-five years old and wanted to tell Anastasia that she and her husband never stopped believing in her authenticity. Dominique Auclères, a journalist who had written many articles and even a book about her, met them in Paris and took Anastasia to restaurants, nice boutiques, even to the Eiffel Tower. They said that she had a wonderful time there, but when she came back from France she was disappointed – the meeting with the ballerina couldn't take place, as her son Vova had forbidden it. She also found out that most of the cats and dogs had been put down by some of the farmers and became very angry with everyone here. Then Prince Frederick Ernst told her that the mayor of Unterlengenhardt and the district board of health were ordering him to clean the premises. Anastasia became furious and threatened him by saying the she would move to America."

"Interesting," I said. "So, she was planning that trip in advance?"

"I was told by Frau Mayhoff that none of them really believed her. Then her relationship with the Prince and poor Baroness Miltitz went from bad to worse. At that time Anastasia was only on good terms with a Russian named Alexis Miliukoff, who used to visit her and record all their conversations. She seemed to have a strong temper!"

"Quite some temper!" I interrupted. "It was nice that Luise Mayhoff told you so much about her."

"Certainly, Luise knew many things. She told me that because Anastasia was angry with everybody, she did not go out to the garden anymore. For the one hundredth anniversary of her father Nicholas II, in May 1968, all her friends wanted to cheer her up and organized a small party outside. She only looked through the window. Then she said that she didn't need anybody's help, and for several weeks didn't let any of the ladies into the house. Luise Mayhoff also told me that one day she forced the entry gate, tore the front door down and found the Grand Duchess very ill, almost unconscious. Anastasia had to be rushed to a hospital, where she stayed for several weeks, and from there she fled to America with the help of Alexis Miliukoff. She gave him the keys to her house and told him what to pack. He did it quietly and then they left. That took everyone by surprise!"

"I'm sorry to ask so many questions. Everything you tell me is so fascinating. Do you know what happened to all the things she left behind?" I asked.

"Yes, Frau Mayhoff kept some of Anastasia's possessions, others were taken by the Prince, and Ian Lilburn took some boxes to London. I remember a conversation about one box that she forgot with documents and letters that were very important and had to be preserved. Luise Mayhoff maintained contact with the Prince, even after we bought the house. He continued coming to visit his old friends in Unterlegenhardt and did some archaeological excavations in the area. One day he confessed to me that Anastasia had not spoken to him for several years. That made him very sad, because he loved her like a sister. I was very happy when he told us about their reconciliation in 1977!"

"Is there anything else you remember, Frau Prömm?"

"Not really," she answered. "I just know what I was told. I am sorry not to be of much help."

"When was the last time you saw the Prince?"

"Ahh, he came with Jack Manahan, the Grand Duchess' husband, after her death. He brought the urn with her ashes and we spent that night here in this living room, sipping tea as they recounted anecdotes from times long gone. Mr Manahan cried most of the time at the emotion of being in this house. He said that she always wanted to come back to Unterlengenhardt, because here she was very happy and loved. It was all rather touching. The next day they took the ashes to be buried in Castle Seeon!"

"Do you know Frau Rosenthal well?"

"Yes of course. This is a very small village and we all know each other very well," she replied. "Why?"

"I went to see her yesterday and she was so chatty and open. She spoke about the past, shared her memories with me, and then suddenly she just became aloof and asked me to leave the house. It seemed to me like she suddenly realized she was saying too much and was frightened. But frightened of what?"

"Herr Mundy, Frau Rosenthal is an old lady and she is paranoid about the Bolsheviks, spies, double agents and things like that. When my husband Otto and I came to live here in 1970, many strange people used to visit the town and ask questions about Anastasia. We thought they were probably soviet spies. They were so easy to spot that they became a joke, and we all knew they were definitely looking for something that probably had belonged to Anastasia, which she had not taken with her. Of course we made sure they left empty-handed, and finally they ceased to come. If you want, I will speak to Augusta and ask her to invite you to tea this afternoon. I am sure I will be able to convince her."

"I am ever so grateful," I responded.

◆ ◆ ◆

I chatted with Frau Prömm and Fritz for a couple more hours, and then invited Fritz for lunch at the Schwarzivaldhof. It was past noon. Astrid saw us come in.

"I'm sorry about Grandma, Herr Mundy," she apologized.

"It's fine, Astrid. She has invited me for tea this afternoon."

"Oh, I'm so glad for you. Riesling?" she asked, smiling.

While we drank a glass of the delicious chilled wine, I started making polite conversation with Fritz with the aim of discovering more about this odd character.

"I really appreciate you introducing me to Adrianne Prömm. She is a charming lady."

"A pleasure, Herr Mundy."

"Please, call me Rodney."

"Very well, Rodney, why are you so interested in Anastasia? Your interest seems to go well beyond that of an amateur historian," he asked.

During the meal I told him about my mother's distress over the fate of Frau Anderson and how my late wife and son were fascinated by the case. He listened to my story in silence, and I felt him observing all my expressions and listening to my words with utmost interest.

"So your family has lived here for years?" I asked.

"For generations, Rodney."

"And what do you do for a living?"

"I am an artist. If you have time I would be happy to invite you to my studio and show you my work."

"That would be a pleasure but I am returning to Stuttgart tomorrow. Maybe next time."

I tried my best to get him to confide in me, to give me some hints as to his motives so I could unmask him, but he was being cautious and kept the conversation strictly to mundane matters. Maybe he was just a local artist, as he claimed to be, but if he was something else or was working for an organization, he seemed to be quite well trained.

✦ ✦ ✦

At five o'clock, after having visited with Fritz the site Prince Frederick Ernst had excavated in the seventies, I rang Augusta Rosenthal's doorbell. Astrid opened the door.

"Grandma is waiting for you, Herr Mundy."

I walked into the living room where the gracious lady was sitting down. She smiled and raised her hand to be kissed. "Welcome, Rodney," she said in the friendliest of tones. "So where were we, when you suddenly had to leave yesterday?" she asked impishly, and laughed.

"You were telling me that Crown Princess Cecilie had no doubt about the real identity of Anna Anderson."

"That is absolutely true," she said, recalling where we had left our conversation the previous afternoon.

Astrid left the room and Augusta continued talking.

"Do you remember any other visitors?" I dared ask.

"A Romanov prince named Alexander also came to visit her, in 1964. He was the grandson of her aunt, Grand Duchess Xenia Alexandrovna. There is a picture of him with Princess Margaretha outside Anastasia's house, in the garden."

"I find it very interesting that members of her close family travelled here to see her. That must have made her very happy, I guess," I said.

"Absolutely," she agreed. "I was amazed over and over again at how many people found space in the cottage. The Grand Duchess felt truly in her element when a circle of dear friends was around her. How her personality sparkled! And with what bewitching charm she could always be the center of the conversation – and how totally natural!" Augusta expressed, emphasizing with her hands to be more convincing. "But they always came quietly. When Princess Margaret brought Crown Princess Cecilie, she wanted to keep the visit a secret, but somehow one of Anastasia's lawyers found out and told the press. That made her very angry and she complained a lot. Some time later, Crown Princess Cecilie wanted her daughter-in-law Kira Kirilovna to meet Anastasia, and they indeed met but they disliked each other immediately. Anastasia said that Kira was conceited and arrogant, very different to the lovely Crown Princess. I remember very well."

"So," I asked, "the aristocratic and royal persons who came to visit wanted to remain incognito?"

"Yes. In those days all the members of her family that visited her were under tremendous pressure from all the attention that the media was giving to her court cases, and some were closely related to those who maintained adamantly that she was a fraud. They were villains. How could they treat her in such a shameful way?" Augusta was clearly upset at the thought. "In 1957 two very important people came to visit her. One was Frau Lili Dehn, a former lady-in-waiting of her mother the Tsarina. She came with Prince Frederick Ernst who had located her in Venezuela, where she was living."

"And she recognized Frau Anderson as the legitimate Anastasia?" I questioned.

"Oh yes, entirely. Frau Dehn spent six days here. They talked about

Anna Anderson (later Anastasia Manahan) in 1952, around the time she met with Crown Princess Cecilie and her daughter-in-law Kira Kirilovna Romanova (Anastasia archive, Germany).

people and situations that only both of them knew. They laughed and cried looking at pictures, and the Grand Duchess said that Lili Dehn reminded her of her own mother, the Tsarina, in her bearing, elegance and manners.

"The other visitor was her cousin Prince Sigismund of Prussia. He was a member of our Imperial family. It was in the spring, and he arrived with Baron and Baroness Gienanth in a big Mercedes Benz! I clearly recall that year because I was pregnant with Astrid's mother. They had not seen each other since 1912 but they had been very close then. You see, the Tsarina and the Prince's mother were sisters. Her Imperial Highness mentioned to me that her mother and her aunt Irene were very close because they both had haemophiliac sons."

"That make sense," I said.

"Grand Duchess Anastasia also told me that her sister, Olga, and Prince Sigismund had fallen in love in 1910, when they spent a summer holiday together. The Tsarina discovered the affair and didn't approve of it, because they were still very young and they were first cousins. Anastasia said that the two young lovers would take walks together and often she had to go with them, accompanied by a chaperone who was also an accomplice."

Augusta paused, lost in thought, and then she gave me her hand, as she looked into my eyes smiling warmly.

"Prince Sigismund stayed for several days and talked with her for hours. He brought from Costa Rica, where he was living, many old pictures of family reunions. They talked about their relatives and she enjoyed recounting stories and episodes shared by both. They seemed to be very happy in each other's company. Another Princess of one of our royal houses was with them but I can't seem to remember her name. They sat in the garden, went out for walks and enjoyed being together. It was a true family reunion."

"Well I guess they had a lot to talk about," I said, trying to make her remember more things.

"I also remember that the following year, Prince Sigismund's charming wife, Charlotte Agnes, came to visit us. She was Prince Frederick Ernst's sister."

"Augusta, I have just been in Costa Rica where Prince Sigismund and his wife lived! I tried to meet their son, Prince Alfred, but he was out of the country."

"They were lovely people and always supported the cause of the Grand Duchess, which was the source of constant quarrels with many members

Grand Duchesses Olga and Anastasia with Prince Sigismund of Prussia, and accompanied by Anna Vyrubova, in 1910 (Romanov Collection, Beinecke Rare Book and Manuscript Library, Yale University).

of their family, even his mother, Princess Irene, and their own daughter. They had no doubt that Frau Anderson was Grand Duchess Anastasia because in 1932 Prince Sigismund had sent Her Imperial Highness a questionnaire with fourteen very personal questions that only she could have answered, and she answered all of them correctly. They wrote to each other frequently – I personally filed his letters."

"Yes, I read about that and I know that their support for Anna Anderson made their lives quite difficult."

"When Prince Sigismund left from here, I overheard him say that he was going to Italy to meet Grand Duchess Olga, who had also survived. I clearly remember the conversation and Anastasia's excitement at the possibility that one of her sisters was still alive. It was all to be a secret. Of course, I never told anyone until today."

"It would be fascinating to know if Olga indeed survived, and why she remained hidden," I said, clearly intrigued by that last revelation. Then Augusta had an even bigger surprise for me.

"I have a box that Prince Frederick Ernst gave me for safe keeping in 1968, which I have never shown to anyone. He said that one day someone would come to pick it up, but I've had it now for twenty-six years. Some Russians came poking around when the Grand Duchess left to America, and also when she died ten years ago. I refused to meet or talk to them. They were communists, and I know what they were looking for," she confided. "But you are different," she added.

"And you think they were looking for that box?"

"Not exactly. In fact, I think that they were looking for a precious icon, a historical relic that belonged to the Romanovs."

"Really?" I asked doubtfully.

"It was given as a lifetime loan to Grand Duchess Anastasia by Grand Duchess Elizabeth of Saxe-Weimar-Eisenach in 1946, when she became the godmother of her son, Prince Michael Benedict, together with Queen Juliana of the Netherlands. It was to be returned to the Saxe-Weimar-Eisenachs after Anastasia's death," she said, lowering her voice as if someone might be able to hear us.

"Well, if true, that in itself is proof enough of who she was. The miracle many people had been waiting for! The Dutch queen would have never agreed to share such an honour with an impersonator. And the Saxe-Weimar-Eisenachs would never ask a swindler to be godmother of their heir. I find absolutely impossible to believe that they would give something that significant, an heirloom, to an impostor. To me, this is powerful evidence in her favour. Did you see the icon?" I asked.

"Sure! It was beautiful, a small and elaborate painting on metal, with a silver-gilded frame. Grand Duchess Elisabeth of Saxe-Weimar-Eisenach is still alive. Maybe you should go and talk to her. Anastasia told me that the icon had belonged to Grand Duchess Maria Pavlovna of Russia, daughter of Tsar Paul I. She married Charles Frederick, Grand Duke of Saxe-Weimar-Eisenach in 1804, and moved to Germany."

"What a romantic and powerful story!" I exclaimed.

"Rodney, that icon meant a lot to Anastasia. She always believed that the holy relic protected her during her escape from the Soviet-occupied zone in December of 1946, and kept it beside her bed when she lived here. It was also very precious to her, as it had been with the Imperial family for many generations, and she used to pray to it every day," Augusta explained.

"How fascinating!" I said, encouraging her to go on.

"I think the Communists wanted it because it was very valuable."

"Those greedy bastards!" I exclaimed, making her laugh out loud.

"Maybe it is not just the money they were after," Augusta whispered, staring at me with a strange look in her tiny eyes.

"Ah!" I said, confused. "So why did they want the icon?" I asked.

"It hides a secret, some secret!" Augusta answered dramatically.

"A secret! What secret?"

"I really don't know, Rodney, but I heard Anastasia confide in Prince Frederick Ernst that she had hidden a document in it, something that was supposed to be revealed to the world only after her death."

"But surely those Russian spies couldn't have known that," I said, trying to reassure her. "The Soviets believed that all the property belonging to the Imperial Family belonged to the Russian people and that is surely the reason they wanted it back."

"When the Grand Duchess left for America, she took it with her," she said. "It was so important to her that she would never abandon it. After she died some people came here asking questions. No one in the village said a word. They wanted to meet Frau Mayhoff and me, as we were the only living persons that had been close to her. But we refused. We did not see them. Those wretched horrible communist murderers!"

"Good for you, my dear." I was amazed at her resolve and strength and just imagined the pressure she must have been put through. "You surely have an amazing memory!" I exclaimed as Astrid entered the room with freshly brewed tea.

"Thank you *liebe*!" she said as she smiled to her granddaughter.

"Do you have any idea where the icon might be now?"

"Who knows where it is…" She sighed deeply.

"Maybe it was returned to Grand Duchess Elisabeth," I speculated, trying to reassure her.

"No, it was not. When Anastasia died, Prince Frederick Ernst was very distressed. He remembered the promise and called a close friend of her in Charlottesville, who was a neighbour and knew about the icon. He also told Mr Manahan that he had to bring the icon with her ashes back to Germany. Apparently, when they went to get the relic it was already gone. The icon had disappeared, probably stolen."

"How could that be possible?" I exclaimed.

"Nobody knows. It is a tragedy; Prince Frederick Ernst was shocked when he found out. It makes me so sad, because Grand Duchess Anastasia was so honourable that she always wanted to keep the promise of returning the icon to its owners."

"Indeed it is a big tragedy! I'll have to look into that!" I said. "We don't want that historical treasure falling into the wrong hands. Especially if it is true that it carries a secret."

"It's probably too late, Rodney!" she said sadly. "I suppose the KGB was behind the theft."

Augusta sipped her tea. For a few seconds she seemed to be lost in her thoughts. Then she breathed deeply and facing to the kitchen's door she said, "*Liebling*[3] please bring the box I have under my bed."

"Yes, Grandma," Astrid replied obediently.

"This box was mistakenly left behind when the Grand Duchess left in haste for America. I told Prince Frederick Ernst many times and he said he would collect it and take it to her someday, but he never did, so I have kept it safely all these years," Augusta explained.

We finished our tea as Astrid entered the room with an old, large wooden box. Was it the box that Frau Prömm had talked about with Prince Frederick? I had to assume it was. What a stroke of luck!

"So let's see what the Grand Duchess left behind. I have never looked inside the box," she said excitedly. "Please Rodney, do the honours and open it."

I stood up and got on my knees, close to Augusta's feet, where Astrid had deposited the box. She was standing beside me, looking in nervous anticipation at her grandmother as I opened the brass locks: two in the front and two on either side, and then I opened the lid like a trunk. The first thing I took out of the wooden box was an object wrapped in a colourful embroidered cloth.

"Oh my God!" Augusta exclaimed, her face reddening. "That was embroidered by the Grand Duchess. How marvellous! She had her left arm paralyzed from the elbow down, but she still managed to do something she loved since childhood; she said she inherited that talent from her mother, who also loved embroidery. Rodney, let's see what is wrapped in it." Augusta's eyes filled with excitement as she transformed into a much younger woman.

I carefully unwrapped the object. It was an old cuckoo clock. Augusta looked at it with surprising intensity and tears started to roll down her cheeks. She took a handkerchief out of her pocket and dried them delicately.

"What is it, Grandma?" Astrid asked, showing concern for Augusta's emotions.

"That was a gift given to the Grand Duchess by your grandfather. My dear Lupold! He made it himself. Every time the clock struck six or twelve, small figurines representing the Imperial family marched out through this little door and went in through this other one to the music of *God Save the Tsar*. What a surprise! I always believed she had taken it to America!"

"Well," Astrid said, "it was packed. Obviously Miliukoff missed it, Grandma."

"This is a treasure. Let's see if it works!" I said, fiddling with it. It did not work. "You need to get it fixed. It's beautiful," I said as I admired the clock.

"So what else is there?" Astrid impatiently asked.

I took out a leather bag containing some notebooks dated from 1948, which I showed to Augusta.

"These were her diaries. I think they are childhood memoirs!" She said.

I opened them and saw they were written in Russian.

"And what's this?" asked Astrid, opening a small book with a cover made of golden paper. The pages were held together with a mauve ribbon. It had *"Das Goldene Buch"*[1] written on its cover.

"Ahh! We all had copies of that. I still have mine!" Frau Rosenthal answered. "Gertrud Lamerdin wrote it during the fifties. She was another good friend of Anastasia who met her at the hospital, when Prince Frederick Ernst brought the Grand Duchess here. Frau Lamerdin was a lovely lady, very educated, refined and intelligent, and soon had a

---

[3] 'The Golden Book'

deep affection for our fragile Grand Duchess. She, Frau von Miltitz and the Prince always met with the lawyers that were working on Anastasia's court case. In *Das Goldene Buch* she writes about many episodes nobody has ever mentioned or published before about the life of Grand Duchess Anastasia here in Unterlengenhardt. She gave us a copy of the book as an Easter gift, as Easter was a very special time of the year for the Grand Duchess. Probably that was Anastasia's copy," Augusta remembered in reverence.

I held and examined the book. The paper was very thin and yellowed. Pages were typed in German but some notes were in English, and included several original photographs. The rest of the box contained some unopened letters and other documents, even a blank cheque signed by Anna Anderson.

"Rodney, I think you have to examine these things carefully. Would you like to take it all with you?" Augusta asked after we had gone through the contents.

"I have been asked to deliver them to you," she said mysteriously. "I am sure Prince Frederick Ernst would have agreed with me. We gave so much of our lives to this cause! Someone has to continue our work."

"I don't understand," I exclaimed, perplexed. "Of course I will be very happy to be responsible for these historical treasures, but who has asked you to give them to me? Why?"

"When the time is right, you will know. That is not important now, but you have been chosen. The important thing is that from now on, they will be your responsibility and not that of a senile, romantic old woman like me." She said, smiling. "I will, of course, keep the clock," Augusta added as an afterthought, laughing joyfully as she passed the weight of responsibility to me.

"You have been so kind. I will be forever so grateful, Augusta."

"It is destiny, Rodney. It is your destiny!"

That night I decided to take a walk and get to know a little of Bad Liebenzell. I needed to clear my head, as so many thoughts were spinning in it. Certainly I was astonished by all the information I had gathered in just this trip. I ended my walk dining in a cosy restaurant named *Gasthof zur Sonne*. I ordered a scotch and the house special that a young lady from the Kohnle family had suggested. Sipping my scotch, I could not stop thinking about the nice people I had met here and imagining the future of this case. Now I was also convinced that all I had experienced was not mere coincidence. Augusta's last words resounded in my ears: "It is destiny, Rodney. It is your destiny!"

## 9. BRIDGE, KENT, UNITED KINGDOM, 1ST APRIL 1994

I returned to Madrid with my precious documents. On the flight home from Stuttgart I could not help but wonder at my fateful encounter with those extraordinary women. I felt totally absorbed by the mystery of Anastasia, the lost icon and its compelling secret. Miles was certain to be as fascinated as I was by the documents I was able to find, which would undoubtedly help us proceed with our investigation. So I phoned him and asked him to spend some time with me the next day examining some fascinating documents I had just found in Germany. I went to Carlos' office to update him on my latest "scouting" trip. He was over the moon as he looked at the supposed diaries of Grand Duchess Anastasia, the Golden Book and all the letters.

"Please call me as soon as you go through all this with Miles," he urged me. "I wish I could go to London with you, but Tatiana is arriving tomorrow and we have so much work to do."

"Don't worry, Carlos. I promise I'll call you as soon as we figure out what to do next. Miles was going to speak to a couple of ex-KGB mates of his."

So I left the office and took a taxi to Barajas airport for the afternoon flight to Gatwick, where Miles would be waiting for me.

✦ ✦ ✦

Miles and I were on our own, his wife having gone to visit relatives for a couple of days. I had declined his invitation to stay in his elegant home close to Bridge's parish church, instead booking a room in the bed and breakfast above the White Horse pub. After settling in, I walked to Miles' home. As we sat in his living room in front of an open fire sipping scoth, he began telling me what new information he had about the DNA tests of the Romanov bones. Apparently Professor William Maples, a forensic anthropologist from United States, had obtained some bone and tooth fragments from the alleged Romanovs in Ekaterinburg the year before, and taken them to US for DNA testing. He was disappointed that Dr Mary Claire King, the specialist he chose to perform the DNA tests, had still not presented the report with her results. According to Miles, relations between scientists in London and those in America were "tense and difficult."

Then we decided to examine the documents found in Unterlengenhardt that I had brought with me. After discarding some personal letters, bills and post cards, we focused our attention on a sealed envelope. Captivated, Miles read it carefully, picked up a magnifying glass and then pointed at the signature.

"Look Rodney! Do you see the same thing I see?"

The letter was written in English and signed "*Papa.*"

"This is incredible! It seems to be a letter from the Tsar to his daughter, dated 5th June 1951!" I cried out in astonishment, and began to read it aloud:

"*My dear precious daughter,*

*First of all you must forgive me for being so far from you for all these years. I know of your suffering and how difficult it has been for you. Believe me, my little one, it has been extremely difficult and painful for all of us, too. I send you these pearls, one for each birthday that we have not been together. I remember how happy you and your sisters were when I gave you one or more pearls every birthday for your necklaces and the bracelets that you seemed to adore. Every 5th of June, your birthday, my darling, my heart has bled. It has been now thirty-three years since the tragedy that separated us. I know my final day to be with the Lord is near, and I wanted to tell you how much I love you and how much I have suffered from this separation.*

*My darling and sweet Anastasia, I bless you, and I beg your forgiveness. Please also forgive all those that have remained silent. You know it was necessary to protect our lives and the lives of those who saved us. Our fate is a state secret, and it is still essential that everyone believes we were all murdered that night. Maybe one day, when it is not dangerous, the world will know the truth. Keep your faith in our Lord Jesus Christ. He will give you the strength to overcome this ordeal. Pray for your poor Mamma, she loved you dearly and suffered more than anybody. She is and will always be watching over you. I love you with all my heart, my sweet and dearest little child,*

*Papa.*"

We both looked at each other in total bewilderment, quite unprepared for the content of the letter.

"Rodney, if this is genuine, we have a time bomb on our hands," Miles said, worried. "I wasn't ready for this kind of thing when I agreed to help you. If this has been a cover-up it has been the work of our government in conjunction with many others. This is dynamite. I thought we were just trying to put some historical facts together. I had something much lighter in mind."

"What shall we do now?" I asked him, very confused.

"We first have to confirm that this is not a forgery. I have another letter that I received this morning from a former retired KGB friend. I thought it was a joke when I first read it but now that we have this other one, it might be plausible that the Imperial family was not murdered after all. Look at it, Rodney."

Miles handed me a copy of a small note. It was dated the 6th January 1919. I read it aloud: "*My dear Fox, I need not tell you how indebted I am for all that you have done towards consummating my escape. I feel that you will do all you can to maintain my state secret.*"[1]

I was dumbfounded. The letter was signed "*Nicolas.*"

"What is this? Is it genuine, Miles?"

"It might be. Who knows? I was told that the original exists and is said to be in the United States," Miles answered.

We looked at the handwriting in both letters and they definitely appeared the same. The strokes seemed nearly identical, though many years had elapsed between them.

"Again, the Tsar speaks of a state secret, and there are thirty-two years between the letters!" Miles pointed out.

"This is just unbelievable. I can't even tell my son. We are dealing here with state secrets at the highest level and probably swimming in murky waters. Miles, you must get one more sample of the Tsar's handwriting while he was in power and then we must have an expert examine all the three letters and see if they were written by the same hand," I said.

"That should be no problem. We must be very careful though, Rodney."

"Is your friend from KGB reliable?" I asked, as I wondered what my next move should be.

"I think we can trust him. I just told him I wanted to help a friend's daughter with her university thesis. I think he believed me. But in hindsight, he was quite jumpy when I discussed the case with him. Now I understand why it is so sensitive."

"Good, let's keep it that way. My letter mentions pearls. There were no pearls in the box I opened in Germany where these documents came

---

[1] Thank you note published in *The Hunt for the Tsar*, by Guy Richards. See picture.

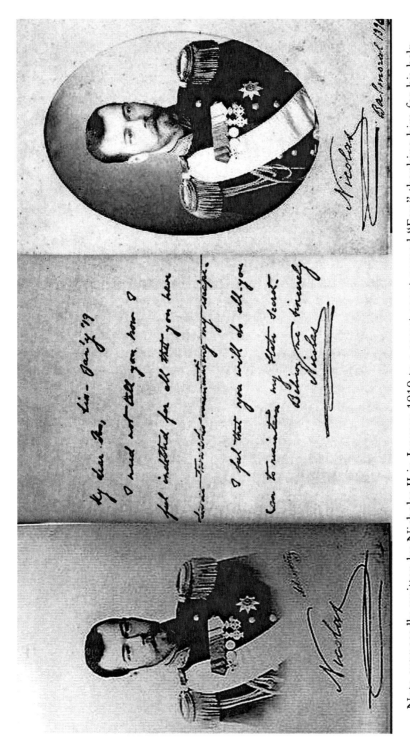

Note supposedly written by Nicholas II in January 1919 to a secret agent named "Fox," thanking him for his help during Nicholas' escape from Russia. Two pictures of the Tsar with his signature are shown here for comparison. (Note published in *The Hunt for the Tsar* by Guy Richards, Doubleday & Company, Garden City, New York, 1970.)

from. I wonder if they ever existed or if it's all part of a big hoax. Maybe it's true the KGB worked hard to sow confusion among the exiles. Do you know who Fox was, Miles?"

"He is believed to have been working for us. Somebody at the firm told me that there were rumours of a secret rescue operation led by Captain Stephen Alley, second in command of the British intelligence mission in Petrograd – now Saint Petersburg."

"That is new to me!" I exclaimed. "I used to believe what I was told: that Britain had abandoned the tsar, his wife Alexandra – a granddaughter of Queen Victoria – and their children. But if evidence ever emerges proving that both King George V and the government of David Lloyd George were willing to rescue the family, the news will cause a historical revolution," I said, thinking quickly.

"Well Rodney, Stephen Alley was an expert. You know he is considered one of our top agents of all time. He would definitely be the best man to organize such an operation to rescue the Romanovs. Did he participate? Was he successful? I don't know, and I doubt it, but the story deserves to be investigated. Maybe his family has some of his documents or diaries, because I learned that his files in MI6 and others in the US are classified. All this is very shady, but maybe in the future they will see the light of day."

"Indeed! Why would they have to keep those documents classified?" I asked.

"I don't know. All this is so strange! To me it proves that there has been a cover-up for decades."

"You are right. Perhaps soon we will discover something big, my friend. So who was Fox?"

"I told you, Rodney, there are several theories about his identity. One says that he was an American working with other British and American agents in an attempt to rescue the Imperial family, but so far nobody has found evidence of his identity."

# 10. MADRID, SPAIN, 3RD APRIL 1994

It was a wet spring day and I got to the agency early. I was sitting in my office looking at photocopies of the documents I had left with Miles. God knows I hate to wake up early, but I couldn't sleep the night before so I decided to benefit from the privacy of the empty agency. I arrived at eight in the morning, made myself some tea and settled down to look at Anastasia's diaries. I couldn't believe I had them to myself. I had decided not to tell Carlos the scope of the matter at hand. I needed to protect him in case this affair exploded in my face. MI6: if there was a cover-up, they would likely have been complicit. At that point I was full of doubts and I really did not know what path to follow. I had decided that my top priority was to search for and locate the lost icon and its secret, but I had no clue how to go about it. I had to think and plan my moves carefully and raise no suspicion. And there was the matter of the expense of it all to consider. It was just before ten when I heard the door open and Carlos say "good morning." He must have seen my raincoat. I yelled back and he came into my office.

"So?" he asked.

"Nothing new, I'm afraid," I answered, hating myself for having to lie to him. "Miles has all the documents and is going to look them over. By the way, did Tatiana arrive?" I asked, changing the subject.

"Yes, she did. She's quite beautiful. I sent her to a very good photographer and she is having some great pictures taken. She needs them desperately. She's going to make lots of money, don't worry!" Carlos joked, knowing how I reacted to the cash advances we gave the models, which on many occasions were never recovered.

"So I did a good job, then?"

"Great, Papa. She is coming to see you in about an hour. I told her you had gone to London to look into the Anastasia case. She seemed surprised!"

"Why did you do that? The less people know about this the better," I said, trying to hide my concern.

"But she is, after all, supposed to be the Tsar's godson's daughter…"

"That's crap!" I said, slightly irritated. "Please, don't speak about this with anyone or I'm out. Understood?"

"I'm really sorry. I just wanted to engage her in a conversation about the Romanovs, but anyway she just blanked me out. I promise I won't talk to anyone about this again."

"Fine. I'm sorry to have snapped at you. Maybe I've been too involved with the story lately. I need to get back to work and distance myself from the whole affair."

✦ ✦ ✦

I was going over some figures with the accountant when I heard a knock on the door, and in came Tatiana. She looked even more beautiful than when I had seen her in Warsaw. I asked her to sit down and the accountant left us alone.

"I'm happy to hear that you are doing some test pictures tomorrow."

"Yes, Rodney. Carlos is so charming and I'm very grateful that you have given me this opportunity."

We chatted for a while and I suddenly noticed that she had caught a glimpse of the documents on the table. She realized that I'd seen her looking.

"So, Carlos told me that you are looking into the Anastasia case. You don't believe my father, then?"

It was just what I had not wanted. If only Carlos could have been more discreet. By now I knew of so many people who, over the years, had devoted their lives to proving that Anna Anderson and Grand Duchess Anastasia were one and the same person. People who had selflessly dedicated their time and resources to this woman who had never wanted to prove anything herself. This thought distracted me for a moment.

"Sorry, Tatiana. I was just thinking about something. It's not that. I'm sure your dad believes that his godfather was the Tsar. Maybe he was. There is so much mystery surrounding this story. What I do know for a fact, though, is that that Mrs Smith was not Grand Duchess Anastasia. That is the reason I doubt your dad's story."

"But how can you? You never met her or anyone else related to the family," she said in a sudden defiant tone.

"Darling, I just know. Let's not make this a bone of contention. You're here to have a great time, become a great model and make lots of money. Isn't that what you want?" I asked.

"Yes, Rodney. Sorry. It's just that my dad is so certain his godfather was the Tsar and knows the entire story."

"That's fine. No problem. It has nothing to do with me anyway."

"So why are you looking into the Anastasia matter, then?"

"Tatiana, I'm not. I'm fascinated by the story and so is Carlos, so I have a friend in London who is an expert in Russian history and I went to tell him that I had met you and your dad and what you had told me. Only that. I'm just curious."

"I see. In Poland they say that curiosity kills the cat!"

"We say the same thing in England," I replied jokingly.

"Well, Rodney, if you need any help, as a translator or whatever, please let me know. This story also fascinates me and concerns my family, too. Promise?" She offered winningly.

"Promise!" I answered, trying to finish the discussion.

✦ ✦ ✦

"Señor, the telephone for you!" the maid announced while I was relaxing at home with my wife and my evening scotch.

"Who is it, Esperanza?" I asked.

"I don't know, Señor. I did not understand her name. It's a long distance call," our Filipina housekeeper said.

I picked up the phone. "Hello. Who is it?"

"Rodney, it's Augusta from Germany. How are you my dear?"

"How nice to hear from you. I'm fine. I have just returned from England and have decided that I'm going to try to trace the lost icon. We need to find its secret. I feel I now owe it to you, to my family and to the memory of the Grand Duchess," I said.

"I am very glad, my *liebe*. I just wanted to tell you that something marvellous has happened. Do you remember the cuckoo clock that my husband made for Her Imperial Highness?" Augusta asked.

"Yes, of course. How could I forget such a beautiful piece?"

"I took it to a shop to be repaired. The reason it did not work when we found it and you could not see the Imperial family parade was…" I heard her giggle youthfully. "Do you know why?" she asked excitedly.

"No, why? Tell me, please!" I asked.

"On the back of the clock, within the machinery, a little velvet bag had been concealed in the mechanism, and inside were thirty-three of the most beautiful pearls I have ever seen."

## 11. LONDON, UNITED KINGDOM, 10TH APRIL 1994

Thirty-three years had passed since the assassination or disappearance of the Imperial family in 1918 when the Tsar's letter to his daughter had been signed, in 1951. He had mentioned a gift of pearls, one for each birthday during their separation. Augusta had found the pearls. For me, there was now no doubt that the letter was genuine, as I could not believe anyone would have planted those pearls in the clock or given an impostor such a valuable gift. I needed scientific confirmation now, and as soon as I had time, under the pretext of another scouting trip, I flew to London.

I booked a suite at Claridge's, one of my favourite hotels in the heart of Mayfair. I used to come often for meetings and for tea in my early days with MI6 during the war and its aftermath.

Miles had agreed to meet me for a drink at the Fumoir, which was elegantly decorated in an art deco style that very much appealed to me. I ordered a glass of champagne as I waited and reflected on all the things that had happened in the last weeks. I always believed the story that the whole Imperial family and some of their servants had been murdered in Ekaterinburg, in the cellar of the Ipatiev House, during the night of 16–17th July 1918, when they were prisoners of the Bolsheviks. But I'd thought it possible that one or two could have survived, Anastasia being one of them. Now stories surfaced that other members of the family had survived and lived in Poland, or Italy, or that there was a state secret involved. All that seemed too big to remain hidden all this time. Of course there had been rumours over the years, and different people had sprung up here and there claiming to be one Grand Duchess or another, or even the Tsarevitch Alexei. Only Anna Anderson had been taken seriously. Anyway, to me it was still inconceivable that the Imperial family had been rescued and the secret kept for so many decades. At that point of my investigation, I believed with certainty that Anastasia escaped, went to Romania and was mentally unstable when she appeared in Berlin in 1920 and tried to kill herself. To me her erratic behaviour was. She never tried at all to convince any of the visitors that went to see her or made any effort to defend her identity. She just went on living.

"Hey, mate. How are you? How was your trip?" Miles dragged me from my thoughts. He arrived at the bar accompanied by a tall middle-aged man whose face was disfigured by smallpox. We were supposed to meet alone.

"I'm fine, my friend," I replied, slightly startled as his companion fixed his unpleasant gaze upon me.

"Please meet my friend Anatoly Levkov. He is the graphology expert who compared the handwriting on your original, the copy of the "Dear Fox" note and a letter Nicholas II wrote to Queen Marie of Romania in 1915.

I did not feel too comfortable with his presence but I greeted Anatoly civilly.

"Shall we have a drink?" I asked, trying to hide my feelings. I was cross at Miles as we had agreed to keep this as secret as possible. Why had he considered it necessary for me to meet this Anatoly, to whom I had taken an instant dislike?

"Scotch?" I suggested.

"Vodka for me." Anatoly barked without any pretence of civility.

I ordered the drinks and when they came both Anatoly and Miles drank theirs in one gulp.

"So what do you have?" I finally asked.

"Something absolutely incredible, Rodney," Miles said excitedly.

"And?" I asked impatiently.

Anatoly looked at me. He opened his briefcase and took a document out of a file, which he handed to me.

"It is my conclusion that the same person has written these three letters."

"You have no doubts about that?" I asked excitedly.

"None whatsoever. In this document I have authenticated the signature in the three letters. So there is no doubt. The Tsar survived. He was the author of all the letters!"

"Oh! We should celebrate." I exclaimed with mixed feelings.

I ordered a bottle of champagne. Although I'd expected this positive result, I somehow would have preferred the letters to have been fakes. The discovery would have tremendous implications once it was made public. It took me a while to react.

"Mr Mundy, with this discovery you have opened a very dangerous Pandora's Box, and the consequences are unpredictable, maybe even unpleasant. I wanted to come and warn you in person, and if you are interested in my opinion, go home and forget the Romanovs. You better drop it all," Anatoly said sternly without changing his hideous expression.

"My original interest was to find out the truth about Anastasia. I swear it was only that!" I said, still in shock after all the new developments. "Then I learned about the missing Romanov icon and wanted to know what happened to it. I never meant to get involved in anything else."

"But knowing you, Rodney, I suppose these new findings will encourage you to go ahead. Probably you will have to go to Charlottesville and start tracing the lost icon," Miles said cheerfully as he sipped his second glass of champagne.

"Yes Miles, I guess that's my next stop! But maybe I will follow your friend's advice, go home and forget it all." I was terribly upset with Miles. Why on earth had he hired a Russian for this job when any good graphologist would have come to the same conclusion?

# 12. CHARLOTTESVILLE, VIRGINIA, USA, 15TH APRIL 1994

I of course had not listened to Anatoly's warning and had no time to tell Miles what I thought of his *faux pas*. If anything it just made me more determined to get to the bottom of this affair. Was it just plain old curiosity, or madness?

There I was, driving from Washington airport to Charlottesville in Virginia, where Grand Duchess Anastasia had lived for sixteen years with her husband Jack Manahan. I felt elated. It was refreshing to have a mission again. It was like being back with MI6, but now I was my own boss. Miles and I made a good team, and I still had it in me to get to the bottom of this matter, find the icon and reveal its secret.

I had booked a room at 200 South Street Inn, a beautiful building from 1856. It was charming, discreet and in the middle of the historical district, not far from Monticello, the mountain home of Thomas Jefferson. Tired from the long flight, I decided to stay in the hotel and to check my schedule for the couple of days I would spend in this lovely town.

◆ ◆ ◆

I woke up early. It was a splendid spring day. The sun was shining and there was a soft pleasant breeze. After a hearty American breakfast, I strolled out of the hotel and went straight to the office of Cross & Associates, a private investigation firm that had been highly recommended by an FBI friend of Miles. Their office was just two blocks from my hotel, so I arrived a few minutes early. James Cross was waiting for me in his office with a hot cup of coffee. He was about my height, strongly built, and had an amicable air about him. Down-to-earth as many Americans are, he was probably older than I was, maybe in his seventies, but was fit and energetic.

"Tell me what you know about the Manahans," I said, without much preamble, as I had already briefed him prior to my arrival.

"I'm happy to help you in your investigation, Rodney. I knew Jack Manahan quite well. He was a gentleman: always courteous and very considerate. He was a kind man and totally devoted his wife, whom he took good care of as long as he was able to. He was an important man in our community, but with old age they became more and more eccentric, and eventually a big mess."

"What do you mean by a big mess, James?"

"In 1978, ten years after Anastasia arrived, the house was overflowing with trash, the garden wild and untended, full of cats and dogs. The stench was unbearable and it became a health hazard. The conditions both inside and outside the house were shocking. They never heated the house so they had a fire burning all day and night. Things became worse after she underwent surgery and ended up practically paralyzed. The authorities appointed an official guardian, but both were always complaining about him. Then she was taken to a psychiatric ward, but Jack smuggled her out and both were at large for several days. When captured, she was transferred to a nursing home, where she died on 12th February, 1984. It was all very sad."

"Can we visit the house?" I asked.

"Unfortunately not. I called Althea Hurt, the current owner. She inherited everything when Jack died. There was a big court case. Some members of his family claimed that she had talked him into changing the will, but she won the claim in the end. The truth is that it was all very bizarre. At the end of his life Jack wanted to marry her but he had lost the plot by then, as you English say. The controversy around that poor woman seems to be endless, and right now there is another legal battle going on, as you are probably aware."

"Yes, I think I read something in the newspapers. But you can tell me all the latest developments, being in the eye of the storm."

"A tissue sample ostensibly belonging to Mrs Manahan was found at Martha Jefferson Hospital. Apparently, it is hospital policy to keep these samples in case of complaints. Because of the news about some bones discovered in Russia, which could belong to the Romanovs, several strong supporters of the claim of Mrs Manahan to be the real Grand Duchess Anastasia requested DNA testing of the sample. But now other people have surfaced, including the Russian Nobility Association, claiming the right to test it themselves. A real battle has taken place, and Richard and Marina Schweitzer have being trying to gain access and take it to a good lab for the genetic analysis. Marina is the daughter of Gleb Botkin, a childhood friend of the Imperial children. His father was one of the physicians of the Romanov family, and he had recognized Mrs Manahan as the real Anastasia since 1927. Richard Schweitzer is a prominent lawyer here. He and his wife were always very close to the Manahans; to them, it is a matter of family honour to try their utmost to fulfil her lifelong wish to have her identity as Grand Duchess Anastasia recognized."

"And how do you think all this is going to end?" I asked, really interested in this parallel investigation.

"This new year brought good news for us who believe in the authenticity of Mrs Anastasia Manahan. In January, a German Baron named Ulrich von Gienanth became a part of the court case. He was Mrs Manahan's last legal representative. He had her last will and still holds power to be the executor of that will. To make the story short, Mr Mundy, last March the judge granted Baron Gienanth access to the tissue sample. However, the Russian Nobility Association did not accept that decision and they are going to appeal. The case is getting more complicated. Nobody knows for sure how or when all will be resolved."

"I see. Actually I was not aware of this conflict surrounding that tissue sample. Please, keep me informed about future developments," I told James. "And now, can you show me where the Grand Duchess lived?"

"I will be happy to show you the house, but it has changed a lot since then."

"And do you know what happened to the objects that belonged to the Grand Duchess?" I asked, trying to lead him to the icon.

"Many things were sold to collectors, but they also had a great deal of junk, and piles and piles of documents, magazines and old books. It was all very controversial. Mr Mundy, I have written a list of people and places you should visit here. I suggest we start with a visit to Marlen Jewels. She was Mrs Manahan's neighbour and friend. She visited Mrs Anderson regularly and might be able to tell you a bit more."

James drove me to the home of Mrs Jewels, a nice big Italian-style house. As we walked to the porch the door opened and a charming old lady in her seventies welcomed us. She was tall and thin and still stood erect in spite of her age. She served us a glass of lemonade and we sat on the porch to enjoy the spring air, warm and pleasant.

"So what can I do for you?" she asked sweetly.

"James says you visited the Manahans' residence often."

"Yes, I did, I even met Maria Rasputin, the daughter of the infamous mad monk Gregori Rasputin, when she came to visit in 1968."

"Oh, did you!" I exclaimed. I was practiced in putting potential sources at ease.

"It was Tuesday 13th August. Maria came with another woman. When Anastasia saw her, she called her "Mara," a name that was only known to them. First they talked in private, then they joined us and continued the conversation in front of us, a group of friends who had gathered to witness that historic encounter, including a journalist, Rey Barry. Maria said she was convinced that the fragile woman – Anna Anderson, as she was called at the time – was the real Anastasia. She remembered things they had done together and nobody else could know, such as the time when Maria dressed up as a Red Cross nurse. Maria's endorsement that day was unambiguous and public. Both women left and later sent an invitation for Anastasia to join them in Los Angeles, California. But the Grand Duchess did not accept it. She wanted to be left alone, in peace. I think she was afraid for her own safety. To make things worse, the two women came back east in November and tried in person to convince her. She still absolutely rejected the invitation, and they threatened to withdraw Maria's endorsement if the Grand Duchess would not go with them to the west. As you probably know, they left very disappointed and called a press conference at Washington DC airport, where Maria denounced Anna as a fraud. What a traitor she was…"

"I did read about it. Do you know why she changed her mind?" I added, trying to stir her memories a little bit.

"Well, apparently she wanted Anastasia to move with her to California, write books, participate in TV shows, and maybe even a movie. That didn't go over well with the Grand Duchess. She was already sixty-seven years old, and after so many terrible experiences, I bet she just wanted to live quietly," concluded Mrs Jewels.

I was really happy that James had introduced me to this lady; she seemed to know about Anastasia Manahan's life in Charlottesville. Sources had not disappointed me so far during my investigation, and, eager to know more, I asked her if she remembered any special anecdote.

"I have a lovely story to share with you. Jack and Anastasia did not have a television at home, but they always nipped over to our place when there was something important on. They came the evening the Apollo 11 landed on the moon. Anastasia was in awe and she ordered us all to stand up. She said the astronauts deserved our respect. I love that story!" Marlen recounted, as I saw her eyes filling with tears.

"Mrs Jewels, maybe you can help me. I'm trying to find out what happened to a Russian icon that Anastasia brought from Germany."

"Oh yes, I remember the icon perfectly well. She treasured it. It was an image of the Virgin Mary with the child Jesus, painted on metal in a gilded silver frame."

Bingo! I now had a description of what I was looking for. A great start. "How big was it, Marlen?"

"About six by eight inches, more or less. Anastasia said it was over two hundred years old and had been in her family for many years. She was very fond of it, and of the German royal family that had given it to her. She said she was the godmother of their heir. Actually, I now remember something else; she kept her godson's wedding invitation inside a portrait next to the icon. She always said the icon had protected her in difficult times, and had to be returned to that family after she died. But it was stolen."

"How do you know that?" I asked.

"When she died, Prince Frederick Ernst called Jack Manahan and asked him to honour Anastasia's promise. He went to get the icon and found that it had vanished, there was only a dustless spot were the precious icon had been placed. I remember Jack first said it was the KGB, and later accused MI6. Both of them always believed the KGB was spying on them and wanted to kill them, but if you want my opinion about the lost icon, anyone could have stolen it. Jack and Anastasia used to keep the doors of their house open, unlocked even when they weren't at home. It was all so sad."

"Would you have a photograph of the icon by any chance, Marlen?" I asked, pushing my luck.

"As a matter of fact, I might. I will look and if I find it I'll call James. Thanks for dropping by."

James took me to see the Manahans' headstone at the University of Virginia cemetery, though Mrs Manahan's ashes were buried at Castle Seeon, the home of the Dukes of Leuchtenberg in Germany. As she had wished and as the Duke of Leuchtenberg had promised, Anastasia's ashes finally rest in the churchyard of the property of a member of the Russian Imperial family. We also drove by 35 University Circle, their former home. It was smaller compared to the rest of the elegant Italianate houses. University Circle was one of the best residential areas in the city, with beautiful stately homes carefully placed amid immaculate gardens and lawns. After our tour, I invited James for lunch and let him choose the restaurant. He suggested Farmington Country Club, where James said Jack and Anastasia had been many times. While eating, James told me many good memories of his longtime friends.

"I used to go with them to Ken Johnson's Cafeteria, one of her favourite places. We normally ate inside, but in later years Anastasia stayed in the car and Jack would take her food there. In the end she only ate mashed potatoes with onions and drank coffee with tons of sugar. I think she was addicted to the stuff," James recalled.

✦✦✦

After lunch, I was ready for the next adventure. James took me to Martha Jefferson Hospital, having arranged a meeting with the director of medical records. My interest was to know how certain the hospital was that the tissues of contention did belong to Anna Anderson, or Anastasia Manahan, as they called her.

I don't know how I would have done it without James. It seemed he had the keys to all the doors in Charlottesville.

The director was a lady in her mid-forties. She wore no makeup and hair pulled back severely.

"So, what can I do for you, Mr Mundy?" she asked, looking directly to my eyes, seeming reluctant to speak. It was thanks to James that she relaxed a bit.

"I am just curious about this entire affair," I said, trying not to show too much interest.

"This whole 'affair', as you call it, has cost this hospital much time and resources. I'm not sure if you are aware that there has been a fierce legal battle to gain access to the tissue sample, dragging on for over eight months. I hope the results prove that she was the Grand Duchess," she said. The last statement really surprised me.

"Why?"

"It is just such a romantic story. I also feel that the Russian Nobility Association have had some sort of hidden agenda with their litigation in this case. It is just a gut feeling."

"I just wanted to ask if you are one hundred per cent sure that the tissue samples came from Mrs Manahan and if so, if there has been any chance of manipulation or a switch?"

"We are one hundred per cent sure they belonged to Anastasia Manahan. They were taken when she had an operation in 1979 to remove a gangrenous bowel obstruction. We kept the pathology samples, as we always do, to use for comparative studies or in the case of malpractice lawsuits. In other words, we do this routinely to cover our backs. I really hope that the judges soon decide who is going to get the right to test the samples, and then the hospital will release them. That's all we can do. Believe me, Mr Mundy, we also want to know the results!"

After that visit, James took me directly to the hotel. As I opened the door to my room I immediately realized that someone had been there and gone through my things. I noticed that my copy of the James Blair Lovell book on Anastasia lay open on my bed and not on the side table where I had left it. The drawers were open and my things were scattered all over the room. As Anatoly Levkov had warned me, the cat was out of the bag, but much sooner than I had expected. I sat on the bed and picked up the book. It seemed intact, with all my notes inside it.

"Don't move or I'll shoot." I heard a husky male voice with a heavy Russian accent from behind. I froze.

"What do you want?" I asked without turning around.

"Place the book and your notes beside you," the voice ordered. I did as I was told and as he was taking the book and notes from my side, I swiftly grabbed his hand and turned around. The man was tall and very strong. He was obviously young, as he was extremely well built. His face was covered with a balaclava but he did not have a gun.

I pinned his hand down on the bed with my right hand as he firmly gripped the book and with my left I took a gamble and pulled the balaclava. For a split second I took a good look at his face. The eyes were dark and full of anger at having been caught. His hair was light blonde and had a military crew cut and the nose of a boxer. He pushed me back with great force and I fell from the bed onto the floor. In the confusion, he ran out of the room with the book and my notes.

Seconds later the receptionist was helping me get up.

"Mr Mundy, are you all right? The maid saw someone running out of your room and I saw this tall man leaving the hotel in haste. I have called the sheriff. This has never happened before," she said excitedly.

The sheriff was soon over and we accompanied him to the room.

"Any ideas?" asked the sheriff. "Have they stolen anything?"

"Not a clue, but nothing has gone missing," I lied.

"But someone was looking for something?" he asked, as his assistant went through the room looking for clues.

"I assume it was a regular thief, or a junkie trying to find some cash." I replied in a matter-of-fact tone.

"Did you see his face? Would you be able to recognize him?"

"I am sorry sheriff; I didn't as he was wearing a head cover," I lied again.

"He was no junkie," the sheriff said. "He was well dressed according to the people who saw him leave the premises. So what business has brought you to Charlottesville, may I ask?"

"I'm just a tourist. I'm going back to Washington tomorrow."

"Please, are you sure nothing is missing from your belongings?" The sheriff asked again.

"My watch and my money are with me, and my passport is in reception, so it seems they have not taken anything."

"So, there is nothing much more to do here. Have a good day, Mr Mundy," the sheriff said as we shook hands and we went down to the reception.

"Oh, my God! This is terrible! I am so sorry. We won't charge you for the room," the receptionist apologized once the police had left.

"It's not the end of the world. Don't worry. Please just give me a new room and all will be fine."

"OK, Mr Mundy. Thank you. By the way, your wife called and left a message. You should call Miles in England as soon as possible."

I collected my things that were scattered all over the room, packed with the help of the maid, and moved to a new room. Then I called Miles.

"Someone knows I'm here." I explained to him what had just happened. "Your friend Anatoly gave me the creeps with his warning. He must have spoken to someone about my trip here. Miles, why on earth did you get a Russian involved? You were careless." He did not know very well what to say.

"…But he was recommended by my friend from the KGB!" he replied, trying to justify himself.

"So we have two Russians onto our secret now. I am not surprised that they are here."

"I am sorry, Rodney. I probably made a mistake, but how do you know it's the Russians?" Miles asked apologetically.

"The accent gave him away and he stole my notes. Nothing to worry about, as they were only a few photocopies and notes that I scribbled on the book."

I gave him the update on the icon, and then asked him why he needed to talk to me.

"Rodney, a friend in London has just sent me a newspaper article which I think is important to the case. I don't know if you have heard of Mother Pascalina Lenhert. She was the governess and close confidante of Pope Pius XII. In this old paper from November, 1983, it is said that Pope Pacelli knew well that the Romanov women had survived, and he received Grand Duchesses Olga and Maria at the Vatican. It was all kept a secret. Rodney, the survival theory is most plausible. Maybe Rome is your next step. I'll fax you the article. But please, be very careful."

# 13. MADRID, SPAIN, 18TH APRIL 1994

Just as I was leaving the hotel, James had rushed in, carrying an envelope. Mildred had found a copy of the photograph where the icon was visible. The colours had faded with the passing of time. She was standing beside Anastasia, who held the icon proudly in her hand. It was a beautiful object and, more importantly, this was proof that it really existed. James also gave me a newspaper clip from The Daily Progress dated the 7th of April 1991, where the icon was mentioned together with other heirlooms that had disappeared from the Manahan's house. It was priceless and now I had to find out who had stolen it and why. I now had something to work with.

He knew about my assault and apologized for the bad experience I had had in his town. He took me to the airport and offered to cooperate with the police to find the perpetrator and keep me informed of all the new developments related to the tissue sample.

I arrived home early in the morning and took a good nap to recover from the Washington night flight. I had hardly slept on the flight. Not only did I have Blondie's face on my mind as I wondered whom he might be working for, but as I was checking in at the airport, I noticed a familiar face not far from where I was standing. It was Fritz. The moment he realized that I had spotted him, he turned around and disappeared into the crowd. What the hell was he doing there? He must have also been sent to keep tabs on me. But who had sent him? Was he working with Blondie? He must have known that I had the documents from Germany, as he had been there. I suddenly felt that maybe Augusta had been forced to speak. I had to call her. The old woman had guarded the box and kept the secret for so many years. Whoever Fritz was, and whoever the people he was working for were, they meant business. I had so many doubts and so many questions. Fritz seemed too clumsy to be a professional agent. Whoever he was, he was rather unskilled at his job.

✦✦✦

When I got up I called Augusta. To my relief, not only was she fine but no one had paid her a visit. I could really not know how much Blondie,

Fritz and their cronies knew. After lunch I went straight to the agency. As soon as I entered my office I sensed there was something wrong. I always kept track of where I left things and how they were placed. It had been a very important part of my training. The cleaning lady never moved things around, yet someone had definitely been looking for something. I only hoped it had been Carlos, looking for information about the models, or photographs from the scouting trips. I went through the copies of the documents I had brought from Germany and carefully placed in a drawer. Everything was out of place. Whoever had gone through the papers had done so in haste. The copies of Anastasia's diaries and the Golden Book were still in the drawer, but the copies of the Tsar's letters had vanished.

"Damn!" I screamed aloud as Carlos entered the room with Tatiana.

"What's wrong, Papa?" He asked.

"Someone has stolen some documents from the office!" I replied, oblivious of Tatiana's presence.

"What documents?" he asked worriedly.

"The copies of the Tsar's letters," I responded, regretting my answer as I suddenly realized that Tatiana was looking at me intently.

"But no one has been in the office, Papa, and no one knew you had them, anyway."

"That's true Carlos, but they're not here. I have had enough. I'm tired, it's costing money and I don't see the point, anyway. The cast have been long dead and who really cares what happened to the Romanovs? I am just going to believe the historically accepted story and concentrate on our business. Don't you agree, Tatiana?" I asked deliberately, taking her by surprise. I could see she felt most uncomfortable. Apart from Carlos, Miles, his KGB friend and Anatoly Levkov, she was the only one who knew I had things belonging to the Romanovs.

"You should continue investigating, Mr Mundy, and then you will discover that my father was right. If you have letters from the Tsar written after 1918, they prove that he survived and that what my father says is also true," she suddenly said.

"What are you talking about, Tatiana?" I asked, unable to conceal my anger. She did not reply.

"Papa, you can't just drop the case!" Carlos pleaded.

"Yes I can, and I'm going to do just that. You and I will speak later. Please come over for dinner tonight, would you?"

"Yes. I'll be there at nine."

That night, Carlos came for dinner with Rosa and me. I did not want to discuss business during dinner and was even less inclined to discuss the Romanov affair, my obsession with which drove my wife mad. She was just not interested and thought that I was going senile. After dinner, she left us to go and watch a film on the television and Carlos and I had the opportunity to chat quietly. I had wanted to keep the details of the story from him but as things had developed, and because of the imminent danger I would be in if I continued with the investigation, I felt I had to give him all the details. I told him to keep an eye on Tatiana, as I had no doubt it had been her who had stolen the letters. She had both motive and opportunity. I reassured him that I was not too worried, as I was certain it had been out of loyalty to her father to prove him right, and I genuinely believed she was not dangerous.

"So, what next, Papa?" Carlos asked when I finished my story.

"I'm going to stay in Madrid for at least a week, as otherwise Rosa might divorce me," I said jokingly.

"And then I'm going to invite her to spend a few days in London. That will make her happy. I have a friend at Christie's who is a specialist in Russian art and an expert on icons, so I'm sure he will be able to help. We'll decide what to do after I see him. But please, Carlos, keep Tatiana out of this. OK?"

He agreed.

# 14. LONDON, UNITED KINGDOM, 7TH MAY 1994

I finally left for London later than I had originally planned, as Rosa had a golf tournament that she did not want to miss and I wanted to be in Madrid for Carlos' birthday. I booked a suite at Claridge's and spent a few days going to the opera, eating, shopping and keeping my wife happy. I invited Miles over for a drink at the hotel and was distressed at the news he delivered.

"Rodney. I'm awfully sorry, but I can't continue helping you."

"But why, Miles? What's the matter?"

"I got a call from the firm. Somehow they have found out I have been poking around into this matter and they've told me to stop. Someone is not happy. In fact, in confidence, I was told they are outright angry."

"But who, Miles?"

"Don't be naïve, Rodney. You are good. Who do you think?"

"The Palace? The Russians?" I asked in disbelief.

"You've said it, not me. Your name hasn't come up yet but it's only a question of time until it does. I really would like to help you, but I don't want to have problems. You are OK for the time being. The bosses don't know you are involved. I stuck to the story of my friend's daughter's thesis, and in the end they seemed to believe me. I brought all your originals. They are safer in your hands. But please, my friend, be careful."

"Well Miles, they might not yet know but either your ex-KGB friend can't be trusted or Anatoly Levkov has a hidden agenda. They know I'm onto something and it's not a university thesis! Blondie is proof of that."

The next morning I went to see João Montereal at Christie's. He was the scion of a Portuguese aristocratic family and his father had been a friend of mine in the old days when I was in Spain during the war. The family had no money, but they had a sophisticated appreciation for the arts, so it had not been a surprise when he had specialized in Russian art and had been offered an important post with the auction firm.

He was delighted to see me.

"I need your help, João," I said, as I showed him the picture of the icon I had brought from America.

He looked at it with close attention.

"What's the scoop on this, Rodney?"

"Grand Duchess Elizabeth of Saxe-Weimar-Eisenach gave it to Grand Duchess Anastasia on loan when she agreed to be godmother to her son, Prince Michael Benedict. Apparently, it has belonged to the Romanovs for over two hundred years. Grand Duchess Anastasia was supposed to arrange its return when she died but someone managed to steal it from her home."

"I can't believe it! What a coincidence!" João exclaimed. "Only yesterday a Russian came to see me and was asking information about this icon. He gave me the same background story, though he just thought that it was a legend. He wanted to know if it had really existed and if so, if we might be able to provide a photograph or know where it could be located. He said he was a collector and was prepared to purchase it well above market price."

To me, that was not exactly a coincidence. They, whoever they were, seemed to be ahead of me.

"How did this man look? I asked. By the description João gave me I did not know who he could be.

"Did he leave a name and phone number?"

"Yes, as a matter of fact he did." João took a card out of his wallet and handed it to me.

"Gregory Dubinkin." I noted his name and phone number. There was no address.

"What would be the market price now that you know it really exists?" I enquired.

"With this story behind it, and from what I can see, it is worth well over two million dollars!" João valued it with certainty. "There is an enormous market for icons now. The Russian tycoons are outbidding each other to recover what they consider national treasures. For them, it's a question of pride and they will go to any length to get them back. Even stealing, if that's what it takes to get their hands on such a valuable piece."

"So that is a possibility, then?"

"Yes, a real possibility. There is an organized crime ring in Russia that steals valuable objects like this icon and then sells them to these tycoons. I heard recently that many very important historical documents, some hundreds of years old, were stolen from the national archives in Moscow," he answered, without a tinge of surprise.

"What should I do next? I need to trace its whereabouts."

"But why? What does it mean to you?" He asked.

"It's a long story. I'll tell you one day over a drink," I replied.

"If it was stolen to be sold again, sooner or later it will resurface and I will hear about it, but if you are desperate to find out more, I would advise you to contact Prince Alexander Chavchavadze. He, if anyone, would know where the icon has gone to, or even might be able to help you trace it. He lives in Tangier. He is an amazing old man."

I could not believe my ears. Dear old Alexander, my friend from the Côte d'Azur. One of the four musketeers! I had not seen him since those days.

"He was a good friend of mine, João. Why would he know about the icon?" I asked.

"He knows everything that goes on in Russia. Here, this is his home number and address. Good luck!"

"One more thing João, please do not call Mr Dubinkin if you hear anything."

"Don't worry Rodney, I won't." João reassured me.

# 15. TANGIER, MOROCCO,
## 21ST MAY 1994

Alexander had been thrilled when I called him. What I did not expect was that he seemed to have been waiting for my call. Not a tinge of surprise in his voice. So many years had passed and so many things had happened in our lives. We spoke for an hour, exchanging stories. The feeling of warmth and friendship was still there after more than five decades. He did not ask the reason for my call, and I did not tell him either, but promised that I would go and spend a few days with him as soon as I found the time. Only two weeks after my meeting with João, I drove to Malaga with my wife and dropped her off at our home in Guadalmina. The next morning I continued on to Algeciras, left the car there and took the ferry to Tangier, where I would stay at Alexander's *ryad* in the kasbah.

I had never been to Morocco, though Carlos had insisted I would like it. My impression was that he was right. Pepita's father had been a big landowner during the years when parts of the country had belonged to Spain, and they had lived in Larache.

Alexander sent one of his servants to pick me up at the harbour. I spotted him immediately, as he stood out in his elegant white *djellaba* and red *tarboush*.

"His Excellency is waiting for you impatiently," Hassan, a very handsome young man, said as he picked up my cases and escorted me to a waiting vintage Mercedes.

It was a sunny, warm spring day. As we drove from the port up to the kasbah, I noticed that the streets were very lively with people going about their daily chores. It was another world, only a couple of hours away from Spain. The car stopped just after the arch, where two more servants dressed in the same uniform as Hassan, Chavchavadze crest on their blue velvet waistcoats, awaited our arrival. I followed them through small winding streets to an inconspicuous large wooden door. As I entered the house, I was not prepared for the opulence of the *ryad*; it was like a palace. Of course I could not have expected less from my friend, who was waiting for me in the patio dressed in a burgundy and golden kaftan. He approached me, and we embraced with affection.

"You look exactly the same!" Alexander said cheerfully.

"You liar!" I scolded him. "It's been nearly sixty years, my old friend. Sixty long years."

"Come along, let's have a drink. We have so much to celebrate," he said, as I followed him to a large living room decorated in traditional Moroccan style with exquisite furniture and Islamic art.

Alexander was around eighty and looked wonderful. He was strong and healthy and had lost none of his elegance and poise. He had always had a sense of drama and here, in his beautiful palace, he moved like an actor on stage.

"Quite a place you have here, my friend. How long have you been living in Tangier?" I asked.

"Since the fifties. It was a fabulous place then. We had a wonderful time. Barbara Hutton[1] used to own a lovely house not far from us. She bought it some years after she divorced Igor. We had some unforgettable parties in those days."

"Whatever happened to Igor?" I asked as wonderful memories of my early years in the South of France poured in.

"He emigrated to Australia and still lives there. We still keep in touch. What wonderful days!" he sighed nostalgically. "We shall call him later. He will be thrilled."

"And Basil Nakashidze?"

"He died in a car crash in the sixties. It was a tragedy. He came to see me a few times. We often talked about you and always wondered why you had not kept in touch."

We sat, drank and talked about our lives. Seeing Alexander again reminded me of how much I had looked up to him during those years when we were getting started. He had always been more of a listener, and sat in awe as I briefed him on all my adventures in MI6 since I had last seen him in 1940.

"Did you get married, Alexander?" I asked, with curiosity.

"No, my dear. I didn't. I finally discovered that I enjoyed the company of gentlemen, and that is one of the reasons I came here. In those days, it was an acceptable way of life in the artistic circles of this fascinating city."

"Well it's an acceptable way of life in Europe now, too. Times have changed, fortunately. It must have been very difficult for you then."

---

[1] Barbara Hutton (1912–1979) was an American socialite and one of the wealthiest women of the twentieth century.

"In our circles it was never a problem, but for the bourgeoisie we were the devil incarnate and they believed we would corrupt the youth. Foolish and ignorant people! I've had a lovely life here and there is a wonderful group of people still living in town. I've organized a small soirée in your honour tonight. Charles Sevigny and his friend Yves Vidal are coming with a couple of other friends. They live in York Castle, which they bought in 1961 and turned into one of the most beautiful houses I have ever been."

"That's wonderful, Alexander. I appreciate it."

"You will like them. Yves and Charles have entertained people from all over the world. Their parties have always been renowned. They were good friends of Barbara's and they have turned Tangier into one of the most captivating destinations. Now, maybe you want to freshen up. I'm going to take a nap; it seems I need to sleep a lot in my old age," he said smiling. "All this excitement has made me a bit tired. If you need anything, Hassan is at your disposal. Maybe you want to take a walk around the kasbah or down to the medina. Please feel at home."

Though Hassan wished to accompany me, I chose to explore the surroundings on my own, so I walked out of the kasbah and down the Rue d'Italie towards the Grand Socco, the lively and bustling centre of the city. I walked past the Minzah Hotel and then stopped in for a mint tea at the Café de Paris, opposite the French consulate. I noticed no women sitting outside. The street was busy with many colourful characters walking to and fro. I had my shoes polished while I took in the action. As I was sipping my tea, reflecting on all the events of the past week, I suddenly saw him again. It was Fritz. He was keeping track of my movements while pretending to read a newspaper. He was a character out of a Peter Sellers film. He seemed so ill at ease at his job that it was almost comical, but now there was no doubt whatsoever: he was on my heels. This time he did not realize that I had spotted him, so I paid for my tea and walked back to the Grand Socco and into the medina. He was close behind, so I picked up my pace. I passed by the food market and walked down the Rue Es-Siaghine. It was very crowded, and I trusted I could lose him. I had no idea where I was heading. I came out onto a charming square and I looked up to see the street sign. I was in the Petit Socco. I walked into the Café Tingis and hid behind a door. Fritz came in, didn't see me and walked out. I saw him go into the Café Central, and I managed to slip out and walk up a small, crowded alley. I was lost in a maze, danger lurking in the shadows. I had no idea where the winding dark alleys were taking me. Suddenly someone grabbed me by the arm and pulled me violently into a side alley. I fell to the ground. Two menacing young men stood above me. Who were they? What could they possibly want? As I struggled with my assailants I felt confused and frightened. I tried to get up, but the younger of the two put his foot on my neck, firmly pinning me to the ground. They spoke to each other in Arabic. I offered my watch and the little money I had, hoping to appease them, as I knew I was no match for them. I was in real danger. My heart was beating fast and I was out of breath. I should have allowed Hassan to accompany me on my walk. How foolish of me to have wandered off alone in unfamiliar territory. As the younger man pulled me up, suddenly the other one fell over me and I was crushed against the ground again. I felt a wave of pain. I could barely move, but managed to turn my head and see Fritz out of the corner of my eye. He was fighting with the younger man who punched him in the face. He too fell to the ground but swiftly stood up and rushed out of the alley. The older of my two assailants tried to get up too as Hassan appeared with a police officer. He was arrested on the spot. There was a lot of screaming and yelling as he was taken from the alley, handcuffed. By then we were surrounded by a large number of people talking excitedly to each other and offering their opinions in Arabic, French and Spanish. What a mess! I was lost for words and confused. They helped me to my feet and I tried to regain my composure as Hassan helped me brush the dirt off my shirt.

"What are you doing here, Fritz? Why are you following me? And Hassan, you!" I exclaimed.

"I work for Prince Alexander," Fritz replied, nonchalantly. "He has ordered me to protect you."

"Protect me from whom, from what? Why?" I asked, trying to put my thoughts in order. "Who were those men?"

"Common criminals, sir. They are drug addicts. You should have not wandered off by yourself into the medina," Hassan replied.

"His Excellency will explain everything when the time comes for you to know," Fritz added.

We walked in silence up towards the kasbah. I had many questions for Alexander. How was he involved in this affair? I suddenly remembered that Princess Nina Chavchavadze, Alexander's aunt, a Romanov by birth, had not recognized Anna Anderson as Anastasia but had clearly stated that she was not a Polish peasant. Her sister Xenia had invited the claimant to New York, believing she was the real Anastasia. Maybe the family had some dark secret that Alexander would soon reveal to me.

✦✦✦

I found Yves Vidal a fascinating character. His friend Charles Sevigny was very polite, but a man of few words, though extremely charming. He was very reserved and in awe of Yves who was very outspoken. I thoroughly enjoyed the delightful, small al fresco candlelit dinner that Alexander had organized in my honour on one of the rooftop terraces of his *ryad* from which we could see the lights of the coast of Spain. The night was star-studded and the moon was nearly full. We spoke of the good old times on the Côte d'Azur and about Igor Trubetskoy, who had been Barbara Hutton's fourth husband. Yves enjoyed the anecdotes, speaking fondly of Barbara's years in Tangier and the extravagant parties given in her home, Sidi Hosni.

"I remember the emeralds clearly," said Yves.

"I sold the necklace to Van Cleef for Princess Niloufer Mourad, who was a daughter of the Turkish Sultan. They were a gift from the seventh Nizam of Hyderabad and each emerald was the exact same tone of her eyes," I recalled. "You should have seen the expression of disbelief on the clerk's face when he saw them. The stones were so large and perfect that his first impression was that it was a piece of costume jewellery!" We all laughed.

"It was one of Barbara's most treasured jewels, and God knows she had many!" Yves cried out merrily.

As we chatted, I observed my old friend with admiration. He had always been very confident, warm, graceful, charming and a complete gentleman. And time had not changed that. It was getting late, and Alexander, who liked to be in bed before midnight, raised his glass of champagne and toasted: "To friendship and the good old times!"

✦✦✦

I woke early to the sounds of the muezzin from the nearby mosque. I was in high spirits and looking forward to speaking with Alexander. We had not even mentioned the incident in the medina. I was sitting at the table prepared for a breakfast of fresh juices, mint tea and Moroccan breads and jams. The sun was shining and a lovely breeze was blowing.

It was a splendid day. Alexander appeared on the terrace wearing a light blue kaftan and navy blue velvet *babouches* with the Chavchvadze family crest. His attention to detail was exquisite.

Hassan brought a tray of poached eggs and smoked salmon and, at a nod from Alexander, disappeared.

"So you had a little taste of the bad elements in the medina, I heard," Alexander said, as he sipped his mint tea.

"You were expecting me, you old rogue!" I blurted out.

"Yes indeed, my friend. We were."

"We?"

"Yes, we; me and my group."

"What kind of group, a political or monarchist group?"

"Not at all. I am a member of the Brotherhood of the White Rose and we are only a spiritual group. We protect humanity's spiritual treasures and fight against injustices and deceit. We promote peace and the end of conflicts without violence. We believe that the whole universe was created by God with the energy of love."

I was speechless. Probably all his experiences in life had led him to this spiritual path, so I encouraged him to continue.

"I have never heard of this brotherhood, tell me more," I said.

"It was founded by Joseph of Arimathea, the grand-uncle of Jesus, when he came to England in the year 62 A.C. Our base is in Glastonbury. We are a secret and hermetic society. That is why you have not heard about us," he explained.

I was looking at him with my eyes and ears wide open. I could not imagine how a Russian prince would end up as member of an ancient secret society. Then he continued.

"We have always existed, since recorded history began. Some of our very first ancestors are mentioned in the Bible and other sacred scriptures: Aaron, Thoth, Hermes, Moses, John the Baptist and Jesus. You must have heard of Glastonbury Abbey and the Merovingian connection?" he asked.

"Yes of course! I have visited the ruins several times. I am a descendant of the Merovingian dynasty on my mother's side," I answered proudly.

"I remember her. A delightful lady, she was. She spoiled you so much!" he smiled at the memory of those days long gone.

"And why is this case of the Romanovs important to your Brotherhood? I need an explanation – for all I could see, the case had only political, economic or dynastic implications; I never suspected any spiritual repercussions."

"It's not your fault to think that way, since we humans tend to consider only material factors, but the spiritual part in our lives is more important than anything else. The planet is ruled by physical laws, but there are also spiritual laws in play, which we call Principles, and can never be destroyed nor ignored, because they deal with eternal spiritual energies."

"And you think that Nicholas II knew that?" I asked.

"Nicholas II was a very spiritual and noble person, a compassionate man of faith. His orthodox faith and his family were the most important things to him; more than his throne and his wealth. His benevolence was misunderstood and taken as a sign of weakness by his enemies, Rodney. And don't forget that he was the head of the Orthodox Church. This is very important in order to understand the current position of the Orthodox Church with respect to the bones found in Ekaterinburg."

"Oh, my friend. I guess I will have to visit you again to talk more about spirituality, but now I need to know about Anastasia's case," I said.

"It will be my pleasure, Rodney. Then I might invite you to become one of us, if you wish," Alexander said teasingly.

"Why not? It would be an honour. Now tell me about Fritz: who is he?"

"He is also a member of the Brotherhood. Because he is a local of Unterlengenhardt, he is stationed there to keep us informed of all visitors searching for information on Anastasia."

"But surely after such a long time he must be very idle!" I exclaimed.

"Not so, my friend! The enigma is very much alive. I believe you are now aware of the controversy in London around the alleged Romanov remains, and the legal battle in Charlottesville over Anastasia's tissue sample. All that craziness has strong motives and great power behind it. You would be surprised."

"So, I assume you know who was behind the ransacking of my room in Charlottesville?" I asked.

"The Cheka, I guess. They have spies in Germany and must have been immediately informed of your presence there."

"The Cheka, Alexander! That was the secret service of the Bolsheviks, and has not existed since 1922."

"You know what I mean, Rodney. The Cheka became the GPU, and later the KGB, and that was dismantled when the Soviet Union collapsed. Same dog, new collar!"

"It's now divided into three agencies: the Federal Security Service, FSB, the Main Intelligence Directorate, GRU, and the Foreign Intelligence Service, SVR," I clarified.

"Exactly," Alexander said.

"You still have some explaining to do, dear friend," I said. "And I am here to listen."

"The Romanov affair is still a very sensitive matter for many people out there. As far as the Russian government is concerned, the bones they unearthed in 1991 have been identified as those of Nicholas II, Empress Alexandra and three of their daughters. But there are two missing bodies. For them, they are those of the Tsarevitch and Grand Duchess Maria, but Professor William Maples of Miami University insists it is not Maria's but Anastasia's body that is missing. The Russian government is not pleased with foreigners poking into this matter, as for them is all but a closed case. It's not surprising that they heard about your new interest in this case and are keeping an eye on you until they are satisfied you don't know much or that you are not getting far. But take my word for it: they will not hurt you unless they feel that you are a real threat to national security."

"That's reassuring!" I said, and took a deep breath.

"When you went to Unterlengenhardt and started asking questions, Fritz immediately contacted me and our group in England. I was amazed at the twist of fate: my dear friend Rodney Mundy investigating the Anastasia case! Glastonbury immediately informed me of your old MI6 connection. You were heaven sent! I then instructed Fritz to follow you, protect you and report back to me," Alexander said, laughing at my astonishment. "So when he told us you had met with Augusta Rosenthal, I knew you were on the right track."

"But she was not so easy to start with," I said.

"We know. She is a very stubborn woman. She has always refused to hand us the box that Prince Frederick Ernst gave her for safekeeping. She kept insisting that someone would come one day to collect it and she would know who that person was. Fortunately, as of late she has been worried that no one had come in all these years, and that she was becoming frail and old; so, when you appeared on the scene I personally instructed her to hand it to you. I told her you were the chosen one and she agreed."

"But how did you know about that box?" I asked.

"Prince Frederick Ernst told us."

"And why didn't the Brotherhood take it to your headquarters years ago, even by force?" I added, even more perplexed.

"We knew it was safe with her as no one but us was aware of its existence and we had Fritz there to guard it. The time was not right for any disclosures, anyway."

"Alexander, but that's crazy! She's a very old woman. What if she had passed away? Surely there would have been real danger of the box and its contents being misplaced! What it contains proves the survival of the Tsar!"

"That's the spy speaking!" Alexander laughed. "The box and its contents are safe and that's all that matters."

"So tell me, please. What was in the box?" Alexander finally asked. "My curiosity has been eating away at me for years."

I explained everything in detail, especially the letter to Anastasia.

"And the pearls? Were they in the box?" He asked, unable to restrain himself.

"The pearls? They were also inside the cuckoo clock, but in a separate compartment; hidden in the mechanism! The Grand Duchess surely kept them in a safe hiding place!" I chuckled. "That supports the authenticity of the Tsar's letter."

"That little rascal, dear Augusta!" Alexander exclaimed. "She just forgot to mention the pearls," he added, laughing.

"So what is the truth, who died and who survived?"

"Well, Rodney, this is an extremely complicated situation. Right now I prefer not to answer that question. I can only tell you that it is a huge family drama tangled in state and royal secrets, with the dynastic that you mentioned while ago: political, economic and dynastic. But the truth will reveal itself, you will see. Actually my friend, I am sure that providence chose you to help bring that truth to light."

"So was Prince Frederick Ernst also a member of the Brotherhood?"

"Oh, most definitely! He was an extremely noble person. Honest and good hearted: someone of a much higher spiritual nature than us. His path started when he joined the Anthroposophists in his twenties. He became an active follower of Rudolf Steiner, the founder of Anthroposophy, together with his brother Prince George Moritz, his sister Charlotte and his brother-in-law Prince Sigismund. Years later, when he was already working hard to help Anastasia, he met some people of our hermetic group in England, and his spiritual beliefs matched those of the Brotherhood. He went to Glastonbury several times, both for his archaeological and spiritual investigations."

The more I talked with Alexander, the more I was convinced that there was much in this story that had been suppressed from the public. Some characters around Anna Anderson had been interesting people with extraordinary backgrounds, strong beliefs and unexpected connections. Alexander paused to drink some tea, and I spoke.

"When I went to Poland, someone I met told me that the Tsar had lived and died there in 1952 under the name of Michael Goloniewski. Was this person the Tsar?"

"No, Rodney." Alexander said gravely and without hesitation.

"So where did the Tsar live, then?"

"I cannot tell you for sure. There were rumours of his survival from December 1918, and several credible newspapers reported on that. Some people even claimed to have seen him in Vladivostok with his brother Grand Duke Michael Alexandrovich. But the buzz was wild in France, where many White Russians took refuge, including some of his most loyal generals and members of his secret police. Apparently he lived clandestinely in several places: Poland, Japan, France, Monaco, the Italian riviera. It has also been said that he lived for some years in the US, but I really don't want to speculate nor reveal much more to you at this stage. I trust you will understand."

"Yes, of course. Tell me about the Grand Duchesses then, and the Empress."

"Plenty of facts and misinformation are out there about them. The Tsarina had a long history of health issues and mental imbalance. Sadly, after the terrible ordeal of imprisonment they suffered, she lost her mind forever. She was confined in absolute secrecy to a convent, first in Poland and later in Italy, until her death." Alexander sighed.

"Well, all that is so sad and sounds credible. It was known in her time that she suffered several bouts of depression, probably from the stress of her son's malady!" I interjected.

"Olga, the eldest, was taken to Siberia, under custody of two loyal Cossacks, one of them named Dimitri and employed by the Cheka. Then she boarded a train and arrived in Vladivostok, where an elite German command was waiting for her and, following orders from Wilhelm II, provided her with a forged identity to continue her journey. Some German officers accompanied Olga and her friend Januska to Peking and later to Shanghai. Then the Great War ended: Germany was defeated, Kaiser Wilhelm abdicated and everything devolved into chaos. After a year of wandering she suffered a nervous breakdown in November 1919 and was taken to Hamburg. She was entrusted to the care and guidance of a remarkable woman named Baroness Elisabeth von Schaevenbach. After recovering she lived mostly in Germany, in Potsdam, with Januska and relatives, under the name Maria Bottcher or Marga Boodts. Her passports show that she travelled a lot and lived a lavish life, but was also very compassionate and helped needy people.

Published: January 9, 1919
Copyright © The New York Times

# AGAIN REPORT CZAR TO BE STILL ALIVE

## Grand Duke Cyril Given as Authority for Story That Officer Was Shot Instead.

## HIS FAMILY ALSO LIVING

## News Said to Have Been Conveyed In Letter from Ex-Autocrat's Daughter Tatiana.

LONDON, Jan. 8. (British Wireless Service.)—According to a story sent by a special correspondent of The Morning Post at Archangel—which it is necessary to treat with reserve—the former Emperor of Russia is still alive. The correspondent telegraphs:

"A friend of mine, Prince M——, who has just arrived here from Petrograd, informed me that he had a long talk with Grand Duke Cyril on Nov. 18. The Grand Duke told him that he had just received a letter from Grand Duchess Tatiana, daughter of the Emperor, who wrote that the Empress and her daughters were still alive and that the Emperor had not been shot.

"The Bolshevist officer who was ordered to carry out the sentence of death told the Emperor that it was a matter of indifference to him who was shot. He had orders to produce a corpse—bullets in the head of a victim would make identification impossible.

"Count T——, who was present at the conversation, offered to sacrifice himself, saying he considered it was his duty to lay down his life for his sovereign. The Emperor protested vehemently, but was overruled by Count T—— and the officer. The Emperor escaped, but no one knows where he is at the present time.

"Dr. Botkin has also written to his sister to the effect that 'the greatest crime of the twentieth century has miscarried.'"

An Associated Press dispatch from Warsaw under date of Dec. 24 gave Michael de Tchihatchef, a nephew of General Skoropadski, as authority for the statement that the former Russian Emperor and his entire family were still alive. Count Tatichev, the Emperor's former personal military attaché, was named as the victim who was shot instead of the Emperor.

**The New York Times**

Published: January 9, 1919
Copyright © The New York Times

Article published in the New York Times on 9th January 1919, revealing statements made by Grand Duke Cyril about a letter he received from Grand Duchess Tatiana in November 1918.

After 1939 she settled in Italy. Olga wrote her memoirs in the fifties, but they were not published at that time. Rumours said that the Vatican intervened and stopped publication, fearing her confessions would cause harm to the Catholic Church and the image of Pope Pius XII. Nobody really knows what happened; maybe other unknown forces intervened. Prince Frederick Ernst was in contact with her from 1958 onwards, which is how we know that one copy of the autobiography still exists, and we will eventually arrange for its publication when the time is right."

"You mean Prince Frederick Ernst was in contact with both Olga and Anastasia?"

"Indeed he was, and so was Prince Sigismund of Prussia. He also visited Olga in her villa in Italy in 1957. After that she received his endorsement and that of Nicholas, the Hereditary Grand Duke of Oldenburg. Both provided some monetary help, since her financial situation was critical. In 1953 she claimed a huge deposit of valuables made by her father the Tsar between 1906 and 1914 in the Vatican and met privately with Pope Pius XII, who recognized her from the times they had met when both lived in Berlin, during the twenties. He promised to put everything in order as soon as possible, and give her what had been waiting for her. Meanwhile, he provided her with some money, with the help of Mother Pascalina Lehnert. Eventually, things became very complicated and she was unjustly denied her inheritance. It is a very sad story, Rodney. She suffered immensely and her health and mental state deteriorated. Olga Nikolaevna died poor, though loved and cared for by her loyal lady in waiting and secretary Martha Airoldi, as well as a wonderful and compassionate family in Italy. We know that she left them thousands of documents, including many from the Vatican, which prove that she was indeed Grand Duchess Olga. They will also become public, at the right time."

"This is amazing!" I said in awe. "You just mentioned the Vatican! My friend Miles gave me a copy of an article suggesting that the Vatican has been covering all this story. Mother Pascalina Lenhert admitted that Pope Pius XII met with Olga and Maria, and he knew who they really were."

"Yes, it was Prince Frederick Ernst who first talked with the nun in Rome in 1982. He was aware of Mother Pascalina's role in this story from the very beginning, when she was the governess of Eugenio Pacelli – later Pope Pius XII. Pope Benedict XV appointed Pacelli as nuncio to Bavaria, and since there was no nuncio to Prussia or Germany at the time, Pacelli became the de facto Nuncio to the German Empire in 1918, and held close contact with the Kaiser's government. He was officially appointed in June 1920 and acted as dean of all diplomats. Mother Pascalina was also his confidante: she must have known everything."

"Were he and Mother Pascalina Lenhert the only ones in the Vatican who knew the secret of the Romanovs?" I asked.

"Of course not! The first one implicated was Pope Benedict XV and his secretary of state, Cardinal Pietro Gasparri. They were directly involved in the negotiations to evacuate the Tsarina and her children from Russia; then Popes Pius XI and Pius XII, Pope John XXIII and Pope Paul VI. Also Cardinal Mario Nasalli Rocca di Cornealiano, Cardinal Federico Callori di Vignale and Cardinal Luigi Poggi, just to mention a few."

"Oh my God! Alexander, this is unbelievable! How do you know all that, my friend?"

"Let's say that I am a good researcher," he said, winking an eye.

"And Tatiana and Maria?"

"Dear Rodney, too many questions for one day. I promise that I will tell you everything when the moment is right, but please, I'm not in a position to do so now."

"I understand, Alexander. You know you can trust me when you feel like doing so," I reassured him.

"It's still a secret, Rodney, and we should keep it that way for the moment."

I seized the moment to express a concern. "Alex, I just want to ask your opinion about this issue: there is someone in Madrid calling himself Prince Alexis D'Anjou-Durassow, who claims to be the grandson of Grand Duchess Maria Nikolaevna. He wrote a book claiming his ancestry that caused quite a stir. In Spain many people say he is an impostor. Others believe he is authentic. I heard that the Russian Monarchist League supports him as well as some Ukrainian monarchists and members of the Polish government in exile. What do you know about him?"

Alexander reflected for a moment before he replied. I sensed he was measuring his words.

"We think he might be genuine. Prince Frederick Ernst and other royals privately seemed to believe so, and other people around the prince agreed with him, like Dominique Auclères. We are seriously studying his claim."

"Well, it might be possible. The Russian scientists that identified the bones of the Romanovs said that Maria's skeleton was missing from the mass grave. That could be proof that she survived. Don't you think?"

"Oh Rodney, don't be naïve. The bones found in Ekaterinburg are not those of Nicholas II and his family. Tikhon Kulikovsky, the son of Grand Duchess Olga Alexandrovna, the Tsar's sister, was asked to donate a DNA sample for comparison. He declined, alleging that he would do so when the government and the Orthodox Church formed a commission to investigate seriously."

"I have read Prince Alexis' book and the story is absolutely fascinating if it's true," I said.

"I know all about Alexis' books. Actually I have the French and Spanish versions. The last one in Italian is difficult to find, because somebody bought every copy right after it was published in Italy, to take it off the shelves. Unfortunately, there was never an English edition, which I think would have helped his cause," Alexander said, showing disappointment. "Though I have to admit that when Prince Frederick Ernst told us that Prince Alexis was preparing his first book, we asked him not to publish anything until we had no doubts about his claim. The timing of the book was totally wrong and now he has made many powerful enemies because of it. It is a great shame."

"But what is your gut feeling about him?" I asked.

"He has many interesting documents in his possession including his grandmother's civil and dynastic testaments, notarized in Rome; affidavits from important witnesses; many letters from members of royal houses of Europe; and letters between Lord Mountbatten and Grand Duchess Maria after 1956. Those letters are potentially explosive if they are authentic and we believe they are. To me it seems rather unlikely that someone could fabricate such an intricate story. He has some strong supporters and friends all over the world and within the royal families, and frankly, my feeling is that he is who he claims to be. Having said that, he is too impulsive and he has done great harm to the Romanov cause. The Brotherhood is trying to repair the damage and we hope to rein him in. There are very powerful conflicting interests involved even today. His mother just died three days ago; her name was Princess Olga Beatrice Dolgoruky-Romanov, and although she had been very sick during the last year, she seemed to be on the way to recovery. Then, she died suddenly of a heart attack."

"Olga! Is that another coincidence?" I asked Alexander.

"I don't think it is! Olga is a name closely related to the Romanov family. Her second name, Beatrice, was also one of the names of Alix of Hesse, the Tsarina. At the beginning of this month they announced that both would be giving blood and some hair samples for DNA testing.

Now she is dead and Prince Alexis feels distressed and worried about his future. Maybe it would be a good idea for you to meet him and give him our condolences. Tell him to be patient. He might even listen to you. Try to get a sense of his authenticity. You are good at that, Rodney."

"I will call him when I return to Madrid. Have you met him personally?"

"No I haven't, but from what I've heard he is too flamboyant and tries too hard to push his claim forward. I was informed by some connections at the Russian embassy in Madrid that in November of last year he submitted seven files with documents proving the veracity of his story to the Russian ambassador and to the American consul in Madrid; and as I mentioned, he was willing to provide the samples for DNA analysis. His behaviour is completely opposite to that of Grand Duchess Anastasia, may her soul rest in peace! We have pleaded with him to be discreet and to be patient but he is so stubborn, and just won't listen. If he really is Grand Duchess Maria's grandson, under normal circumstances he would have rights to the throne, but we must abide by Grand Duke Michael's manifesto. He was our last sovereign, even if it was only for a day."

"I'm curious. It will certainly be interesting to meet him and I will do my best to get him to understand the scenario."

"Thanks, Rodney. We would appreciate that."

"So tell me more about Anastasia, then," I asked.

"You know her story; you have read all the books about her. But there are many facts that have never been recorded, like what really happened the night of the alleged murder and why the Romanov women were imprisoned in Perm. Anastasia made a mistake: she was very scared and escaped three times, and after a terrible ordeal she appeared in Berlin in February of 1920. The story of Anna Anderson was a terrible tragedy; she paid a high price for escaping and putting the whole operation at risk. Hopefully soon, in honouring her memory, we can begin to make amends," Alexander sighed.

"I had read something about the women being transferred to Perm in *The File on the Tsar*, but I had no idea of the ordeal that followed!" I mused.

"Yes. The family knew about her escape attempt and that she was captured. They were told that she had been killed by the Bolsheviks and they really believed so. They also thought that the White Army was going to defeat the Bolsheviks and restore the crown, but they failed."

"What a terrible tragedy!" I cried out. "What happened to the Tsarevitch? Surely being a haemophilic he must have died young."

"I promise, Rodney, on my honour, that you will know everything when the moment comes."

"I now remember Igor telling me and making me promise never to reveal that the Tsarevitch had survived. What was the name he was using?" I tried to recall. It had been so many years ago, but the conversation had stuck clearly in my mind. I could see that my questions were making Alexander uncomfortable.

"Never mind!" Alexander said, trying to change the subject. "Please trust me," Alexander pleaded, slightly irritated at my insistent questions.

"OK, my friend. Please forgive me. It is just that this story is so fascinating. I just started investigating the Anastasia affair to satisfy my own curiosity, make my son Carlos happy, and as a token to the memories of both my mother and my wife, Pepita. I think this whole thing is too big for a seventy-year-old," I said, realizing the magnitude of the matter that I had stumbled into.

"I need you to find the lost icon, Rodney. You have been trained for the job. I know we can trust you. You are cunning and brilliant." I noticed a tinge of desperation in Alexander's voice.

"I have been retired for many years, Alexander, and in fact, I came to see you because I was told you might know who had stolen it."

"The truth is that I don't have a clue. You must help us recover it. It is a vital matter, Rodney!" He pleaded, choosing his words with care.

"One last question!" I said. "Is it true that Anastasia concealed a powerful testimony inside the icon?"

"Yes, yes, yes!" Alexander responded, "And that's why this relic is priceless. Anastasia wrote it in 1957 and asked Baroness von Militz and Prince Frederick Ernst to show it only after her death. Both knew where she kept it. Then Baroness Miltitz died and only the prince knew its whereabouts. He actually had planned to write a book telling the whole truth; we talked about it many times. The document was vital to that plan. He also had to return the icon to Grand Duchess Elisabeth of Saxe-Weimar-Eisenach, and when he was informed that the icon had disappeared from Charlottesville, he suffered tremendously. Prince Frederick Ernst thought he wouldn't be able to fulfil one of her last wishes, to show the world that she was indeed Anastasia and let her be buried with her real name: Grand Duchess Anastasia of Russia, the name given to her on the day she was born."

"João told me that a collector called Gregory Dubinkin went to see him the day before I did. He was looking for information on the icon. He wanted to know if it really existed."

"Oh my God!" Alexander cried out.

"What is it, Alex?" I asked with concern.

"He is no collector, Rodney. He is a dangerous ex–KGB agent responsible for the deaths of many of us during the Soviet era. So they are onto the icon. They probably know more than we thought they did. We must move swiftly."

"Who do you think wants to get the icon?"

"The Russian government, the Vatican, your government, unscrupulous collectors and of course, us." Alexander replied, a little nervously.

"But why would the Vatican have any interest? Why would they want it?"

"Well, you will be surprised to know how deeply they were involved in a secret operation in 1918 related to the Romanovs. At that time, it was only known in very high diplomatic circles. They also have good spies. Their secret service is very efficient – probably somebody already told them about your quest. I hope they only want it because of its religious value. Recently they have shown some interest in those orthodox relics. Sometime during the '70s, an icon supposed to be that of Our Lady of Kazan was bought by a catholic group called Blue Army of Our Lady of Fatima and enshrined in Fátima, Portugal. Last year, 1993, the icon was given to Pope John Paul II, who took it to the Vatican and had it installed in his private study."

"Oh, I see; maybe the Pope wants to start his own collection," I added with a little sarcasm.

"After Grand Duchess Anastasia's death, the prince made the arrangements to bury her ashes at Seeon. That was her last wish, too. She wanted to be cremated because of her Anthroposophical beliefs. Prince Frederick Ernst was desperately trying to find the icon, but he didn't want to tell the police because he clearly knew about the secret it was hiding."

"Now I understand why nobody issued an art alert or got Interpol involved."

"Exactly!" Alexander said. "It was a secret. Then Prince Frederick Ernst came here and asked his 'brothers' to start the search, and to also help him find Anastasia's lost child."

"I thought he didn't exist," I said, surprised.

"Indeed, he did! Prince Frederick Ernst had done some research year before. Some clues had been passed to him by someone from the Netherlands. But the last years of his life were dedicated to looking for the missing child and the icon, to honour his promise to Anastasia. Unfortunately, he couldn't find either."

"Alex, do you know someone called Anatoly Levkov? My colleague Miles, who was with me in MI6 years back and has been helping me in my research, contacted him to look at the Tsar's letters. He is supposed to be a very good graphologist."

"Never heard of him, but I can ask for you. Why?"

"As you know, he did authenticate the letters of the Tsar but then warned me to forget everything and I just have a bad feeling about him. Please, ask your Russian contacts, and let me know if you discover anything relevant about him. By the way, when did Prince Frederick Ernst die?" I asked.

"He died in Rosenheim, on 23rd February 1985."

"What happened?" I asked.

Alexander was visibly affected. "Nobody knows for sure. He was a healthy man and full of life, despite being eighty years old. He was very enthusiastic about his investigation. Actually, he told us that he had made good progress meeting with high ranking people at the Vatican. As I mentioned before, he met Mother Pascalina Lehnert, and she told him many things she knew about the negotiations to rescue the Romanov women in 1918, their escape from Russia and their secret lives afterwards. After she died in 1983 he contacted Father Fernando Lamas Pereyra, who had also spoken with the nun on the same topic. The men met several times, the last one being at Castle Duino in November of 1984. Prince Frederick Ernst was a great friend of Prince Raymond of Thurn und Taxis, the second Duke of Castel Duino, and used to spend a lot of time in his beautiful castle near Trieste. He called me to let me know that other royals were present during those days, and the news from around the globe after Mother Pascalina's death was widely discussed. Then he unexpectedly got sick in November 1984, but I never imagined it was something serious. One day a mutual friend, Ian Lilburn, called me with the bad news that Prince Frederick Ernst had suddenly passed away," Alexander explained, while his voice trembled and tears rolled down his cheeks. "That's why we need you, Rodney."

"I understand very well now the importance of this mission: to find the icon and save its secret content."

"We knew we could count on you; I definitely knew I could, knowing you so well. So, thanks. You won't be alone. We will protect you and help you in this great mission," Alexander said, visibly emotional while patting my back.

"I will try my best, my friend. You have my word."

"One last thing. I will ask my brothers at Glastonbury to collect the contents of the box for safekeeping. We have been keeping documents and sacred relics for two thousand years. I trust you are in agreement with these arrangements?"

"You rascal! Of course I am!" I replied grinning.

I had returned to Madrid the day after my conversation with Alexander, leaving my wife in Marbella. I spent less than a week preparing my trip to Rome. I could not believe that I found myself suddenly working on a secret mission for the Brotherhood of the White Rose. I had welcomed the financial assistance that Alexander had offered to cover expenses, but had flatly refused any payment for my services. I was no mercenary.

I went to the office and found a message from James Cross, the private detective in Charlottesville. I called him immediately and he updated me with all the news about the court battle on the tissue sample. New rumours said that even Dr Berenberg-Gossler, the lawyer of Anna Anderson's opposition twenty-five years ago, was trying to exercise some influence over Baron Gienanth to get access to the sample and test it. James said that Marina Schweitzer was probably going to win. It was only a matter of days before the judge's decision.

While in Madrid I followed Alexander's directions and tried to contact Prince Alexis D'Anjou. I phoned him, and a female voice with a Russian accent told me that he was on leave due to the recent passing of his mother, and would return my call as soon he felt better and had some time. But he did not return my call.

I was absolutely sure that my next trip had to be to the Vatican, as it was mentioned by several people in relation to the Romanovs. I told Carlos that I had decided not to speak to Miles about my trip. Then I flew to Rome.

♦ ♦ ♦

I arrived at Fiumicino Airport at noon on the 29th of May and checked into the Inn at the Spanish Steps, a small luxury hotel on Via Dei Condotti. The building was listed as a national monument and had been a stately home in the 1800s.

I was excited about my quest. I felt more elated and full of energy than I had in years, in spite of the dangers. I was on the job again. I was to meet Enrico di Notto for coffee that afternoon, a member of the

Brotherhood who had been contacted to help me with the investigation in Rome. I chose the busy Antico Caffè Greco founded in 1760 and arrived a few minutes before our appointment. I imagined that Fritz was close behind, a sort of invisible guardian angel, as I had not seen him since Tangier. Enrico walked straight towards me, stretching out his hand to shake mine. He smiled. He had a slender frame and was, I guessed, in his mid-fifties. He wore an elegant linen three-piece suit and carried a walking stick with an ivory handle. He was undoubtedly a gentleman of distinction.

"*Benvenuto a Roma, caro signor Mundy!*" He exclaimed, flamboyantly waving his hands, as the Italians like to do.

"It has all been arranged!" he continued, without giving me the opportunity to even greet him. "*Due cappuccini,*" he ordered as we stood by the bar, without asking me what I wanted to have. I laughed.

"*Scusi, Signor Mundy*. I am so excited!" he apologized.

"No problem, Enrico. Don't worry. So what has been arranged?"

"You are to meet one of the librarians of the *Biblioteca Apostolica Vaticana*. His name is Father Elias. He is expecting a historian from England and will be happy to help you on your thesis. We are not sure how much he can do for us, but Alexander is certain that you will be able to squeeze out all he knows. He could lead you to something interesting," he said reassuringly.

"Why have you not been able to do this yourself?" I asked.

"Italians, we don't trust each other!" Enrico exclaimed, with a grand sweep of both arms that made me laugh.

"So when must I go?"

"Tomorrow morning!"

"And where and when shall I see you again?"

"I will call you at the hotel."

✦ ✦ ✦

I took a taxi to the Vatican City to visit one of the oldest libraries in the world, with one of the most significant collections of historical texts. The taxi dropped me off at Saint Peter's Square and I walked past a sentry of Swiss guards into the library complex. I had visited the Vatican on several occasions in the past but for some reason I had never gone to the library. Its grandiosity and opulence surprised me. I walked through the Sistine Hall with its black and white chequered marble floors in which the reflection of the extraordinary paintings of the domed ceilings could be seen. I walked straight to the office, not taking any time to marvel at the treasures surrounding me.

"*Buongiorno!* May I see Father Elias, please? He is expecting me. My name is Rodney Mundy," I told a young handsome father.

"Did you bring your credentials, Signor Mundy?" He asked.

"Certainly!" I replied as I handed him the documents Alexander had given me, identifying me as a historian working for Oxford University.

"Welcome. Father Elias is waiting for you. Please follow me. My name is Father Miguel."

"*Eres español?*" I asked.

"*Sí.*" He replied as he smiled, also asking me if I came from Spain.

"Yes, I live in Madrid though I work for a British university," I replied, as I followed him through the immense library.

"This is Father Elias," Father Miguel said, as we approached a fragile man in his seventies who was seated in a little corner desk, focusing all of his attention on several documents. He slowly got up, removed his glasses, and shook my hand.

"What can I do for you, Signor?"

"Are you familiar with the Romanov case, father?" I asked.

"Vaguely," he replied, not showing much interest.

"It's a fascinating mystery, Father Elias," Father Miguel said with a sudden excitement that surprised me.

"There is a lot of controversy about some skeletons disinterred in the city of Ekaterinburg, in Russia," I said. "Scientists and anthropologists from different parts of the world are now testing the DNA of those bones, since rumours of deceit and secrecy have abounded. Also, possibly, very soon a tissue sample from Anastasia Manahan will be tested. She was the woman who claimed to be the youngest daughter of the Tsar, who miraculously survived the assassination of her family. For this reason, Oxford University has asked me to investigate the allegations of Mother Pascalina Lenhert: that surviving members of the Imperial family visited the Vatican in the past, and were received in private audience by Pope Pius XII. So I am wondering if you can help me find any relevant archives that could be in this library," I inquired. Father Elias seemed tense and uncomfortable.

"There is nothing on the Russian Imperial family here! Nothing at all! Mother Pascalina burnt all personal documents belonging to Pope Pius XII immediately after his death. She justified herself by saying that she was following the Holy Father's orders but it is a tragedy for history! She was expelled within twenty-four hours from the Vatican for this disgraceful action." He sighed nervously.

"But father, this is an enormous library. We should check on the computer," Father Miguel said, trying to be helpful and undoubtedly interested in the matter.

"Father Miguel, I know this library inside out. I have been here for over fifty years. You are only an assistant, so please don't tell me what to do. Anyway, if any documents survived she must have taken them with her." Father Elias was losing his patience with me.

"I'm sorry, Signor Mundy. Though I'm certain you won't find anything here in the library, you might want to look in the secret archives, just in case any document survived the perfidious destruction of that nun; but you will need special permission from Cardinal Luigi Poggi, the archivist and librarian of the Holy Roman Church, or from the prefect of the secret archives, Father Jozef Metzler. This permit must be requested in writing, far in advance, and you must clearly indicate what you are looking for and the purpose of your investigation. Then the Holy Church will or will not grant you permission. In my opinion you are wasting your time. I insist, I have never heard of such records. Have a good day!" He bluntly dismissed me as he slowly sat down, put on his spectacles and picked up the documents he was studying with so much interest that he did not even glance back at me again.

I followed Father Miguel back to the office.

"That did not go too well, father, but thanks for your help, anyway," I said gratefully.

"I have a friend from the seminar who works in the secret archives. He is Russian and he seems to have some special interest in the Romanovs. That is why this story fascinates me, too. I will speak to him and see what he really knows and if he is willing to speak to you."

I could not believe this serendipity.

"How can I contact you, father?" He scribbled his phone number on a piece of paper and handed it over to me.

"Call me tomorrow afternoon."

As I was walking into Saint Peter's Square, I heard Father Miguel calling my name. I turned around and saw him running towards me.

"Signor Mundy, Cardinal Poggi wants to see you!" he yelled, slightly out of breath.

"News seems to travel fast here," I said. I followed Father Miguel back to the library and into the magnificent office of the all-powerful archivist and librarian of the Holy Roman Church: the custodian of all the church's secrets. As I walked in, he rose from his richly decorated desk and gave me his hand to kiss. I knew from Alexander's brief that he was seventy-seven years old and had held many posts of power under different popes. He had worked for twenty years at the Secretariat of State and rose to the rank of domestic prelate in 1960. Moreover, he had been papal nuncio in central Africa and according to Alexander, he had played some murky role in negotiations with the communist-ruled nations of the Warsaw Pact. He was both steeped in knowledge of the Eastern Orthodox Church and well-versed in political intrigue, having been sent to Warsaw by Pope John Paul II and later to the Kremlin to negotiate with Moscow.

Poggi was of medium height and clearly a man who enjoyed good food and good wines. He invited me to sit down. I gazed at the frescoes on the ceiling and the magnificent tapestries on the walls.

"So, Signor Mundy, I hear that you are interested in the Romanovs," he said as he smiled. He came across as a gentle man with a friendly manner, but I knew I was sitting in front of the most powerful man in the Vatican and I could not allow myself to succumb to his charm. I immediately sensed that our conversation was being recorded by the deliberately way he spoke.

"Yes, Cardinal Poggi. I am. And now that I have the privilege of meeting you I would like to directly request your authorization for me to check the secret archives for files on the last Russian Imperial family."

"You don't miss a beat, signor." The cardinal replied. "I am afraid that I cannot grant you that permission because there are no files on the Imperial family in the secret archives."

"That is hard to believe, Your Eminence," I teased him.

"The Romanovs must interest you very much, signor, for you to have gone back to your old profession," he said with sudden scorn.

I ignored his insinuation as I had him exactly were I wanted him.

"So then, Your Eminence, you affirm with total certainty that such documents do not exist in the secret archives?"

"Yes, I do. I know all the nooks and crannies of this library, but even if those documents did exist we would always keep them secret," he added mysteriously.

"Would you?" I asked provocatively, waiting for his reaction. "I thought you said they don't exist," I insisted.

"They don't, caro signor, and for your own safety, please take my word for it!"

✦ ✦ ✦

I had not liked the veiled threat. The Cardinal knew who I was and that I had been in MI6. I had to assume he also knew that I was looking for information on the icon. It was now an open race and I had to be the winner and find it first.

As I left the Vatican City I had the sensation that I was being followed. I thought I had caught a glimpse of Blondie. There were many tourists around and I could not be sure, but instinct was telling me he was in Rome. The cardinal was also not going to let me out of his sight. I could not know whether Fritz was around so I felt rather vulnerable and alone. I rushed into the hotel and went to my room to rest and plan my next move. I had a message from Enrico. I was to meet him at nine for dinner at a small restaurant in the Trastevere called the Taverna Trilussa. I took a shower, freshened up and was pouring myself a scotch on the rocks when the phone rang.

"Signor Mundy!"

"Yes, it's me. Who is it?" I asked.

"This is Father Miguel."

"*Buenas tardes, padre*," I said, happy to receive his call.

"Please listen carefully, signor. Meet me tomorrow at noon at the Church of Santa Maria della Pace. There will be a mass at that time. Just join the congregation. Go straight to the Capella Chigi, the first one on the right. I will be waiting for you inside the first confessional box. I have a message for you. Please do not be late."

"I'll be there, but father, how did you know where I was staying? I didn't tell you," I asked with concern.

"You must know that the Holy Church has eyes everywhere!" he replied. "Please don't worry. I want to help you."

"I will be there," I said as Father Miguel hung up.

✦ ✦ ✦

I arrived at the Taverna Trilussa five minutes before nine and Enrico was already sitting at the table. I loved being in the Trastevere, the old world of the Romans. Homes were decked with flower boxes and clinging ivy, and laundry lines hung from terracotta buildings in a maze of cobblestone streets.

The place named after the famous Roman poet was crowded, noisy and lively, as are most Roman restaurants. I noticed that the ambience was much more formal than I had expected: the name taverna had probably been linked to its tradition rather than to its present-day reality. Enrico had already ordered a bottle of Chianti and we toasted as he explained that the restaurant was famous for its traditional local cuisine. He took charge and ordered a selection of its most famous dishes: pumpkin flowers, crostini with artichokes and homemade ricotta then a plate each of rigatoni alla'amatriciana.

"So how did your day go?" he asked, as we drank some more wine while waiting for the meal.

I told him about my meeting with Father Elias and how I was followed out of the building and asked to go and see Cardinal Poggi.

"They both insisted that there was no information whatsoever on the Romanovs in the Vatican archives. The cardinal subtly threatened me and asked me to forget my investigation! He knows who I am, Enrico," I acknowledged with concern.

The waiter brought the starters.

"It looks delicious, Enrico. Good choices," I said.

"Try the artichokes. They are sublime!"

"Artichokes are about the only thing I don't eat, but no worries as there is plenty to eat!" I said merrily, taking another sip of the delicious Chianti.

"You must know that the cardinal is very close to the Black Pope, who oversees all clandestine activities of the Vatican secret service," Enrico confided as he took an artichoke. "Delicious! A shame you don't like them."

"Who is this Black Pope?" I asked.

"The head of the Jesuit Generals of the Society of Jesus. He is a very powerful man. The Jesuits are in fact a secret society very close to the Pope!"

"Enrico, they are probably here. Someone is following me everywhere. Do they know you?" I said with concern.

"But of course, *caro amico,* but they don't know what I do!" he exclaimed theatrically.

"That is reassuring, Enrico," I said.

"Let's drink to it," he proposed, as he raised his glass of Chianti and took a big sip.

"Are you alright?" I asked, as I saw his expression suddenly change. He downed the rest of the glass in one gulp.

"I don't know, Rodney, I have a tingling sensation in my mouth and my throat is on fire."

"But the food isn't spicy! Drink some water," I suggested.

"I feel dizzy!" he said.

"Do you want us to leave?" I asked. Enrico looked very pale. He seemed to be suffocating. He started loosening his tie and unbuttoned his shirt. Sweat was dripping from his forehead.

"Rodney, please, I don't feel well… I can't breathe!"

"Waiter, waiter, call an ambulance," I cried out as everyone's attention was drawn to us. I got up to try to help Enrico. I took his pulse and it was completely erratic. The *maître d'* and someone sitting close to our table who identified himself as a doctor came to our aid and helped Enrico lie on the floor. He asked a waiter to bring some tablecloths to cover him as he was now shivering. His muscles started to twitch. He was clearly in agony and could barely breathe. The doctor gave him mouth-to-mouth resuscitation. He was frantically trying to save his life. And then I saw Enrico's eyes go blank. Less than twenty minutes after we had sat down for dinner, he was dead. I was utterly shocked.

There was a huge commotion in the restaurant. Most of the horrified diners were starting to leave just as the ambulance arrived.

What had happened? I asked myself. It could not be the food, as I felt fine.

I heard the doctor say that it must have been some sort of seizure or an allergic reaction to something.

"Did you know the victim?" the policeman asked me.

"Very slightly. His name was Enrico di Notto. We were business associates and we had just met today."

I told the police where I was staying, left the restaurant, and lost myself in the Trastevere as I reflected on all the things that had happened since I had arrived in the eternal city. No one seemed to be following me.

◆ ◆ ◆

I could barely sleep. The events of the night had been very disturbing. I called the bellboy at eight in the morning, gave him money and a generous tip, and sent him to buy me a wig, some make-up and some women's clothes. He looked at me in disbelief, but I explained I had a fancy dress party that evening and I wanted to go as an Italian *nonna*.[1] I told him I had a hangover and did not feel well and that I was checking out at eleven. He laughed conspiratorially.

"Too much Chianti, signor!"

I gave him my sizes and he promised to get me everything. He cheerfully told me he would ask his mother to do the shopping on my behalf. After what had happened I had to take precautions and I could not risk my life or Father Miguel's. I called Alexander to inform him of Enrico's death. Though the police suggested it had been a heart attack, I knew there had to be foul play.

"Good morning, Alexander."

"Rodney, are you alright?" Alexander asked anxiously. So he already knew. "What exactly happened?"

"We were talking and he suddenly felt unwell and died within minutes."

"What were the symptoms?"

"He complained of a tingling and burning sensation in his mouth. He drank water and wine desperately and soon after became incoherent, which is when I asked the waiter to call an ambulance. Before the ambulance arrived his muscles began to twitch and then he couldn't breathe and just collapsed and died in front of me." Alexander took his time. "Alex… are you there?"

"He was poisoned with tetrodotoxin," Alexander finally said.

"Never heard of it."

"It comes from the Fugu fish. The bastards! It's nearly untraceable and surely the police will record it as death from natural causes."

"Enrico ordered the food for both of us. He ordered *crostini* with artichokes for the middle of the table, and it just so happens that artichokes are not my cup of tea, so I didn't touch them. It must have been that dish! He ate most of it, and within twenty minutes he was dead. I now realize whoever did this wanted us both out of the way," I recounted, shocked at this realization.

"What's going on here? Who do you think is responsible for this, Alex?" I asked. "How could they know we were in that restaurant or have the chance to tamper with the food?"

"Rodney, most people have a price. I'm sorry, but I don't have a clue. This is getting out of hand. You must be very careful. You had better leave Rome as soon as you can."

---

[1] Grandmother.

"I'm meeting a young priest at noon, who says he has some information for me. I'll try to fly out this evening."

"Rodney, Fritz is there to protect you."

"I am glad to know. I have to admit he is good at his job as I haven't even felt his presence or seen him. I'm being followed by the Russians and probably also by Vatican agents."

"By the way, I do have information on Anatoly Levkov," Alexander said.

"Tell me," I said, eager to know.

"He is indeed a top graphologist and historian. He works freelance, and is often hired by the Vatican and other religious and military orders."

I was now even more confused.

"Please leave Rome as soon as you can!" Alexander ordered.

✦ ✦ ✦

By ten thirty, I had granny's clothes in my room. The bellboy laughed as he placed everything on the bed: a blouse, a skirt, a pair of stockings, a headscarf, a shawl, a handbag and a white wig. Everything else was black.

"*La mia mamma* says that a true Italian grandmother must be dressed in black. They are always mourning the death of a loved one!" he said teasingly, leaving the room.

I went downstairs, paid the bill and returned to my room to finish packing. My plan was to check out of the hotel, leave my bags with the concierge, find a busy café and transform myself into a *nonna* before I went to meet Father Miguel.

Just as I was leaving the room after having packed my small bag with my disguise, the phone rang. I answered, and heard a shrill voice asking for me.

"Signor Mundy, this is Prince Cyril Vaganoff, a historian of the Sovereign Order of Malta. I was wondering if you could come and see me at four this afternoon."

"I'll be there," I replied.

"Very well then, at four o'clock at the Palazzo de Malta, Via Condotti, 68. It's very close to your hotel," he said, and hung up without another word.

By now it was no surprise that all of Rome knew where I was staying.

In view of the new circumstances, I decided to stay until the next day, but to move to another hotel and fly back to Madrid first thing in the morning.

As planned, I transformed myself and looked in the mirror at my unrecognizable reflection. I arrived just after noon and ran into the chapel. Mass had already started, but not many people were attending. The Capella Chigi had a beautiful fresco by Raphael of the four Sybils, each of them receiving a revelation from an angel. Was this symbolic of the revelation I was just about to receive? I saw the confessional box and knelt. The little wooden window opened as I heard Father Miguel say, "May God be with you, signora."

"Father, it's me. It's Rodney Mundy."

"*Dios mio!*" Father Miguel exclaimed. "What is happening?" he asked.

"I'm being followed and a friend of mine was murdered last night. This disguise is for both our protection. So, father what do you have for me?"

"May his soul rest in peace!" Father Miguel said as he handed me an envelope, which I immediately opened. I lit my small torch to read the paper it contained.

I could not believe my eyes. The paper had the seal of the *Archivio della Segretaria di Stato*,[2] and it seemed to be the cover of a file dated 1918. It was signed and stamped and had a series of protocol numbers written on a left-hand column. Handwritten under the name of the file were the magic words: *Imperatrice di Russia e figlie*,[3] while below was written *Interessamento dal S. Padre*.[4] I was speechless, and could only try to imagine why they had these files on the Imperial family. And why was the Vatican so adamant about hiding the existence of these files? What were they trying to keep secret, and for what reason? Father Miguel spoke interrupting my thoughts.

"Signor Mundy, as I told you, my friend who works in the secret archive is a Russian Catholic priest. He has asked me to tell you that there are over twenty files on the late Imperial family. This is just the cover of one of the files, but he will photograph everything for you," Father Miguel said in a hushed voice.

"Why would he do that? Surely it's not safe," I asked with concern.

"He is devoted to discovering the truth about what happened. He says he owes it to Russia. He is obsessed with the matter. He claims you have been sent by the Almighty Father to reveal the truth."

---

[2] Archive of the Secretariat of State.
[3] Empress of Russia and daughters.
[4] Interest of the Holy Father.

"How will he contact me?" I asked.

"Please give me your phone number in Spain and he will call you."

I handed Father Miguel my business card and he blessed me as I left the confessional box. I looked around to see if someone was following me and did not notice anything out of the ordinary. I decided to sit for the rest of the mass and contemplate the beauty of this church before I returned to the hotel with my little treasure. I certainly had been very fortunate to meet Father Miguel.

I took a taxi and drove to another busy café where I changed into Rodney again.

I walked to the Piazza Navona. It was a lovely warm day and I decided to have lunch at a pretty terrace before meeting Prince Vaganoff. I felt good and satisfied with myself.

✦ ✦ ✦

Though it does not have territory, the Catholic Sovereign Military Order of Malta is recognized as a sovereign country by some nations and even has diplomatic representation, which I found quite remarkable.

The order had been founded in the eleventh century in Jerusalem, where it built a hospital to care for pilgrims during the crusades and while the Knights of Malta waged wars against Islam. After fleeing from Malta when the country was invaded by Napoleon, the organization finally found a home in Rome in 1834. That was where I was heading: to the Palazzo di Malta, seat of the legendary Knights, to meet one of their historians, Prince Cyril Vaganoff.

Alexander had given me some information on the Prince. He had been born in Saint Petersburg and like the Chavchavadzes, he belonged to a prominent Georgian noble family. After the revolution, he fled Russia with his family, first living in Paris and then in North America. I was quite intrigued as to why I had been summoned to meet him.

The Palazzo di Malta is a two-storey building on a popular shopping street, housing a number of luxury stores on its ground floor.

As I was escorted to the Prince's office, to my utter surprise I saw Anatoly Levkov coming out. He acknowledged my presence with a nod but did not say a word. He smiled at me mischievously as if he knew what would happen in my meeting with Prince Vaganoff, who was waiting for me in his richly decorated office. In his eighties, he was a frail old man with a reedy voice. He explained the

ARCHIVIO
SEGRETERIA

DELLA
DI STATO

| Anno | Rubrica | Località |
|---|---|---|
| *1918.* | *211 — D. 5.* | *a. b.* |

| NUMERO del PROTOCOLLO | NOME |
|---|---|
| | *Imperatrice di Russia e figlie* |
| | **Oggetto** |
| *51996. 20617. 70557. 2. 80369. 81143 — 82843. 83029* | *Interessamento del S. Padre.* |

Cover of one of the files in the secret archives of the Vatican, showing
"Nome: *Imperatrice di Russia e figlie*" (Empress of Russia and daughters).
"Oggetto: *Interessamento dal S. Padre.*" (Interest of the Holy Father),
containing documents about the ex-Tsarina of Russia and her
daughters, dated 1918 (from *Io Alessio Pronipote dello Zar*,
by Prince Alexis D'Anjou. Mursia Editores, 1989, Italy).

history of the Knights of Malta to me. He had a sharp mind and a condescending manner.

"Excuse me! I get carried away. Would you like a cup of tea, Signor Mundy?" He asked politely.

"Thank you," I replied with formality. "I am sure, Your Excellency, that you have not asked me to come to talk about the Knights of Malta," I said, as he tried to resume his history lesson. "It is rather a coincidence that Signor Levkov was here."

"Ah, so you know dear Anatoly!" he said, trying to feign surprise.

"Indeed I do," I added seriously.

He looked at me with a rigid expression. He did not appreciate my interruption. The door of his office opened and a young priest came in carrying a tray with a silver teapot and some porcelain cups.

"This is Father Dimitri Mishkevich. He is a Russian Catholic priest and very interested in history. He has very kindly volunteered to help me with my workload," the prince said as we were introduced.

The young priest, a tall, good-looking young man with deep blue eyes and auburn hair, acknowledged the introduction and served tea. Without another word he left the room.

"He is of great help to an old man like me. So I imagine that you are wondering why you are here, *caro amico*?"

I stared into his eyes, expecting a clear answer.

"It has come to my attention that you are trying to trace a lost Romanov icon." he finally said, as we both studied each other.

"How do you know, Your Excellency?" I asked.

"We have eyes that no one can see, and ears that can hear through walls. Our friend Anatoly has also informed me of your interest in the Russian Imperial family. May I ask why?"

I told him exactly the same story I had told the cardinal.

"In fact, I'm writing a paper for Oxford University about all the contention surrounding the bones of Ekaterinburg – soon a tissue sample from Anna Anderson is going to be tested for DNA comparison."

"That impostor!" Vaganoff shouted angrily.

"Please calm down. I'm sorry to disagree. I'm certain she was the Grand Duchess Anastasia. The fact that she had this icon is further proof of her identity," I said with some scorn.

"If ever those tissue samples are tested, the results will prove me right," the prince said with a little smile.

"They might if they are manipulated!" I added defiantly.

"So, if the results are not what you expect them to be then you will say they have been tampered with!" The prince laughed sarcastically. "I want to be clear, Mr Mundy: I hate the Bolsheviks. They destroyed my country and murdered my relatives, just like they murdered the whole Imperial family. I don't appreciate foreigners meddling in our affairs, so you better believe that nobody survived; absolutely nobody. Anastasia died with them, and that is that!"

Vaganoff was fidgeting in his chair and was visibly upset.

To try to soften the tense atmosphere, I said: "I also find that there is something romantic about my quest. If I find the icon, I would like to return it to its rightful owner, the Grand Duchess Elisabeth of Saxe-Weimar-Eisenach."

"Signor Mundy," he finally said, "I have spoken with Cardinal Poggi and he has informed me of your credentials, so please, let us cut the crap, as you say in your country. I am not happy about the request I'm going to make because I believe this is a Russian matter that should be handled by Russians. The cardinal and the general of the International Military Order of the Society of Jesus want you to work for us. You must find the icon and bring it to us."

"Why would I do that, Your Excellency? If I find it, I will hand it back to Grand Duchess Elisabeth of Saxe-Weimar-Eisenach, to whom it belongs. That was the wish of Grand Duchess Anastasia, and if I can, I will honour it."

"You are unwise, signor. You will be handsomely rewarded if you work for us."

"Your Excellency, please tell the cardinal and the general of the Jesuits that they have misjudged me entirely. I am an old man now and I have many defects, but I am loyal to my principles. I am not a mercenary, and my involvement in this case is personal. I want to make it quite clear that I'm not working for anyone. I just want to honour the memory of the late Grand Duchess Anastasia," I replied calmly.

"You mean the memory of an unscrupulous fraudster. Clearly a very talented actress, I must admit!" the prince said with disdain. "Then may I advise you to return to Spain and forget this whole affair. You have a lovely family and a successful business. Forget this conversation, forget the days you were a spy and enjoy your old age. We will find the icon ourselves for the good of the Catholic Church and its protection."

"But why would the Vatican have an interest in the icon, Your Excellency?" I wanted to provoke him.

"That is none of your business!"

"I insist on knowing," I demanded, wondering what he meant by protecting the Catholic Church. Did he know what it contained, and if so, what did the church fear? If the family had indeed survived, by this time they would all be dead.

"Let's say the Holy Father would like to give it to Patriarch Alexis II as a gift. Church diplomacy!" he replied, as he stood up and terminated our brief meeting on a most disagreeable note.

I flew back to Madrid the following day. I had not seen Fritz. On the flight, I reflected on my visit to Rome. Again, more questions than answers. As my investigation progressed more leads opened up. The characters I had just met knew much more than they let on and were certainly more than what they appeared to be. They, as I, were masters of deceit. I decided to take it easy and do nothing for a few days in the hope that things would calm down. I was amazed that the Vatican had asked me to work for them. That only proved that they had no idea where the icon was, which was good. I was not sure if they knew that it contained something important. The cards were on the table and there was more than one player with interests. By now, the secret services of both the Vatican and Russia knew what I was looking for. And they wanted it too. From now on it would be a race to find it first. Together with the Brotherhood of the White Rose, I was up against two powerful secret services with access to large sums of money. The odds were definitely against us. If I was to be successful, I would have to be very cunning, and I was whether at my age I was a match for the powerful Catholic Church and the Russians. It was obvious to me that they were trying to cover up the truth about the survival of the Imperial family. Why? So much time had passed and there seemed no logical reason for it. I was reassured by the fact that at least they were not working together. I had two formidable enemies, but they were also each other's rivals, and that was where my strength lay.

I spent a quiet weekend with my wife at our country home in Las Matas, outside Madrid. I played golf and relaxed, and realized how much I had needed a break. The Romanovs had taken over my life, but I was determined to succeed in my quest.

During the week I went to the agency in an attempt to push recent events out of my mind and concentrate on the work. I felt that it would do me good to keep a low profile for a few days.

One morning Carlos called me into his office.

"Papa, would you like to go to Costa Rica again?"

"Why?" I asked. "Is it related to our quest?"

"No, not at all," he laughed. "We are producing a swimwear catalogue shoot. We have organized it all: the photographer, the makeup artist, the model and I have chosen the location. Though you know I love Costa Rica, I have other claims on my attention here and cannot go. It's a one week job."

"Do I know the team?" I asked.

"Tatiana has been booked as the model and Sandra will be doing hair and makeup. The rest of them you don't know."

I was delighted to travel again to that paradise, with Tatiana and with my daughter Sandra, who was one of the top professionals in her field in Spain. It would be fun, and maybe I would have the chance to finally meet Prince Alfred of Prussia, so I did not hesitate to accept.

"I would be delighted to go. It will do me good."

"Great, Papa. So I'll arrange everything. You leave on the 15th."

The days before my departure to Costa Rica passed by quietly. I did not speak to Alexander nor did I have any news from anyone. I decided to call João at Christie's. I reasoned that as the Russians had ransacked my room in Charlottesville, and the Vatican wanted me to work for them, neither had a clue to the whereabouts of the icon. It was clear to me that someone had stolen it with the aim of selling it for a large sum of money to a corrupt collector, as João had speculated.

"How did it go with Alexander Chavchavadze?" he asked, happy to hear from me.

"It was lovely to see him but he was not much help. I need a favour from you, João. You mentioned that if the icon were put on the market you would know, so please call me the moment you hear something."

"These criminal gangs are very well-organized and won't be contacting us. They are concerned with the art alerts, so you can imagine that they are extremely cautious. But I have a colleague in Saint Petersburg and if it reaches the market, I'm sure he will let me know. I'll tell him I have a buyer with money to burn. Rest assured he will notify me if it surfaces."

"That's wonderful. I'm going to Costa Rica in three days, but you can call my cell phone if there is any news."

"You remember the collector that came to see me about the icon, Gregory Dubinkin?"

"Yes of course. What about him?"

"Well he is a very insistent man. He has come to see me twice. He confirmed that the icon did exist and even showed me a photograph. It was the same as yours and he has made the exact same request. I am to call him immediately if I know that the icon is put on the market. But Rodney, don't worry, you will be the only one to know. I trust you and your good intentions. That precious object should return to where it belongs."

✦ ✦ ✦

On my last day before departing for Costa Rica, I decided to stay home, relax, and take my time to pack. My wife had gone to play golf, as she liked to do when the weather was good, and she had left early, to avoid the heat. As I was about to have breakfast, Esperanza brought me the phone. It was Father Miguel from Rome.

"*Buenos días, padre*! Any news?"

"Signor, my friend needs to see you. He has photographed all the documents related to the Romanovs in the secret archives. He wants to fly tomorrow to Madrid, but needs you to arrange his ticket," Father Miguel said excitedly.

"Padre, I'm flying to Costa Rica tomorrow, where I'll stay for about ten days."

"Signor, this is urgent. He has asked for a week's leave. You must see him immediately. He says it's dangerous for him to keep the documents."

OK. I have an idea. It's probably better if he flies to Costa Rica. It will be less suspicious than him coming to Madrid. They know I live here. I will arrange everything. What is his name, padre?"

"Dimitri Mishkevich."

I was stunned. This was the same name as the young priest who worked for Prince Toumanoff. It was too much of a coincidence. Was I being set up? I was hesitant, but sensed that somehow I had to trust Father Miguel.

"Padre, is Dimitri trustworthy? He also works for the Knights of Malta. I met him when I was there," I said.

"He is my best friend, signor. You can trust him with your life. The only reason he has volunteered to work with Prince Toumanoff is because he wants to discover the truth about the Romanovs."

"OK, padre. I will arrange everything and will call you back with instructions."

# 18. COSTA RICA, THIRD WEEK OF JUNE 1994

We arrived, rather exhausted, in Flamingo beach in Guanacaste that Friday evening. We had chartered a small plane to fly to Liberia, where the hotel staff were waiting to drive us to the resort. The weather forecast was excellent and I expected a smooth shoot, as Carlos had arranged the production down to the smallest detail. With me was my daughter Sandra, the photographer and his assistant, the stylist, and of course Tatiana, our beautiful model who was very excited about her first big job.

The client had booked rooms at the Flamingo Beach Resort, a beautiful hotel visibly designed to please American tastes: big, modern and comfortable. It was located on a beautiful Pacific beach of pure white sands, surrounded by majestic mountains and national parks. That weekend we were supposed to rest, recover from the jet lag, and prepare everything for the intense work of the coming week. I had booked flights for Father Dimitri, who I expected to arrive in San Jose on Thursday evening. I also reserved a room for him at the Hotel Irazu, close to the airport, where he would spend that night. On Friday morning, he was supposed to take a small commercial plane to Liberia and the hotel driver would take him to the Flamingo Resort, then we would meet for dinner at eight o'clock. That was expected to be the last day of the shoot. So I had decided to stay on for the next two days and had invited him to do so as well. He had taken a big risk in photographing the documents and I wanted at least to offer him my hospitality after the long journey. I told Sandra that I had invited the Russian nephew of an old friend.

The shoot went smoothly. The photographer was delighted with Tatiana's look and how professional she was. The stylist seemed pleased at the beautiful photographs and informed the client in Germany. So the five days flew by. We woke up at sunrise to get the best light and took long lunch breaks before continuing the shoot until sunset. The evenings were relaxed and merry in the company of Sandra, Tatiana and the crew, but deep down I was eager to meet with Father Dimitri. Before I knew it, it was already Friday morning, and in a few hours Father Dimitri would be arriving. Tatiana and Sandra had asked me if they could stay on for the weekend and, with some hesitation, I had agreed after their excellent work. I was not too happy that Tatiana would meet him, but there was not much I could do.

We were enjoying a delicious poolside breakfast when a bellboy came over.

"Señor Mundy. You have a call. They say it is urgent," he said.

I walked to the pool phone.

"Yes, who is it?" I asked.

"It's Father Dimitri, signor!" He sounded very alarmed and nervous.

"Hello father, I am glad you arrived safe. Are you alright?" I asked, concerned.

"No, I'm not. Some minutes ago, when I came up to my room after breakfast, it had been ransacked. The room is a mess, but I did not tell anybody. I am scared, Signor Mundy! Someone knows I'm here and why."

"Did they steal the documents, father?"

"No, fortunately I had left them in the safe deposit box. I am not going to Liberia. I think it's too dangerous!"

"Who do you think is behind this?" I was really worried by now. Things were getting out of hand, and whoever these people were, they were too close on our heels.

"Maybe the Vatican secret service, the Russians? Who knows?" Father Dimitri sighed.

"Why have you been helping me with this, father? You have put yourself in danger. What is in this for you?" I had been asking myself this question ever since he had offered to copy the Romanov files from the Vatican secret archives.

"One day you will know, but let's say that I want to put the record straight. It's a family matter," he replied mysteriously.

"Family matter!" I exclaimed, surprised. "Were members of your family working for the Imperial family or stationed in Ekaterinburg?" I asked.

"In a sense, Signor Mundy."

"So what do you want me to do?" I asked.

"I met a charming young journalist called Victoria on the plane yesterday, during my flight from Miami to San José. No one can connect her to me. I have asked her to collect the package at the reception desk and deliver it to you. Sorry we could not meet, Mr Mundy. I truly hope the photos help you with your investigation. She will contact you as soon as she has the parcel. She seems to be a nice woman. I didn't know what else to do."

"But father, do you think that was a sensible idea?" I protested.

"I had to follow my instincts, Signor Mundy. I could only do that. I have explained to her that something happened requiring my immediate return to the Holy See. I did not lie, as I told her that the documents are only of historical value for your research." He tried to sound convincing, though I could hear anguish in the tone of his voice.

"I am also sorry, father; I appreciate your interest in helping me."

"Now I have to leave; I will try to catch the next flight back to Rome."

"Very well father, I trust it is as you say. Have a safe trip home, and please be careful. I will contact you when I get back to Madrid."

"God bless you, Rodney. May the holy angels protect you in your quest." He hung up.

✦ ✦ ✦

At 6:30 pm we were back in the hotel after a long session of pictures in a beautiful yacht that we rented for that purpose. The sunset was wonderful and everything went according to plan, except that I could not stop thinking about what had happened to Father Dimitri that morning.

Back in my room, I was getting ready for dinner. After taking a bath, I poured a large scotch and switched on the television to watch the local news. I had half an hour before joining Sandra and Tatiana at one of the hotel's restaurants. Suddenly, my attention was drawn to the screen by a photograph of Father Dimitri. I was horrified as I listened on. The news anchor was explaining that an unknown gunman had shot and killed a young man as he was getting out of a taxi at Juan Santamaría airport that morning. The victim died at the scene and had been identified as a priest from the Vatican named Dimitri Mishkevich. The apparent motive had been robbery, as his luggage had been stolen. The police were following several leads.

I drank my scotch in one gulp. I was stunned, scared, utterly devastated, and felt responsible for the death of Father Dimitri. Whoever had murdered him knew he had copied those documents and wanted them badly enough to kill for them. The stakes were high and now I felt that even my family could be in danger. If the assassins were still in Cosa Rica we were all at risk. I called Alexander.

"Father Dimitri has been murdered!" I blurted out.

"Do you have the documents?" he asked.

"No, but supposedly a journalist called Victoria is going to contact me. Father Dimitri was very cautious and he prevented the documents from falling into his murderer's hands, unless she is one of them too. They know he copied the documents. Who are they, Alexander? They are ruthless!"

"We don't know yet, Rodney. But we will find out."

"But surely if the Vatican knew he had copied the documents, he would not have been allowed to leave Rome. They would not kill one of their own! Anyway, who was this Father Mishkevich? He said he had a family interest in the affair."

"Rodney, you don't need more distractions for the moment. And now I have to call to Glastonbury and give them the bad news. You are watched and protected by us, but anyway, be extremely careful."

I was so shocked by Father Dimitri's murder that I called my daughter and with the excuse of a headache stayed in my room to plan my next move. I ordered room service, and before the meal arrived the phone rang.

"Is this Señor Mundy?" A soft-spoken woman asked.

"Yes, it's me. Who is it?"

"This is Victoria Alba. A friend of yours gave me a package for you. I'm frightened, Señor Mundy. Did you see the news?" She asked as her voice quavered.

"Yes, it's a tragedy!"

"I opened the package when I heard the news. Sorry! I needed to be certain that I was not the messenger of anything illegal. There are many documents with the Vatican seal," she said nervously.

"I understand. Are you from Costa Rica?"

"Yes I am. I'm a journalist and I work for Channel 4 TV. Don't worry, Señor Mundy, you can trust me. The documents are safe and I will hand them over to you. I promise," she said reassuringly.

"Thank you. When can I see you?" I asked.

"When are you leaving Costa Rica?"

"I will fly to San José tomorrow, spend the night there, and return to Madrid on Sunday. Let's meet tomorrow afternoon. I'll call you."

Victoria gave me her phone number and hung up. I felt unsure. Could she be trusted? I decided to call Rita Stern and asked her if I could spend the weekend at her home with Sandra and Tatiana. It felt like the right thing to do, as her husband Antonio Blasco was a high-ranking police inspector. I would invite Victoria to her home and would ask Antonio to investigate her.

✦ ✦ ✦

The next morning we packed our things and cut our stay short. Sandra and Tatiana were not too happy and I could only give them an evasive explanation for the sudden change of plans.

On our short flight to San José, I noticed Tatiana reading the newspaper *La Nación* with interest.

"Someone murdered a Russian Catholic priest at the airport yesterday," she told me.

"Yes, I know. I saw it on the news last night."

"It's odd, don't you think?"

"What's odd, Tatiana?"

"It says here that he had only arrived in San José from Rome the day before. He was only in the country for a few hours and was returning to Rome, and then he was murdered," she continued.

"I don't know. He must have been here on church business," I speculated, trying to sound uninterested.

"No, Rodney. The Apostolic Nuncio in San José issued a statement saying that they had no idea that Father Mishkevich was in the country or what he was doing here, for that matter. And his hotel room was ransacked. He must have been here on a secret mission."

"What makes you say that?" I asked, not knowing where she was going with this conversation.

"The paper says he worked in the Vatican Secret Archives, so there is something fishy going on. This is excellent material for a spy novel!" she exclaimed teasingly, winking.

✦ ✦ ✦

Rita had been more than surprised when I had called her and asked if we could spend Saturday night at her house. She had no idea that I was in the country. I apologized for the short notice and explained everything. She was delighted that we would spend at least one night with them, and thrilled to meet Sandra. She organized for Rodney, her delightful son, to take the girls out for lunch and show them the city so that I could meet with Victoria quietly.

Our plane arrived at Pavas airport at 10:30 am, and we were at her doorstep fifteen minutes later. Soon after exchanging pleasantries, Rodney Jr. and the girls left the house.

When Antonio Blasco heard my story, he immediately looked into it and confirmed that Victoria did indeed work at Channel 4 TV and was a rising star with an impeccable reputation, and highly respected despite her age. He offered to join me in the meeting, as he had some questions he wanted to ask her about Father Dimitri that might help solve the case. I agreed.

During lunch I explained to Rita and Antonio my deep involvement in the Romanov case and the lost icon.

"Rodney, I think you should stay for a couple extra days," she said.

"Rita, this affair is extremely dangerous. It has already left a few corpses in its path. Since I have become involved, there are powerful forces that want secret to be kept. I think at this stage, it's better to leave and return home as soon as possible."

"As you wish, Rodney. You are probably right," she agreed.

"So how did you meet Father Dimitri, Rodney?" Antonio asked. I explained the story. They both listened in awe.

"The documents he gave Victoria suggest that other members of the Imperial family might have survived the massacre in Ekaterinburg, at least the women," I concluded.

"Not only Anastasia and Olga then, as Prince Sigismund claimed?" Rita asked, surprised.

"Apparently other members of the family also survived. I guess that the files contain clues to this effect. I believe that's why he was killed. Someone does not want the truth revealed."

"But why? It all happened so long ago. Who cares now?" Antonio asked in bewilderment.

"There are still many open wounds, political and dynastic issues: too many conflicting interests, my friend."

"You Europeans are mad with all this royalty stuff!" Rita exclaimed.

"So you are implying that Father Dimitri was murdered because someone was after the documents he brought for you?" Antonio asked gravely.

"I am absolutely certain and I'm going to ask a big favour of you. When Victoria comes, I will give you the documents she brings me. Please send them by courier to Madrid. I can't risk them falling into the wrong hands. Whoever killed Father Dimitri must know who I am and what I'm after."

✦ ✦ ✦

At exactly four o'clock the doorbell rang and Victoria Alba arrived. Rita escorted her into the living room where I was sitting with Antonio. She was a slim brunette of medium height with soft features and a pretty face. Though Antonio had said she was young, I was still surprised at her youth. She could not be a day over twenty-five, so I understood that she seemed a bit overwhelmed as we exchanged pleasantries. She had obviously expected this to be a private meeting. Antonio Blasco introducing himself as a police inspector had not helped her relax. He immediately recognized her from the television and this made her feel a bit more at ease.

"You are among friends, Victoria. Please don't worry. I have asked Inspector Blasco, my host, to join us, as you have information that might help him get to the bottom of this. But all this will remain private."

"Yes, Señorita Victoria, we want to catch the people that have given our country a bad name. You see, Rodney believes they are foreigners."

"First of all, I want to hand these documents over to you as promised, and then you can ask me whatever you want – but I'm afraid I know nothing. I met the priest on the plane; we had a nice and friendly conversation. He told me he lived in Rome and came here to meet somebody who was doing historical research. Then we exchanged phone numbers. That's all. I was very surprised when he called me the next morning and said he had to return to Rome on the first flight and asked me to immediately go to the hotel and pick up a package to be delivered to Mr Mundy. And that is why I am here, Inspector."

Victoria handed me the package that she'd already opened. I took out dozens of documents. Many of them carried the Vatican seal, others were marked *"Memoriale Reservatissimo"*[1] I gave them to Antonio. The package also contained a few rolls of film.

"I'm a journalist and I know that someone has been murdered for these documents. When I opened the package to examine the contents I immediately knew that they were copies of very important documents. I could understand what was written because I speak Italian. So, I think

---

[1] Very private memorandum.

I have an idea about the substance of your investigation, Mr Mundy, and however unwillingly, I am now part of this case. What is all this about?" Victoria looked at us, perplexed.

"Father Dimitri was a good person; he secretly photographed these documents that are of vital historical importance from the Vatican secret archives. I'm doing research on an murky period of European history and it seems some people don't want me to succeed. That is as much as I can tell you. I am most grateful for your honesty. I can only imagine your shock when you saw the news!"

"I must admit that I was terrified. You meet someone on a plane, the next day he hands you some documents and then he is shot! That only happens in the movies," Victoria exclaimed.

"I am afraid, my dear, and I speak from experience, that often reality is stranger than fiction!" Antonio sighed.

I deliberately led the conversation to mundane matters, and after a cup of tea, Victoria and I exchanged business cards and she left. Something inside told me that it would not be the last time we would meet. I could see in her beautiful green eyes that the story had captivated her. If she was as good a journalist as Antonio said she was, she would undoubtedly investigate further now that she knew of the Romanov connection.

It was hot and stuffy in Madrid. My wife had already left for Marbella and had been upset that I hadn't gone with her. I could sympathize with her, as of late I had been immersed in the Romanov affair to the neglect of everything else.

I felt I was close to solving the case and I couldn't just leave. God knows how much I needed a holiday, to go to the beach, play golf and just relax. I was not a young man anymore and this was definitely exhausting me, but I had made a promise and I was going to honour it.

When I went to the office I found another message from James Cross, urging me to call him as soon as I arrived. I phoned him immediately, since I thought that he might have news about Blondie, my assailant in Charlottesville. He knew nothing about him; the police had been searching, but two months later they had no clues. The organization was obviously very professional. However, there was good news about the tissue sample. Finally the last court hearing on Anastasia Manahan's tissue took place on 11th May 1994: the Russian Nobility Association was dismissed, and on 19th June Dr Peter Gill travelled quietly to Martha Jefferson Hospital and with the help of its pathology staff collected tissue samples, while a TV crew recorded everything.

"The Schweitzers finally won the case," he said, excited. "Now Dr Gill is going to get the DNA that will solve this mystery. However, during a brief press conference Gill said that he was not sure if external factors, like the age of the sample or the formalin used to preserve it, would affect the process of extraction. He hoped to have some results within three to six months."

"That is great news, James! We are getting closer to discovering the truth. Thanks, and keep me updated."

"Sure Rodney, I will call you when I get more news."

✦ ✦ ✦

Antonio Blasco had kept his word, and a week after my return from Costa Rica I had the privilege of studying the documents that had cost Father Dimitri his life. I read the letter Father Dimitri had written explaining the content of the negative. After that, I rushed to develop all the remaining rolls at the studio someone I could trust. Sergei Nazarewicz, Carlos' best friend, came to mind. It was he who had introduced Carlos to the Anastasia saga before tragically dying in 1988. He would have been the perfect person for this job: a trusted friend and a great photographer. And undoubtedly he would have been thrilled at my discoveries.

Finally, three days later, I examined all the documents. Father Dimitri's notes stated that he had developed roll number 1, and those 36 pictures belonged to the file "*Imperatrice di Russia e Figlie.*"[1] Rolls numbered 2 and 3 were from the same file. Then he noted that rolls 4, 5 and 6 corresponded to a file named "*Gran Duchessa Olga Nicolaievna di Russia,*"[2] containing documents from 1953–1976. The next two rolls, 7 and 8, corresponded to a file named "*Imperatore Nicola II,*" and the last three, 9, 10 and 11, were from a file named "*Documenti importanti sul l'Imperatrice Alessandra Feodorovna e figlie, incarico speciale de la Regina Helena d'Italia.*"[3] It was a large dossier prepared by Signor Francesco Lequio, a distinguished Italian diplomat. I recognized that the cover with the words "*Imperatrice di Russia e Figlie,*" was the same one Father Miguel had given me in the Church of Santa Maria, only this time I had its contents. It was a big surprise to find a letter from Cardinal Gasparri, the secretary general of the Vatican, instructing the Nuncio Valfre in Vienna to pressure the government of Austria into securing the liberation of the Tsarina Alexandra and her children from the Russian territory. It was dated August 1918, a month after their supposed murder! As far as I was concerned, this was yet again another sign that they had survived their documented deaths. The next paper that caught my attention was a letter from Nuncio Pacelli in Berlin, dated 29th August 1918, which specified, "For the ex-Czarina of Russia and her Family." Pacelli, who later became Pope Pius XII, was sending Cardinal Gasparri at the Vatican the translation of a letter dated the 27th from Baron von dem Bussche, assistant secretary of state for foreign affairs in Berlin. In it, he also referred to the negotiations of the King of Spain to help the unhappy "ex-Czarina and her closest relatives, assuring them, if that would be possible with the support of Germany, a refuge in Spain."

---

[1] Empress of Russia and Daughters.
[2] Grand Duchess Olga Nikolaeyna of Russia.
[3] Important documents about Empress Alexandra Feodorovna and daughters, special request made by Queen Helen of Italy.

I spent over a week at home going through every single document. I did not even go to the office. Fortunately, I had the apartment to myself, though my wife called me every day wanting to know when I would be joining her in Marbella. I was overwhelmed by so much information, despite no mention of the icon. What I did find, to my absolute surprise, was a file titled, "*Deposito valori fatto dal Zar Nicola II*"[4] – a detailed list of precious objects that the Tsar had sent to be deposited in the Vatican for safekeeping after the first signs of revolution in 1905. The list included tiaras, rings, bracelets, emeralds, diamonds, rubies, gold bars, gold roubles, gold dollars, several other pieces of jewellery and Fabergé eggs. Now I understood the reluctance of Cardinal Poggi to accept the existence of these documents. It was not in their interest for the official version of the massacre to be questioned. Surviving descendants of the Tsar would have the right to claim these treasures, which the greedy Vatican had unlawfully kept. Now it all made sense. Pius XII had given covert financial aid to Grand Duchesses Olga and Maria, who had indeed visited him in the Vatican, according to Mother Pascalina's statement. I saw copies of letters from the *Nunciatura* in Switzerland mentioning funds to be transferred to Grand Duchess Olga's bank account in Italy, under her assumed name Marga Boodts. It was now clear to me why the Vatican did not allow her to publish her memoirs in 1956, despite the fact that she had already signed a contract with a publisher, and would do anything they could to prevent that document becoming public. They must have known that Father Dimitri had copied them. On the other hand, the Russian secret service might be suspicious of one of its own citizens working in the Vatican, unless they knew something else about his past. The pieces of the puzzle were starting to fit. I went back to my daily chores at the agency, waiting for the call from London that would decide my next move.

✦ ✦ ✦

Finally on the morning on the 14th of July, Bastille Day, I received the call that I had been expecting. It was João Montereal, my friend at Christie's.

"Aren't I glad to hear from you," I said cheerfully.

"I have news for you, Rodney. My contact in Saint Petersburg has informed me that a very valuable icon is up for sale on the black market.

---

[4] Deposit of valuables made by Tsar Nicholas II.

It's your icon, Rodney. I have arranged for you to go as the expert representative of an anonymous buyer. The whole operation is very shady, as you might well imagine. They are asking two million dollars for it and I have assured them that after you inspect it, if it's what you are looking for, you have authorization to close the deal. You don't want to mess with these people, Rodney. The Russian mafia are ruthless."

"Thanks, João."

"So who shall I say you are, Rodney? I mean what will your name be?"

"Let me get back to you on that. I need to speak to someone and I'll let you know!"

❖ ❖ ❖

I phoned Alexander and he assured me that his organization would be able to raise the two million dollars if the icon was genuine of Saxe-Weimar-Eisenach. I was very excited, as my quest was reaching its end. I would be receiving a British passport within the next few days. Meynell Phillips would be the name of my new identity – my middle name and my mother's maiden name. I spoke to Sandra and explained everything to her. She was astonished, but she agreed to disguise me with makeup for the new passport photo. I was delighted by her work. I could not even recognize myself when I looked into the mirror. She was a great pro. She had changed my hair colour with a very convincing wig. She also made my nose aquiline which changed the rest of my facial features. I organized my trip to Saint Petersburg and spoke to Carlos about my plans. Somehow, Tatiana found out about the trip and convinced me to take her as my personal translator. I spoke no Russian and I believed that her assistance would be quite valuable, so I would be travelling with her and Sandra. Because of my new identity, I also had to confide in Tatiana, so I told her about the icon I was trying to buy from the mafia to return to its rightful owners. I omitted any reference to the secret it contained. I was sure she believed that it was just a transaction, though she was aware it was a dangerous one. She admitted enjoying challenges, and seemed to be very excited about being the translator for such an expedition. I felt she would be an asset, as by now she felt at ease in Spain and in our company. She was making good money, working nearly every day and seemed relaxed and happy.

# 20. ST PETERSBURG, RUSSIA, THIRD WEEK OF JULY 1994

As scheduled, I flew to St Petersburg in the company of my daughter and Tatiana. She was a charming and intelligent girl and I felt that in her company and Sandra's, not only would we enjoy the city, but the trip would be a success.

Fortunately Rosa was in Marbella, as she would have thought that I had gone totally mad had she seen me in disguise. Tatiana was shocked when she saw me. The transformation had been so good that she did not recognize me. My disguise worked perfectly.

During the flight, Tatiana was most chatty and excited. She rambled on, insisting that I was mistaken about Anna Anderson and that Eugenia Smith had been the Grand Duchess Anastasia. She persisted in arguing that the Tsarevich was her dad's godfather's son, Colonel Goloniewski, the Polish spy. Her dad knew, and she did too, so she was at a loss as to why I was so stubborn. I tried to reason with her to no avail. I explained the icon's story as another proof of Anna Anderson's true identity, but she was not impressed and refused to accept any other version than what she had been told since childhood.

I was glad to arrive at the extraordinary Grand Hotel Europe, where Carlos had booked us rooms. It was a landmark that had played a central role in St Petersburg life for over one hundred and thirty years, located in the heart of the city in Nevsky Prospekt. The neo-baroque façade had been restored to its former glory and the building was most impressive. I was excited to be in the capital built by Peter the Great, and I was planning to explore it before my appointment with the people that had the icon. We had a long weekend ahead of this meeting and I was going to immerse myself in the history of Imperial Russia.

Tatiana and Sandra shared a room and, to my delight, I had been upgraded to a suite.

After lunch I organized a visit to the Moika Palace, which had been the residence of the Yusupovs. The palace had been originally built in 1770 by the French architect Jean Baptiste Vallin de la Mothe and had much work done to it over the years, making it a hodgepodge of architectural styles. The immensely wealthy Yusupovs bought it in

1830 and made it the grandest palace in Saint Petersburg. It was here that Prince Felix, with the help of Grand Duke Dimitri Pavlovich, his lover in those days, murdered the infamous Rasputin. The Soviets had converted it into a museum, which had a permanent exhibit on the famous murder. We spent a couple of hours exploring the palace and Tatiana seemed enthralled. She had never been to Russia before and she talked incessantly about the Tsar and the conspiracy to cover up the truth. I found it all quite fascinating, as she, without knowing it, was spot on.

As we left the Moika Palace and hailed a taxi to return to the hotel, I saw Blondie out of the corner of my eye. As we drove to the Grand Hotel Europe I looked back and saw him with another man in a black suit in a car behind us. How could they know my every move? I had a new identity and I was in disguise, but there he was. I felt uneasy and rushed into the hotel with Sandra and Tatiana in tow to find Fritz, of all people, waiting in the lobby for us. I felt relieved to see him and was glad he had booked himself into our hotel. It made me feel safer.

"Couldn't be happier to see you Fritz!" I said as I approached him. He looked at me in disbelief, as he too did not recognize me.

"My God, Rodney." Fritz cried out laughing.

"This is my daughter, Sandra, who is responsible for my new look, and Tatiana, my interpreter."

"What a great job, Sandra." Fritz said, unable to conceal his surprise.

"But not good enough it seems. Blondie and another guy are following me." My disappointment was visible.

"You and I should go to have a drink; maybe you are tired and are just imagining things. Let's go, you need to relax," he said, pulling my arm and practically dragging me to the bar, while waving goodbye to the girls.

"We need to discuss a plan," Fritz suggested.

✦ ✦ ✦

Fritz ordered drinks for us both. He already knew my preferences. It was the first time I had seen him so confident and persuasive. He appeared to be taking his role as protector very seriously, something I had not seen since Tangier, when he defended me from the two criminals. We got our drinks and immediately began to discuss the business at hand.

"This is getting more dangerous by the moment. As the Russians know you are here we have to change the plan," he said, taking command.

"What do you suggest, Fritz?"

"For starters I think you should leave this hotel until we get the icon. It would be best to ask your daughter to completely change your appearance again."

"The problem is that this is the appearance I have on my passport so another hotel is out of the question."

"OK, then I will call Alexander and ask him if one of his Russian friends here can shelter you until the icon is in our possession. Now go to your room and wait for my call. I'll arrange everything."

One hour later Fritz phoned and asked me to be ready to move.

"And the girls?" I asked, worried about their safety.

"They will stay here. Call Sandra to say you have the flu, as then you will be free to move around the city undisturbed. You must change the meeting with the sellers to tomorrow at 9:00 am; I will be your driver and take you there. You are to request to inspect the icon in private, as you need to be one hundred per cent sure of its authenticity. This will seem reasonable and hopefully they won't suspect anything.

"But I was planning to take Tatiana as my translator," I told Fritz, "that's why I brought her here!"

"That is out of the question now," he said emphatically.

"It is best she believes you are unwell. Only let your daughter in on this please. Not a word to Tatiana. She might be beautiful, but I don't trust her. I will pick you up in four hours. I'm sure she will have time to create a fascinating new character!" Fritz said.

✦ ✦ ✦

I called Sandra to my room and told her that I was not feeling well so that she could relay the news to Tatiana. I asked her to be very discreet but to bring all her makeup stuff. She understood. Luckily she had brought all her stuff just in case she needed to retouch me or change my appearance once again. I loved Sandra, as she never left anything to chance.

It took over three hours of intense work on her part but when I looked myself in the mirror I was aghast. She had taken over twenty years from my face and had transformed me into some sort of middle-aged Irish farmer: redheaded and with freckles. I couldn't help but laugh.

"You are a genius!" I exclaimed in delight as I hugged her.

"They pay me very well for my work," she replied with a broad grin on her beautiful face.

"Sandra, listen to me carefully. You and Tatiana will stay here until I return tomorrow. You have to inform the hotel that I have the flu and that I am not to be disturbed. Order some room service for me and stay in my room for a while. Tatiana must not know the truth and you must behave normally. Understood?"

"Yes, Papa, but where will you go? I'm really worried about you. Don't you think this has gone too far? Why don't you just forget it and we return to Madrid?"

"I can't, Sandra, but this will be over soon and all will be fine." I looked at my watch; Fritz would be in the lobby to take me to the safe house. I dressed casually and kissed my daughter goodbye.

Fritz once again did not recognize me but this time he kept a straight face when I approached him and nodded. We left the hotel and hailed a taxi. Blondie was there in a waiting car but, unaware of my new look, he did not even glance at me and we managed to leave the hotel unnoticed.

✦✦✦

As planned, Fritz, disguised as my driver, picked me up at 8:30 am from the place where I had spent a sleepless night.

It was a glorious warm sunny summer morning. We drove through the city. I admired St Isaac's Cathedral as we drove past it. We crossed Blagoveschchensky Bridge over the Neva and drove to what seemed to be the outskirts of the city. The surrounding buildings were a reminder of the Stalinist era. Fritz and I drove in uneasy silence, lost in our own thoughts.

We left the city and drove through a pine forest, finally arriving at a small farm. The car stopped in front of a picturesque large country cottage. Fritz got out of the car and opened the door for me. Two thugs were waiting for us and invited me to follow them into the house.

The living room was nicely decorated and had many feminine touches including several vases with flowers. We sat down as the men left the room. Shortly afterward, a pudgy short middle-aged man with an unfriendly sneer on his face came in, trying hard to be amicable.

"So you are Mr Phillips," he said as I rose to greet him.

"My name is Boris."

"May I see the icon now? I will need a few minutes on my own to examine it."

"That should be no problem, Mr Phillips, but I assure you it's an excellent piece. It used to belong to the Romanovs. Please follow me."

I followed him into the dining room. On the dining table I saw the icon. I felt a surge of excitement and walked towards it, pulled out a chair and sat in front of it. I looked up at Boris.

"Please can you leave the room for some minutes?"

Boris obliged. I picked up the icon. I finally had it in my hands. It was an image of the Madonna and child painted in very dark colours in a gilded silver frame. Its size was approximately 16 by 22 cm. I was overwhelmed by excitement as I knew it was the one: the lost icon of Grand Duchess Anastasia the Saxe-Weimar-Eisenachs. I fiddled with it, trying to find where the secret it carried might be hidden. I heard voices speaking Russian coming from the living room. I started to sweat but I was determined not to fail. The back of the icon seemed to be very well sealed. I tried my best to open it to no avail. I was shaking and I heard Boris' voice as he returned to the room.

"So, Mr Phillips, are you satisfied?" he asked. "Because if you are not I have another client that has shown interest."

"Yes. I am satisfied. I will now return to the hotel and will call my client and the deal can proceed as agreed."

"Very well then. When we have confirmation of the transfer we will arrange for the handover of the icon."

"The transaction will be immediate and the funds will be in your account before midday," I said.

We shook hands and Fritz drove me back to the hotel.

Blondie and his pal were in the car where we had left them the day before. They had not suspected anything. Fritz's plan had worked perfectly.

✦✦✦

Back in the room I called Sandra, who came immediately to see me.

"I'm so glad that all is fine, papa. Do you need me to switch you back?" she said jokingly.

"Not yet, darling. I have to meet a gentleman this afternoon. He has seen me like this. After that I will need you again. How is Tatiana?"

"Don't worry. She is fine and has not suspected anything. Let's order a big breakfast now that you are feeling much better from the flu!" Sandra suggested mockingly.

At about four o'clock in the afternoon, Boris called my room. The transaction had gone through as planned and he had brought the icon. I invited him up. He handed it to me, we shook hands and he swiftly left. It had all gone smoothly and without any problem whatsoever. I was very satisfied with a job well done and Fritz had played a big part in its success. I was beside myself with excitement. I had in my possession the famous lost icon hiding a momentous secret shake the world. For security reasons I decided I had to take the concealed secret from the icon and transport them back to England separately. I again fiddled with it to no avail. I took my nail file and forced it into its back. I put pressure on it and suddenly it snapped. The silver back opened and there it was: a folded old yellowish sealed envelope. It had the name Anastasia written on it in Russian. It was very similar to the envelope containing the letter about the pearls. Could it be possible that it contained a copy of that letter? All this trouble just to find a copy? I was very intrigued. What kind of explosive information could be inside that sealed envelope? My hands started trembling, and I did not dare to open the envelope. I thought that such an honour was fitting only for Alexander. I fixed the back on the icon and placed it and the envelope in the safe in my suite, along with money and our passports.

◆ ◆ ◆

After my transformation, I called Tatiana and told her I felt much better. We all went to Volga, one of the best restaurants in town, with Blondie and his friend in tow. The evening was merry and we enjoyed ourselves; for the first time in quite a long time I finally felt relaxed. We had planned an early night on the pretext that I was still recovering from my short bout of flu, and as I was preparing for bed I heard a knock on the door.

"Yes. Who is it?" I asked.

"Tatiana."

I opened the door.

"Can I come in, Rodney?" she asked in a flirtatious tone that took me by surprise.

"Please do, Tatiana. What is it?" She came in and closed the door behind her.

"Can we have a nightcap, please?"

"Ok, just one, and then you will be a good girl and go to sleep. What would you like?"

"A vodka tonic please!" I went to the minibar and got us two drinks and sat down.

"*Na zdorovie!*" I toasted as I lifted my glass and looked searching into her eyes.

We chatted about the beauty of the city and the greatness of the Moika Palace, and then she started talking about the Romanovs and moved on to the icon.

"May I see the icon, please? You did get it. I know you were not sick, Rodney." She caught me off guard.

"I was sick here in my bedroom, Tatiana. And unfortunately I was informed that our deal did not go through," I lied.

"Really? I assumed you did not want me to go with you. So did someone else buy it, then?" She asked.

"Yes, someone outbid us and offered way too much money; my friend was not prepared to raise his bid."

"Why would your friend want to pay such a hefty price for it just to return it to its owners? It is hard to believe. I think, Rodney, that you have not been truthful with me. There is something else. Isn't there?"

"No. Why should there be something else?" I replied. "My friend is a romantic millionaire, but his fiscal restraint won out," I said convincingly, taking another sip of the cold vodka.

"May I use your bathroom, Rodney?" she asked.

"Tatiana, it's late. You should go back to your room. You can use your bathroom there," I said.

"Relax. It will only be a moment," she teased me as she walked into my bathroom.

I waited for a couple of minutes. The door of the bathroom opened and Tatiana walked out completely naked. Her figure was outstanding. Her breasts were small and firm. I momentarily felt aroused. I felt tempted as I stood there paralyzed, unable to utter a word and too nervous to make a move. She walked towards me, swaying her hips provocatively. I looked into her eyes, bewildered. She got close to me and I shuddered as she put her lips on mine and tried to kiss me. I felt her warm wet tongue against my lips as she tried to part them. I came to my senses and softly pushed her away as I took a sheet from the bed and covered her up.

"Are you crazy, Tatiana? What do you think you are doing?"

I could see that she felt embarrassed at my rejection but she remained cool.

"I like you, Rodney. You are an attractive man and I like older men. You look very sexy in your disguise," she said.

"But I could be your grandfather. It's just not right."

"I know you like me. I saw lust in your face just now." She was a real temptress.

"You are a beautiful woman, but not only am I married, I'm responsible for your wellbeing. What would your father say? I'm grateful for the offer but I'm going to pass, so if you don't mind get dressed and return to your room before there's anything to regret."

Without a word she returned to the bathroom, dressed and left the room.

So this was what it was all about. She was prepared to sacrifice her body for information about the icon and I had nearly succumbed to her enchantment. What was her game?

◆ ◆ ◆

Sandra called my room at about ten the next morning.

"Papa, I'm going to the pharmacy and to take a stroll. Do you need me?" she inquired.

"Why don't you wait for me? I would like to go to the State Hermitage Museum this afternoon and we can have lunch later too."

"I will be back by noon then. Promise!" she replied.

"Are you going with Tatiana?" I asked, worried that she would go out alone.

"No, she's sleeping. I'm down at reception. Last night after we got back from dinner she suddenly left the room. It was weird: she wouldn't tell me where she was going."

"I know. She came to see me for a nightcap."

"Papa!" Sandra exclaimed. "You didn't?" she asked.

"Of course not darling, though I confess, I had to restrain myself." Sandra laughed.

"When she returned from your room she called someone. I pretended to be asleep but she was whispering in Russian or Polish. I heard her mention your name."

"Mmmmmm…. She told me she doesn't know anyone in Saint Petersburg. I'll check with reception to see which number she called."

"Maybe that is a good idea, Papa."

It was nearly two in the afternoon and Sandra had not returned. I imagined she had got lost in the marvels of Saint Petersburg. It was a splendid summer day and from what I had seen, the city was probably one of the most beautiful in the world with its baroque and neoclassical architecture. A jewel from the mind of an enlightened ruler: Peter the Great.

I called Tatiana and we went to the coffee shop for a quick lunch.

"I was told by Sandra that you called someone in the middle of the night, Tatiana? I thought you had no friends here!" I took her by surprise.

"Well, it's a friend of my father." She blushed and I knew she was lying. "She has a gift for me to take back to him."

"Ahh. That's fine."

"What's the plan for today?" She asked.

"We were going to visit the Hermitage, but now I am worried that Sandra is not back."

"She probably went shopping," she said without much conviction.

I did not go to the museum. Instead, I spent the afternoon in my room waiting for Sandra. At about half past five I was almost desperate. I called Tatiana to the room and she had no news. I called Fritz's room and shared my concern. He came to my room, as he also wanted to see the icon.

"Fritz, I would never forgive myself if anything happened to my daughter. Now I realize that none of this was worth it."

"Sandra is a big girl. I am sure she will be fine. May I see the icon?"

"I hope you are right, Fritz. I just have a bad feeling. I know my daughter and she would not change her plans without calling me."

I took the icon out of the safe deposit box and showed it to Fritz. I did not mention the envelope.

As he was admiring it, the phone rang. I picked it up.

"What? Who are you? Is she OK? Please don't hurt her!" I pleaded in desperation. The phone went dead.

"What's wrong, Rodney?" Fritz asked, gravely concerned.

"They have Sandra. Someone has kidnapped my daughter, Fritz!" I was desperate.

"What do they want?" he asked.

"I don't know. They are calling in thirty minutes. They want to speak to Tatiana. Why Tatiana? How do they know who she is? This is crazy."

"You'd better ask her to come to the room and please keep calm. They will only want money and the Brotherhood won't let them harm your girl. Kidnappings are fairly common in Russia," he said, trying to comfort me.

I called Tatiana and she immediately came to my room.

After I recounted what had just happened, she did not look panicked. Strangely, she seemed calmed. Was I imagining it?

Exactly thirty minutes after the first call, the phone rang again. This time Tatiana picked it up and spoke in Russian. After a few minutes she hung up and looked into my eyes.

"They want the icon for Sandra's life. I am really sorry Rodney!" she said meekly.

"But I don't have the icon!" I said, trying to perpetuate the lie and hoping she would give away her involvement.

"Yes you do, Rodney, and they know it." They are not joking, believe me." She was grave.

I looked at Fritz.

"The police are totally out of the question. This transaction was illegal. We have paid a large sum of money for a missing icon and have dealt with a criminal gang. Too much explaining to do," Fritz added.

"But who are they?" I said in exasperation. "How do they know I have it?"

"They might be the same mob you bought it from. If they have another client, they might want to sell it twice," Tatiana responded.

"That sounds logical, but how do they know you, Tatiana?"

"I don't know, Rodney! I only know they said if we call the police Sandra is dead," Tatiana said, starting to cry.

"I'll give them the icon." I said decisively. "I will call Alexander and tell him we have lost it again, and that's it. End of story."

Without hesitation I called Tangier. We had played and we had lost. The icon would be used to buy my beloved daughter's freedom.

"So where do we have to deliver the icon?" I asked.

Tatiana was surprised at my sudden calm.

"I need to be sure that Sandra is OK before we proceed."

"They are calling back with instructions," Tatiana replied.

"How do they know who you are?" I demanded again.

"I don't know, I promise."

"I don't believe you. You are lying."

"You are the one that lied to me. You said you did not have the icon and you do." She was suddenly furious.

"Please calm down, you two." Fritz ordered, taking control of the situation.

The phone rang once again. She picked it up, said something in Russian, then passed the phone to me.

"Papa, Papa!! It's Sandra."

"Are you well my darling?" I asked, full of emotion at hearing my daughter's voice.

"Yes I am. They have not hurt me but please do as they say. All will be fine if you give them what they want. They know everything. I guess I am not so good after all with the disguises," she joked, trying to ease my pain. I was so proud of my daughter, of her inner strength.

"Don't be silly, darling. You are wonderful. I will give them what they want. Be brave. I'll see you later, my love." A man's voice came on the line and barked something in Russian so I passed the phone back to Tatiana, who scribbled something on a piece of paper and hung up.

"We are to meet them at this address in an hour. I am to go with you. We give them the icon and they free Sandra. They don't want anyone hurt."

"Why would they want you to go?" I was so confused but I did not care anymore. My child's safety was paramount.

Was it Boris and his mafia that had taken Sandra?

They now had the money safely in a Swiss account. Not a bad *coup*. I could not think of anyone else. They were the only ones that could know what was going on. But how did they know Tatiana? That really bothered me.

"I will drive you and wait outside the building to make sure all goes smoothly. Don't worry, I'm sure all will be fine," Fritz tried to reassure me.

It was already past seven. I put the icon in a bag and we left the hotel for an unknown destination to free my beloved daughter.

The address was only fifteen minutes away from the hotel. I did nothing to hide from Blondie. If he was Russian Secret Service, as I suspected, perhaps he would follow and intervene. During the drive I was lost in thought. I would never forgive myself if something happened to Sandra. Nothing in the world would be worth paying such a price.

The building seemed deserted. Fritz inconspicuously stayed in the car in front of the building as planned. The instructions were specific; I had to arrive alone with Tatiana. We took the elevator to the eleventh floor. Tatiana was very nervous. She seemed to be as frightened as I was. I knocked on the door. An armed man invited us in and took us into an empty living room.

"*Tatuś!*" Tatiana exclaimed, as her father Nikolai Przedziecki came into the room with Sandra by his side. They kissed. She did not seem surprised. My jaw dropped. What the hell was going on?

"Nikolai! What are you doing here? Who are you? Why did you take my daughter?" I was at a loss.

Before Nikolai had time to answer, another door opened and Anatoly Levkov entered with two armed thugs.

"Good evening, Mr Mundy," he said with an ugly smirk on his face. "We meet again. You will recall that I did warn you to drop this affair, but you chose not to listen." I wanted to punch him in the face.

"Do you have the icon, Mr Mundy?" Nikolai asked.

"Yes, I do." I handed him the bag and Sandra moved towards me, hugged and kissed me on the cheeks. I was amazed that she kept her cool.

Nikolai took the icon out of the bag and inspected it.

"Is it the one, *tatuś*?" Tatiana asked her father.

"Yes, it is. Good work, Tatiana."

"Who are you two working for?" I asked again, anger seething inside me. Tatiana had been working against me all this time and I had not seen it.

"That is none of your business; I can only tell you that they pay us extremely well," Anatoly Levkov replied, leaving with the icon and a smug look.

"Why, Tatiana*?*" I asked her, still stunned with the disappointment. "We've been so good to you!" I exclaimed.

"For the money, Rodney." Tatiana replied coldly, without a hint of her former charm.

"For truth and for our family," Nikolai added. As he was speaking, we heard a shot and the front door crashed open. In the corridor we heard male voices. Blondie and his pal suddenly stormed into the room. One of Nikolai's men, the one on his right, pulled the trigger and missed. I heard another shot. I pushed Sandra to the floor and covered her with my body. The other man shot at Blondie and his friend but missed. More shots. Blondie was hit but continued shooting. Out of the corner of my eye, I saw Nikolai lying on the floor in a pool of blood. Tatiana was trying to revive him, screaming hysterically and crying. More shots were fired.

"*Tatuś, tatuś!*" she cried in desperation. The room was full of smoke. Blondie's pal was shouting orders in Russian I could not understand. Tatiana tried to stand up and was hit on the head. She gasped and fell forward on top of her father. She died instantly. Sandra was crying, terrified. The room went suddenly silent. The odour of the gunshots and fresh blood was unbearable. I was dragged to my feet by Blondie.

Sandra and I had survived the shooting but Nikolai, his accomplices and Tatiana lay dead.

Anatoly was not in the room, perhaps shot outside.

Then other men came in, Blondie's backup.

"Mr Mundy, my name is Gregory Dubinkin. Where is the icon?"

"Finally we meet." I said sarcastically. "I assume you work for the Federal Security Service of the Russian Federation."

"Yes, and you have something that belongs to us. I am not in the mood for games," Dubinkin said darkly.

"Your reputation as a cold-blooded murderer precedes you," I said defiantly, now that the game was finally over.

"I am not here for compliments. Where is the icon?"

"There was another man here who took it in a bag. You must have passed him. Actually you must know him: Anatoly Levkov. I'm sorry but that is the truth."

"Levkov, Anatoly Levkov?" he shouted, infuriated.

"Yes, he just left with the icon two minutes before you arrived."

"I don't believe you," he screamed.

Sandra was shaking and I hugged her.

"I'm sorry darling. Had I known...please forgive me," I pleaded.

She did not react. She was still in shock. Dubinkin gave some orders to Blondie, who made a call. Sandra and I sat in silence as Dubinkin searched the house. Ambulances arrived to take the bodies and treat the injured. After a while, Dubinkin admitted defeat. The search had been unsuccessful.

"So it seems that those bastards have beaten us," he finally said.

"Which bastards?" I asked.

"It's all your fault! Only your fault!" he yelled at me.

"I purchased the icon for a client of mine who only wanted to return it to its owner," I said.

"Cut the crap!" Dubinkin shouted angrily. It was obvious he was a man not accustomed to defeat. "We know very well that you are working for Prince Alexander and his acolytes, a bunch of nostalgics who want the Romanovs restored to the throne. But rest assured, no such thing will ever happen. If it was up to me, I would have disposed of him and his kind long ago."

"Fortunately for the world, the Soviet era is no more, and it would be up to the Russian people to decide if they want the monarchy back," I said provocatively, waiting for a reaction.

"The revolution of 1917 killed the monarchy's hopes forever. There will never again be a Tsar in Russia!"

"So that is why you don't want the truth to be known. Now I understand!" I said, visibly upset.

"You, Mr Mundy, have friends in high places. If it were up to me, I would throw you in jail and dump the key in the Neva. You have not only committed a crime in dealing with thieves but your worst crime, as far as I'm concerned, is interfering in Russian affairs. The icon belongs to the Russian state and the fate of the Romanovs is none of your or the world's business."

"The world has the right to know the truth," I retorted. "Why is this matter still so sensitive for you people?" I asked with rear anger. This quest had nearly cost the life of my beloved daughter and this criminal was giving me a lecture. He ignored my question.

"Now we'd better drive you and your daughter back to the hotel," he suggested.

"There is no need for that. I have my driver and car outside the building."

# 21. GLASTONBURY, UNITED KINGDOM, 1ST AUGUST 1994

I flew from Saint Petersburg to London without returning to Madrid. Sandra was so shaken that she flew with me and then continued back home. She wanted to go to the north of Spain with her husband and daughter and try to forget what she had gone through. She was still very shocked after her ordeal and I had insisted she stay with me, but she just wanted to get away. I'd had no right to expose her to such danger. I would never have forgiven myself if something had happened to her. I loved Sandra dearly. I stayed with her and Fritz at the airport until her flight was ready for boarding.

During the flight I asked Fritz why he had not stopped Anatoly as he left the building, but he insisted he had not seen him. We had to assume he had left through a back door.

We spent the night in London and call Miles to relay the story.

"I know, Rodney," he said.

"What do you mean you know?" I asked.

"The Russian government has made a complaint. Luckily we were able to convince them that you are not MI6 anymore. That is why you were allowed to leave."

"Who was your ex-KGB friend you got in touch with when we started with this?"

"Gregory Dubinkin."

"You fool, Miles. He is still active! That is why he knew most of my moves."

"Rodney, I thought he was retired. That is what he told me!"

"You have been very careless, Miles. He is a cruel fanatic and still very much active."

Miles was embarrassed and apologized for his imprudence. He then gave a brief report of the progress around the Romanovs' bones and Anastasia Manahan's DNA. Dr Gill had reported experiencing serious problems in extracting the DNA. Buckingham Palace was following all the developments and pressing for results. They were concerned that controversy over Anastasia Manahan's true identity would overshadow the Queen's scheduled visit to Russia on 17th October.

"Believe me," Miles added, "my contacts here think something big is going to happen, as the royal family would be very embarrassed if they had to admit that Anna Anderson was indeed Grand Duchess Anastasia, and that they and their ancestors made a mistake."

✦ ✦ ✦

The next morning, a driver sent by Alexander picked us up at the hotel and drove us straight to Glastonbury where the headquarters of the Brotherhood of the White Rose. Glastonbury, the cradle of Christianity in the British Isles! The small, charming Somerset town still attracted many pilgrims.

Alexander had booked the only three rooms at the charming Hillside Mansion, a wonderful Victorian home below the Tor and a short walk from Chalice Well, Glastonbury Town and Glastonbury Abbey. It offered total privacy for our meeting. Fritz excused himself to run some errands in town.

"The views over the Somerset Levels are stunning," Alexander said over a scotch in the lounge, sensing my tense mood.

"Yes, and the gardens and woods to the foot of the Tor are marvellous, Alexander. Please!" I said, slightly irritated. "My daughter was nearly killed! And I ask myself what for? The icon has been stolen again and will probably be found." I was angry at having failed. "All this for nothing!" I added. "You remember the graphologist, Anatoly Levkov? He walked out of the room before the shooting started with the icon in a bag. I think it must now be in the possession of John Paul II, or the Order of Malta."

"Maybe with the British royal family!" Alexander said. "Don't forget that Levkov has profile in his field. Some of his clients are very powerful but corrupt, just like him. He could be a agent, even a double spy. Who knows! I'm sorry, Rodney, that the icon is lost again. We all are, but we are also very grateful to you for your efforts. You did your best. We tried and we lost."

"It is not yet clear to me what really happened. How did Nikolai Przedziecki end up working Anatoly Levkov, and for who was he working for?" I asked.

"Those two were ambitious opportunists. I'm sorry for the death of the girl. It is tragic but she was as bad as her father and a victim of his ambitions. She gave him information about all your moves. She stole some documents from your office and when she told him about

Tsarina Alexandra Feodorovna and Grand Duchess Anastasia in 1908.
(Romanov Collection, Beinecke Rare Book and Manuscript Library,
Yale University).

the icon's existence, he offered his services to Levkov," Alexander said.

"You might be right. I had left his business card in my desk, and Tatiana probably copied his phone number when she stole my documents."

"And the Russian secret service was on your heels from the very start, because of Miles' bad choices," he added.

"Yes, that's true. Fortunately they were very reasonable," I said. "I was worried that they would not let me leave the country."

"That's because we had promised our full cooperation to try to get the icon back to Russia. A just deal for your freedom, I suppose, my friend. The tragedy is that the hidden secret might be now lost forever!" Alexander sighed.

"Alexander, I have something for you, my friend."

He looked at me, slightly perplexed.

I smiled at him as I took the aged yellowed envelope out of my inside jacket pocket and handed it to him.

"What is it?" he asked.

"The hidden document!" I replied solemnly.

"You old rogue!" he exclaimed excitedly. "You did it. Why didn't you tell me?" Alexander was beside himself with joy. "Bravo, Rodney! I knew you would succeed."

He opened the envelope and carefully took out a document, covered in Cyrillic writing on both sides, and signed "Anastasia." Alexander started reading. He was mesmerized. When he finished he took off his spectacles, carefully folded the letter, returned it to the envelope, looked at me and smiled.

"So?" I asked impatiently.

He got up and embraced me lovingly.

"This document changes everything."

"What do you mean, Alex?" I asked, biting my lips.

"In her own handwriting, the Grand Duchess explains the truth about her escape and her subsequent ordeal."

"But why did she not tell the whole truth before?"

"Once you read it, you will understand everything."

"I read somewhere that she had said to some people: 'There was no massacre, but I cannot tell the rest.'" I tried to recall where I had read it.

"Indeed," Alexander replied. "It was to Anthony Summers and Tom Mangold, the British journalists from the BBC, when they interviewed her in Charlottesville before the publication of their book *The File on the Tsar*. She also told James B. Lovell the truth. She explained to him that the women had been taken to Perm and she had escaped three times. She told him that she felt very sorry to have left her mamma…"[1]

"Oh my God!" I said. "Now I can see the picture more clearly."

Now we were both more relaxed, and Alexander felt eager to tell me some good news.

"During your trip to Russia we were updated about the events in London," he said.

"Yes, Miles told me. It seems that finally Anastasia Manahan's tissue sample is being tested, but no results have been produced yet."

"That's not all!" Our contacts in Germany just alerted us that last July somebody was trying to find any other samples from Anna Anderson to be tested. Dr Stefan Sandkuhler, a former haematologist from Heidelberg University, had kept a blood sample of hers. It was drawn for analysis in June 1951, to determine if she was a carrier of the gene for haemophilia, but those results were inconclusive and now that blood is going to be tested for DNA."

"Good, two confirmations of her real identity will be better than one!" I added, now feeling much better.

✦ ✦ ✦

I went to bed but I could not sleep. Too many images of recent events kept me awake. I dozed off and got up at five, having agreed to visit Chalice Well with Alexander, who was waiting for me in the living room. We quietly left the house, walking at a fast pace through the dense fog. Chalice Well is a mythical place surrounded by gardens. People meditated on benches surrounding the well, which attracts many believers in its healing powers. After about an hour strolling the paths, admiring the flowers and the ancient trees, we walked downtown to enjoy a British breakfast.

"Rodney, you did a wonderful job," Alexander said.

"Father Dimitri also did great work. I am very sorry for his death. I wonder if the police in Costa Rica found the assassins. He was young and full of life."

---

[1] James B. Lovell, *Anastasia, the Lost Princess*. St Martin's Press, New York, 1991. pp. 353–4.

"At least this death wasn't in vain," Alexander tried to console me.

"I remember he said it was a family matter for him," I said.

"It is," responded Alexander. "I will tell you all some day. Let's finish breakfast, then I want to introduce you to somebody very special."

We left the cafeteria and walked to a nearby shop called Archangel Michael's Centre for Spiritual Therapies. The scent of incense surrounded its books, postcards and chimes. Alexander talked to the clerk, who guided us to the second floor.

"Good morning, come in, may peace be with you!" said a young man dressed in white with a soft voice.

"Good morning my dear brother," Alexander replied cheerfully.

I was speechless. For a moment I couldn't believe my eyes.

"Let me introduce you to Mikhail Mishkevich," Alexander told me, smiling.

We shook hands. "Father Dimitri!" I cried out in disbelief.

"I am not Father Dimitri." The young man replied as he smiled. "I'm his twin brother," he explained. I hadn't been prepared for this. They were identical.

"Mr Mundy, I understand your surprise. I am in mourning for the loss of my beloved brother, but I want to thank you for what you have done for us," Mikhail said.

"I'm glad I have been of some assistance. I am sorry I failed to prevent your brother's murder," I said, still visibly in shock.

✦ ✦ ✦

We left the building and started walking in direction of Glastonbury Abbey. I still felt like I had seen a ghost. Mikhail Mishkevich was identical to his late brother: only his cornflower blue eyes were different.

"How did you meet Mikhail Mishkevich? When did he come here? Is he also part of the Brotherhood of the White Rose?"

"Too many questions, my dear old friend!" Alexander replied, smiling. "Prince Frederick Ernst brought him here. He came about nine years ago, at the same time Father Dimitri arrived at the Vatican; and yes, brother Mikhail belongs to our group. Tonight we will have a special ceremony the Brotherhood has organized in your honour. Now relax, my friend, let's go and enjoy the beautiful landscape and admire the ancient ruins of the Abbey. We have much to celebrate."

✦ ✦ ✦

When we returned to the hotel before lunch, Fritz was waiting for us. Over lunch and some wine, we talked over our successful mission. Then we went to take a nap and met again at five in the afternoon for tea.

"The Brotherhood wants to thank you, Rodney, for all that you did during this mission. Our ceremonies are for members only, because they involve secrets and rituals that are more than two thousand years old. Sometimes we have what we call open white ceremonies, where we allow special guests like you to attend," Fritz said while he walked to the door. Alexander invited me to follow him and we got in the car waiting for us outside the building.

"You are going to have the privilege of visiting our headquarters," Alexander said.

The car took us to the outskirts of the town, where the magnificent view evoked images of Celts, druids, knights and the legendary King Arthur and his Queen Guinevere. Finally we arrived at our destination. It was an old castle in the middle of a beautiful forest. As we walked in, I admired the chandeliers, pictures and tapestries. It was like an enchanted place out of a fairytale. We were taken to a magnificent room where I recognized the tall and slim figure of Mikhail Mishkevich, all dressed in white like the rest of the participants.

"Here are the lords and ladies of our Order of Knights, who are also brothers and sisters of our Brotherhood," Alexander announced. I was introduced first to a group of twelve people, all dressed in white with long white capes. They seemed to be all of different nationalities and five were women; they were called Masters. Then I met the Grand Master, a man probably in his nineties whose white hair and small eyes radiated peace and benevolence. He was also dressed in white, wearing a long cloak made of white sheepskin. His chest was adorned by a magnificent gold collar with seven embedded precious stones of different colours. He extended his hand and I kissed it while I admired his unique ring. His name was Dairmid. I was impressed by his presence. Alexander told me that he was a holy man. During his childhood he had known Mahatma Gandhi, as his father and Gandhi had been good friends while studying law in England.

After I was introduced to the rest of the members, everybody moved downstairs to another large room to prepare for the ceremony, and filed one by one into the Ceremonial Chamber, greeting the person at its entrance. I stood in line with Fritz and Alexander, fascinated. Once the Brothers were all inside the sacred chamber, the big wooden door closed and we waited by mesmerizing torchlight. It produced a special effect in the black and white chequered marble floor, just like the one in the Vatican library. A few minutes later, Alexander knocked the door three times and somebody from inside answered in words I couldn't make out. Alexander replied with a code phrase. Immediately the door opened and my two friends escorted me inside. The rest I am not allowed to tell.

# 22. MADRID, SPAIN, SEPTEMBER 1994

After my short visit to Glastonbury, I flew to Madrid. I was delighted to know Sandra was fine and with her family. I spent the rest of August in Marbella relaxing and enjoying the beach, my golf and the company of our friends. Rosa seemed to have forgiven my late arrival and we had a splendid summer with a short visit to Tangier to visit Alexander.

I of course called Carlos and told him everything. He was just as impatient as I was to know the contents of the secret letter inside the icon, but despite my insistence, Alexander had not told me. He said the Brotherhood would decide when to make it public, after Anastasia Manahan's DNA results were released.

As soon as I returned to Madrid I called Prince Alexis at Alexander's encouragement, but was told that he was in Zaragoza for the summer holidays and would return in September. The meeting would have to wait.

I went back to my routine work in the agency, I was pleased to leave behind the thrilling Romanov adventure and so was my wife. Though I was still very active I felt that the craziness of the last months had exhausted me and I decided to take it easy and enjoy my family and my life. The days passed as we waited for the announcement.

In mid-September I made another attempt to contact Prince Alexis and was told that he was ill and could not see me. His secretary politely informed me that His Imperial Highness would call me back as soon as he felt better. But he never did.

News came from London again. Miles, always obliging, phoned me to let know that confidential sources working close to Dr Gill reported that the results of the DNA analysis were ready, and apparently both Dr Gill and the Schweitzers mutually agreed to disclose them during a press conference on 5th October. Alexander and I would try to attend.

One day I got a phone call from Victoria Alba, the charming journalist in Costa Rica. She told me that the investigation of Father Dimitri's murder was still open. The OIJ[1] seemed to believe that the perpetrators were Russian gangsters and the Russian Embassy was now involved in the investigation, as there was no record of Russian mob activity in that country. The Vatican Nuncio was following all the details of the case and she for her part was in touch with Antonio Blasco.

---

[1] OIJ (Organismo de Investigacion Judicial – Office of Criminal Investigation).

# 23. LONDON, UNITED KINGDOM, 5TH OCTOBER 1994

The *Sunday Times* had published on the 2nd of October, three days before Dr Gill's press conference, that Anna Anderson had been "unmasked as the conwoman of the century." The article read: "Genetic tests have established beyond doubt that Anna Anderson…was one of the biggest impostors the world has known…The news came at the end of a global race to solve the mystery…"The newspaper reported that the tests has been performed by Professor Bernd Herrmann of the Anthropological Institute of Göttingen University, but gave no specific scientific details.

I flew to London, where Miles had obtained press passes for Alexander and me to Dr Gill's press conference. I had no doubt in my mind as to the results. The decades of secrecy guarded with violence, and my own experience of it, told me that they would never allow the truth to be known. The room was crowded.

"Who are that couple sitting with Dr Gill and his colleague?" I asked Alexander.

"They are Richard and Marina Schweitzer. They have been loyal supporters. She is Dr Eugene Botkin's granddaughter," he explained.

Alexander pointed out Prince Rotislav Romanov, grandnephew of the Tsar. Sitting in the front row was Michael Thornton, who once had power of attorney for Anna Anderson in Britain. Beside them I recognized Ian Lilburn, who had attended every session of the long Hamburg trials as a loyal supporter of the claimant.

Schweitzer introduced himself and his wife, and shortly after Dr Gill revealed his findings: the results indicated that the DNA obtained from the putative samples of Anastasia Manahan showed she was not related to the Tsar or the Tsarina. On the other hand, her results matched the mitochondrial DNA of a man named Karl Maucher, a grandnephew of the Polish peasant Franziska Schanzkwoska, suggesting that he and Mrs Manahan might be relatives. And that was it.

I could see the expression of disbelief in the faces of the Schweitzers and Ian Lilburn, in contrast to those of Prince Rostislav Rostislavovich

Romanov and most others in the room. The journalists were shouting questions at Dr Gill.

"Let's leave. What a charade!" Alexander said.

"What did you expect?" I asked him. "Haven't you noticed how cautious Dr Gill has been with his statement? He has not said once that she was not Grand Duchess Anastasia or that she was Franziska Schanzkowska. Why?"

"Because he can't."

Alexander was irritated and terribly disappointed, and so was I. That we expected such a result did not make us feel better. I invited him to a pub for a drink. I wanted to know what his next move would be.

As we were sipping a glass of white wine I asked: "Why do you think they did it?"

"To totally discredit her, and that, my friend, we will not accept. Franziska Schanzkowska was the Grand Duke of Hesse's trump card. It's all crap: the Berlin police at the time concluded that a serial killer called Karl Friederich Wilhelm Grossmann murdered her. Her family knew about this. Her mother acknowledged it during an interview, and it was not until 1927 that the *Berliner Nachtausgabe* disinterred her to stop people relating her to Anna Anderson/Anastasia. Not only was Franziska taller than the historical Anastasia, but her feet were also larger. Nobody knows for sure if Franziska and Maucher are related; Gertrude Schanzkowska is supposed to be Karl Maucher's grandmother, but her birth certificate has never been found to prove her relationship with Franziska."

"And?" I asked, unsure where he was going.

"If there is no scientifically acceptable proof that Gertrude was Franziska's sister, then the tests have no validity."

"That's marvellous, and just proves the extremes to which they have gone. So what is your next move?" I inquired.

"We will wait until the excitement of this news dies out and then the bomb will explode in their faces." I saw Alexander smile for the first time that morning.

✦ ✦ ✦

It was a typical rainy autumn day in London and I had just put Alexander in a taxi. Despite the rain I was taking a walk to clear my head when two men wearing suits and nearly identical raincoats stopped me.

They identified themselves as officers from Scotland Yard. "Please get in the car and come with us," they ordered.

"What now?" I asked myself as I got into the car. We drove in silence to 10 Broadway, where I followed the inspectors into the building.

I was escorted into a room and left alone for over fifteen minutes. I was getting angrier as each minute passed.

The door suddenly opened and in walked Miles with someone I had not met before.

"Rodney, may I introduce you to the Commissioner of Police. As you know he is under the authority of the Home Secretary," Miles said.

"And?" I asked bluntly.

"Mr Mundy, I am afraid you have stepped on many people's toes with your silly investigation, including a friendly government, and we are not happy." The commissioner scolded me as if I were a child. "You should have known better!"

"I was just trying to help a friend retrieve an icon that was stolen from Grand Duchess Anastasia. My only object was to return it to its rightful owner. Is that a crime?" I asked with sarcasm.

"Grand Duchess Anastasia died in 1918. I'm fed up with this nonsense," the commissioner angrily replied.

"I did warn you, Rodney," Miles added in self-defence. It was obvious he had gotten in trouble for aiding me in my investigation.

"I thought I could trust you, Miles. Your reckless actions have already caused me a lot of trouble. You were the one who brought Anatoly Levkov and Gregory Dubinkin into this. Levkov is the reason the icon is now lost again." I said with bitterness.

"Never mind the icon! You should have informed us. It is your duty as a former member of MI6," the commissioner scolded me again.

"All I did was help an old friend in a private affair that has nothing to do with the interests of our country. In my world, dear commissioner, friends do these sorts of things: we do each other favours and help each other when in need."

I could see he was starting to lose his patience.

"Some parties are not happy!" he said.

"Don't be absurd," I responded.

"Please, I am not a fool. You are in enough trouble as it is, so it would be better for you to tell me everything you know. You have upset our allies."

"I have heard otherwise," I said calmly.

"Please Rodney, tell him," Miles pleaded.

"I think you better speak to His Excellency Prince Alexander Chavchavadze," I said very formally. "He might be in a better position to reply to your questions. Since my friend Miles has kept you well informed of what I have discovered, I have nothing new to say."

"Come on, Mr Mundy. Make life easy for yourself and you can fly back home to your lovely family," the commissioner shouted, losing his patience.

"Is that a threat?" I asked.

"No. It is the advice of a friend."

"Very well. So you want to know what I know. Are you ready? I know that Anastasia Manahan was Her Imperial Highness Grand Duchess Anastasia and that the Vatican has document pertaining to the Imperial family in the secret archives that they do not want revealed. I believe that the Orthodox Church inside Russia is aware of everything. I know that there is an international conspiracy to cover up the truth and…"

"Enough!" the commissioner shouted, beside himself.

"Mr Mundy, I have orders from the Home Secretary to carry out if I am to release you. You have powerful friends but you must take an oath as a former member of MI6."

"What is required for my freedom?" I asked, knowing well what I was going to be asked. I felt sorry for Miles, who was fidgeting guiltily.

"You must swear that you will never reveal to anyone what you know. Are you prepared to do so?"

"I am." I said with solemnity. "I swear on my honour that I will never reveal what I know to anyone! You have my word."

# 24. PARIS, FRANCE, 28TH JANUARY 1995

As I waited for Alexander's bomb to explode I returned to my normal life, to the relief of my patient wife. Christmas came and went merrily, and excitement accumulated for the New Year, hoping that the upcoming events would be remarkable. On the 25th of January I went to Paris for a week with Rosa on the pretext of visiting the agencies. I had a meeting set up with the mythical Eileen Ford, who had become a close business associate over the years. We stayed at the Powers Hotel in Rue Francois I, one of my favourite small Parisian hotels. After lunch at Chez André, I returned to the hotel for a nap. Rosa went shopping in the Faubourg St. Honoré with a friend.

I lay on the bed and flipped through a copy of *ABC*, the Spanish newspaper I always read in Madrid. In the obituaries was the announcement of the death of Prince Alexis. According to the newspaper he had died the day before, January 27th, at the Hospital de la Princesa in Madrid, of an apparent heart attack. He was forty-six years old. The news took me totally by surprise. I knew he had been ill but had no idea of the seriousness of his ailment. No one had bothered to tell me. I had concluded that he had no interest in meeting me and so had not returned my calls.

I called Tangier.

"Alexander, have you heard the news about Prince Alexis?" I asked without preamble.

"Yes Rodney. It's very sad!"

"But why didn't you tell me he was so ill?" I asked.

"We really didn't know. His sickness has been clouded in mystery from the very start and we believe his death is suspicious."

"Why?" I asked, totally surprised.

"He had made many enemies. His claim to be a Romanov was already very controversial, and accepting candidacy for the Serbian crown from an extreme-right political party was another terrible blow to his credibility. What a tragedy!"

"And what about the DNA samples he was going to give?" I asked, remembering his public announcement that everything was to be resolved through DNA.

"I was told that he gave hair samples from his mother Olga Beatriz and grandmother Maria. A laboratory in Madrid already has them, and last October he donated blood for the tests. Also Dr Pavel Ivanov had been in contact with him and with the laboratory. Somebody must have the documents that prove all that."

"Excellent!" I said. "I will make sure we get those results."

"Rodney, I thought you were going to stop here with your investigation about Anastasia. Aren't you?"

"My dear friend, I think there are still many questions that need to be answered. For example: why has the Russian exile community not publicly proposed the possible survival of members of the Imperial family?"

"To be frank, I think it would have been tantamount to questioning the authority of the Orthodox Church-in-exile, which during Soviet rule was the glue of our beleaguered exiled community. They needed martyrs and the Imperial family were the perfect ones!"

"I understand, but what a price to pay!" I said in astonishment.

"Yes it is, but Rodney..." Alexander sighed, paused and then continued: "The Orthodox Church inside Russia has serious doubts about the authenticity of the remains unearthed in 1991. Also, some historians and scientists raised their voices inside Russia, including the Union of Scientists of the University of Saint Petersburg. They demanded answers about the bones and provided documents and testimonies about the survival of the women.

"Tell me Alex –" I tried to say something but Alexander interrupted me.

"The time has come, Rodney. We will publish the document that was hidden in the icon."

"When?" I asked excitedly.

"Very soon, my friend, very soon. And you will be the first one to know."

# 25. MADRID, 12TH FEBRUARY 1995

Carlos and I waited impatiently for Alexander to announce the contents of the document concealed in the lost icon. It was not a coincidence that he chose the 12th of February: the eleventh anniversary of Grand Duchess Anastasia's death.

I had started the investigation a year ago, and after reading the books about her life, talking with people who knew her, comparing her pictures before and after 1918, seeing her diaries, reading Mother Pascalina Lehnert's statements and the documents in the secret archives of the Vatican, I had no doubt that she was the legitimate Grand Duchess Anastasia of Russia. The story of the holy icon given to her by the Saxe-Weimar-Eisenach family was the clearest support of her identity.

I could not deny my strong disappointment at the DNA results, and all the other information concealed or twisted about the true fate of the Romanovs. Who was behind all that?

Alexander had called me the previous evening to announce that the day of reckoning had come. I called Carlos and invited him to my house for breakfast the next day, as he had been partly responsible for my involvement in this affair.

I could hardly sleep with excitement, and woke up very early, thinking that today, finally today, one of the most enigmatic cases in history was about to be solved.

The maid came into the room bringing the day's newspapers and asked me if I wanted my breakfast, but I told her that I only wanted some hot tea, as I was waiting for Carlos to arrive. The temperature was below zero, and it was still snowing heavily outside. The traffic was practically impassable and while I waited for my son, beautiful images flashed through my mind of my youth and different moments of my unusual life. When Carlos finally arrived, wrapped in an elegant coat, he apologized for the delay. As he hugged me I noticed that he was wearing the ancient jade pendant, his talisman of good luck from Rita Stern. I could only smile and hug him back.

We sat at the dining table and Carlos got some tea while I opened the newspapers. There it was: a full page with the transcript of the handwritten text accompanied by a photograph of the original document in Russian and a certification by a prominent graphologist that the signature was that of the Grand Duchess Anastasia of Russia.

This is what it said:

*I, Anastasia Nikolaevna Romanov, declare:*

*I write this document on the same day that I have made my last civil testament before witnesses, which was notarized and given to Baron Ulrich von Gienanth to be executed after my death.*

*Baroness Monica von Miltitz, Frau Adele von Heydebrandt and Prince Frederick Ernst of Saxe-Altenburg are aware of this other one, my confession, which they have promised to keep secret and only reveal its contents to the world upon my demise.*

*All these years I have had a terrible burden in my heart. On many occasions I was encouraged by some close friends or loving and loyal relatives to tell the truth, but I decided to remain silent until the day that the Lord calls me to his divine presence, to finally reveal what really happened to the last Imperial family of Russia, my dear family, in 1918.*

*My youth and immaturity at that time made me behave in such a foolish way that I put my family in great danger. Later, in 1925, while dying in bed and under the influence of some powerful drugs I mentioned facts that were supposed to be kept secret inside my family. All my life I have felt the shame of being unable to ask for forgiveness from my dear grandmother Nina and from my beloved mother Alexandra, to whom I caused a lot of distress and so much pain that, added to her previous suffering, made her lose her mind. My poor loving dearest mamma, how much I missed her all these years!*

*Knowing that my brother and sisters also survived but did not want to see me while they were alive and living all these years without having embraced them again, has caused me one of the greatest sorrows of all my life, only comparable with the very few memories that I keep of my dear little child, my son, who disappeared after I left him in Romania in 1920 to go to Germany looking for Aunt Irene. To all those painful facts, I must add one where human injustice seemed to join the cruelty of my enemies to punish me, as I have been denied of the right to use my own name: Anastasia Nikolaevna Romanov; that beautiful name that was given to me at birth.*

*I never sought recognition because I have always known who I am, and because I thought that in some way I had to pay for the mistakes I made. But today, I want the world to know that I am indeed Anastasia, the youngest daughter of the last Tsar of Russia.*

*Now I want to declare that events in Ekaterinburg did not happen the way they have been told. There was no massacre. During the imprisonment I imprudently escaped several times, fearing for my life. That I have always regretted. My imprudence the first time completely altered the plans made by those who risked their lives to help us. My mother and sisters were taken by train to Perm in the early hours of July 17th. I joined them on the 19th. While in Perm, under the custody of ruthless members of the Cheka, I attempted to escape again, but was caught, and the third time was when my mother, Olga and Tatiana were taken away, and me and Maria left behind. I thought the Bolsheviks were going to kill us, I was terribly scared, and I escaped again, but got captured several days later. The reds tortured me, raped me and severely injured me; I almost died while I was held prisoner in a filthy prison in Perm, and indeed, I wanted to die. But the good Lord saved me, and I was rescued by two young red soldiers who helped me escape to Romania.*

*While in Romania I gave birth to a child, a boy whose father was one of my rescuers. The baby was born on 29th September 1919 and was baptized in a Catholic church because his father was Catholic. He stayed in Romania with his father's relatives when I went to Germany. I tried to find him later, but nobody knew what happened to him. Some said he was taken to Poland, close to Pomerania. Others said he was taken to southern Spain.*

*Today I forgive all the members of my family that have so mistreated me by denying my identity. I suffered a lot, but I feel guilty, because I know that I was the one to blame for their predicament and for placing them in the dilemma that I created. This I realize now after so much suffering.*

*Today I want to tell the truth and thank all the people who have supported me, cared for me and provided spiritual, monetary and legal assistance. To all of them I give my eternal gratitude, because in doing so they also became part of my terrible experience, of my drama; the greatest drama that any woman in history has ever suffered in her body, heart and soul, living like a ghost away from my own country, forbidden to speak my own language and missing the voices, the laughs, the attentions and the loving care of my beloved parents, my sisters and my little brother. Oh! How much I have missed them all these years! How hard and painful it has been to live without them, searching in my memory to revive those long-gone episodes of my life when we were all together in Tsarskoe Selo, playing in its beautiful park, or in Livadia or the Crimea, or the happy times when we visited other places in our motherland Russia.*

*Today, as this document is read, by people who knew me and believed in my story or by eyes that I never saw before, I know there will be people who still won't believe me. To them I can only say that no matter what they think or believe about me, I know who I am, Anastasia of Russia, and despite them, I am now reunited with my loved ones in a heavenly place, and finally I will be happy forever.*

Anastasia Nikolaevna Romanov
Unterlengenhardt, July 10, 1957.[1]
Adele von Heydebrandt, witness.
Monica von Miltitz, witness.

I was speechless and so was my son. This announcement was certainly the bomb that Alexander had predicted, as the case for Anastasia would once again have to be reopened, and the truth of her tragic life finally revealed. History would now have to be rewritten once and for all. I had not broken my oath but surely the Commissioner of Police in Scotland Yard and the Home Secretary would be furious at having underestimated the power of truth.

I could only imagine Gregory Dubinkin's face. I called Alexander in Tangier. I was sure he would be over the moon at his success. The time had come for him to explain everything to me.

"Hassan, may I speak to His Excellency?" I asked.

"Ah, Monsieur Mundy. I have very sad news. Prince Alexander died in his sleep last night. I'm so sorry for your loss!"

I was taken aback by the news. It was a blow. I suddenly felt confronted by mortality, as though my world were slowly ending. Alexander was about the only link to my youth I had left, and our relationship had been very intense during the past months. At least I had helped him to finish his life quest, his *raison d'être*. I felt very sad and also frightfully disappointed. I would never know the whole truth.

"Did he leave anything for me?" I asked Hassan.

"No, sir. He wished to be cremated and his ashes are to be scattered in Cap Spartel. The funeral will be in a week so that his friends can come," Hassan informed me.

"I will be there!" I wanted to honour the memory of my dear friend.

"Very well, Monsieur Mundy. Please let me know and I will collect you. Your room will be ready."

❖ ❖ ❖

I was still holding the newspaper in my hand but my mind played over all the good memories I had of Alexander, especially our exciting final

---

[1] The document with the last will of Anastasia, signed as Anna Anderson, is kept in her archives in Germany.

days. He definitely had a wonderful life, lucky enough to discover his mission and fulfil it. Inevitably, tears rolled down my cheeks. The only thing I resented was that Alexander had died before keeping his promise. I would not know with certainty whether the survival theories of other members of the Imperial family were true. I suspected they were, but without Alexander I could not be sure. I definitely would like to know, if indeed they had survived, what happened to the Tsarevich and the other Grand Duchesses.

Who of the Alexis claimants around the world was the genuine one? Was it Heino Tammet, a man in Canada who briefly made the claim in the seventies? Could it be the one named Nikolai Chebotarev, who my friend Igor Trubetskoy had mentioned so many years ago? And what about the Tsar? Levkov the graphologist said the "Dear Mr Fox" letter of 1919 was authentic; the letter about the pearls was allegedly written by him from Monaco in 1951. Could it be possible that he also escaped? Could it mean that I had to continue investigating?

Suddenly my phone rang and I heard a soft female voice on the other end.

"Señor Mundy, its Victoria Alba."

"Oh, hello Victoria." I was not too interested in speaking to her as my thoughts were lost in Tangier.

"Are you alright?" she asked.

"Not really. My best friend Prince Alexander Chavchavadze passed away last night. It seemed that my day started in a wonderful way and now this news has spoiled it. How can I help you?"

"I'm in Paris and I'm reading the newspaper. What a surprise! I just wanted to touch base with you."

"Amazing, isn't it?" I said. She had become as addicted to the case as I had been, like many others before us who were bewitched by the mystery of the fate of the last Imperial family of Russia. I felt relieved, feeling sure that she would one day find answers to all the questions left unanswered by Alexander's sudden death. Her first encounter with the story had been fairly dramatic and had undoubtedly left a strong impression on her.

"Yes it is. So there is no doubt that Mrs Anna Anderson, I mean Anastasia Manahan, was Grand Duchess Anastasia! However!" she said, "the document published was not among the copies I gave you from the Vatican. Where did you get that confession?"

"Good question! Victoria, I see you pay attention to details. That document was hidden inside the lost Romanov icon."

"Sorry to ask another question, Mr Mundy...which icon are you talking about?"

"Oh my dear, I just realized you were involved in just one episode of this story. Many things happened last year that you don't know yet."

"But I want to know. Just based on my experience and what I read in some books about the Romanovs, I think there are many things that need to be investigated."

"Are there, Victoria?" I asked, knowing well which questions she wanted answered: the same ones I did.

"Indeed!" she said firmly. "First I would like to discover what really happened in Ekaterinburg, and the fate of the survivors."

I smiled inwardly at this latest victim of the Romanov bug. I told her that I was afraid my friend Alexander had taken vital information to the grave, but I still thought I might be able to help her. I mentioned that I had a friend in Glastonbury who might be able to get me copies of all the documents I gave them for safekeeping. That would giver her a start. She could contact me after I returned from Alexander's funeral.

"Thank you Señor Mundy. I am so excited," Victoria said. "I will be very grateful for all the help you can give me."

I could not believe what I was saying. I had promised my wife I would leave the case alone but it seemed I could not. Maybe Carlos, aided by Victoria, would one day be able to follow my footsteps: the footsteps of his grandmother and his own mother, Pepita, who had been so fascinated by the Romanov affair.

Carlos was standing next to me, still astonished by the revelations in Anastasia's confession and the sudden death of one of my greatest friends. He hugged me again and for a few minutes we were just silent, our gaze lost in the white landscape outside the windows. Then he asked: "Papa, what really happened to the Romanovs in 1918? Was the massacre a cover-up? How did they manage to escape and survive all those years living in secrecy? Did they have any descendants? And who would be the rightful heir to the Imperial throne if the Russians decided to restore the monarchy?"

# AFTERTHOUGHTS BY THE AUTHORS

As mentioned in the prologue and during the narrative, the Romanov icon did exist and was given to Anna Anderson when she agreed to be the godmother of Prince Michael Benedict of Saxe-Weimar-Eisenach, together with Queen Juliana of the Netherlands. This alone is quite significant.

Personal letters from Grand Duchess Elisabeth and her son Prince Michael Benedict support the facts, as well as publications in newspapers and stories told by people close to Anastasia Manahan.

It was only after the industrial revolution that Russia's rigid class system started to crumble. Class barriers were impassable; royalty and aristocracy inhabited a distant and hermetic world. Today in a globalized society, with the information we have available on the internet, it would be not impossible to impersonate a well-bred, highly educated, sophisticated person. In the twenties it would have been absolutely unthinkable for a peasant from Poland or anywhere else to pretend to be a Russian Grand Duchess and be recognized by members of her family as such. A farm girl, even today, would have been unable to amass the wealth of intimate details about the person she was impersonating, answer personal questions with accuracy, correct the people who tried to trick her, react with emotion to hidden memories, convince anthropologists and graphologists and know the intricacies of royal etiquette without making the slightest error.

Would it be conceivable for an uneducated rural Briton in 2012 to pretend to be a close relative of Queen Elizabeth and make no errors in strict royal protocol? Surely not, then or now. For example, Princess Nina Chavchvadze, born Princess Nina Georgievna of Russia, in her interview with Peter Kurth, declared that she did not believe Mrs Anderson, the claimant, to be Grand Duchess Anastasia; but whoever she was, she had been brought up in the highest aristocratic circles.

Crown Princess Cecilie of Prussia declared: "Everyone that had the honour of meeting Mrs Anna Anderson and spent time with her recalled that her behaviour was naturally aristocratic, her bearing was regal and this was effortless. Her mannerisms were not that of an impostor. She never tried to push her claim forward. She just knew

**MICHAEL PRINZ VON SACHSEN-WEIMAR**

6800 MANNHEIM
DEUTSCHE BANK AG
P 7, 10-15, TEL. 0621-189320
FAX 0621-169615

July 16, 1991/sc

AIR MAIL

Mr. Robert J. Crouch
2936 Kenbury Court

Richmond, Virginia 23235 / U S A

Dear Mr. Crouch,

Thank you very much for your letter dd. July 2, 1991 which you wrote to my mother, the Grand Duchess Elizabeth.

Most certainly we insist that the icon is being returned to us, especially since the icon was never given as a present but only as a life-long loan to Anastasia.

Proof of the afore-mentioned fact can be given on demand by sworn affidavit by my mother.

We continue to hope that justice will win in this case.

With very best regards,

Yours sincerely,

Enclosure

Letter from Prince Michael Benedict of Saxe-Weimar-Eisenach to Prof. Robert Crouch about the lost icon in 1991 (R. Crouch's collection).

Comparison between pictures of Anastasia Romanov and Anastasia Manahan.

who she was. She behaved totally at ease, as a Grand Duchess would do. Nothing was acted."

The claimant was the same height as the diminutive Anastasia. She had the same feet with *hallux valgus*, same ears, same face, same hair colour, same cornflower blue eyes as her father, same cauterized mole on her shoulder, same forehead scar, same crushed finger, same tone of voice, same way of laughing, same love of animals, same memories (so many memories!) as Anastasia. Many people said so, many who knew the historical Anastasia and gave sworn affidavits supporting their conviction that it was her.

Franziska Schanzkowska, on the other hand, was a poor Polish farmer. After her disappearance, her family had been informed that she was a victim of a serial killer. Her siblings never wanted to sign any affidavit recognizing Anna Anderson as their sister Franziska. They couldn't even remember the colour of her eyes, nor any special birthmark or deformity of her feet. She was taller than the historic Anastasia and had larger feet.

Reports issued by the court's expert Dr Reche (anthropologist) and Minna Becker (graphologist) were not taken into consideration when the court gave its verdict. Both indicated that Anna Anderson and Grand Duchess Anastasia were one and the same person. A very significant testimony was offered by Heinrich Kleibenzetl, a Viennese tailor, in 1960. He declared that he had personally seen Grand Duchess Anastasia wounded but alive in Ekaterinburg, following the Imperial family's alleged assassination. Kleibenzetl's statement was strengthened when he produced documentary proof that he had served in the Austrian army during World War I, had been taken prisoner in Russia and had worked as a tailor's apprentice in Ekaterinburg during 1918. He excused himself for not coming forth earlier with his story by stating that he had only heard of the Anna Anderson's case in 1958. He said that on the night of 16–17th July, a wounded Anastasia was taken to his house, which was located just two blocks from the Ipatiev House. She was almost unconscious. Three days later, a red guard and a civilian fetched her. His mistress recognized them as the same men that brought her the night of the alleged massacre.

Another very interesting deposition was given at the Weisbaden Court by Serge Lifar. This famous Russian ballet dancer declared that the Italian diplomat Francesco Lecquio as well as Mussolini himself had told him that they knew for sure that Anastasia had survived. Moreover, approximately thirty witness testimonies were not heard in Court, because they contradicted the "official" version of the massacre, given by Nicholas A. Sokolov in his report of 1924.

The story of the bones "conveniently" recovered in 1991 has been discussed in numerous books and journals. The most recent, published in Russia in 2011 by Andrei K. Golitsyn, presents all the mistakes made during the excavations and the inconsistencies surrounding the case that lead the readers to believe that the story of the mass grave is a hoax.

Anastasia Manahan was declared a fraud because her DNA did not match that of Prince Phillip, but Dr Gill never mentioned that apparently when his sister Princess Sophie of Hannover's blood was tested, her mtDNA did not match her brother's either. This created much confusion and speculation among the scientists doing the testing. According to Professor William Maples this was due to the fact that mitochondrial DNA was more variable and less reliable, by a mechanism not yet understood, than people imagined.[1]

Another amazing twist in this story is the DNA result from a blood sample which was one hundred per cent certain to have come from Anna Anderson and which had been extracted by Professor Stefan Sandkuhler in 1951. Professor Bernd Hermann of Göttingen University and Dr Charles Ginther tested the blood sample. The results did not match the mtDNA of the tissue sample provided by Martha Jefferson Hospital (which Dr Gill had retrieved from a block of tissue belonging to Anastasia Manahan); the mtDNA did not match that of the Duke of Edinburgh, nor that of Franziska's relative, Carl Maucher, either! We think that this fact deserves more examination.

Of the other DNA tests performed in different laboratories over several years, there is an expert opinion very important to consider. It is that of Dr Alec Knight, former professor at Stanford University. Knight and his colleagues based their claim on molecular and forensic inconsistencies they discovered in the original genetic tests, as well as their independent DNA analysis of the preserved finger of the late Grand Duchess Elisabeth Feodorovna (sister of the Tsarina Alexandra), which also failed to match the mtDNA of the Duke of Edinburgh.[2]

Knight argues that Professor Gill's results were too good to be true. He doubts they could have obtained such long stretches of DNA

---

[1] Michael Gray, *Blood Relative*, Victor Gollanz, 1998.

[2] They were cousins, both sharing the same maternal line from Queen Victoria of England.

sequence from old bones. He declared, "Based on what we know, those bones were contaminated." Professor Knight believed that there was certain evidence that the bone samples were tarnished with fresh, less degraded DNA from a real Romanov, perhaps by an individual that handled the samples. Another scientist, Peter de Knijf, head of the Forensic Laboratory for DNA Research at Leidem University Medical Center in Holland, agrees with Professor Knight that Gill's results are "unrealistically solid."

Along with all these discrepancies is that of Dr Tatsuo Nagai, a well-respected Japanese scientist. On 4th December 2004 the Russian press published the declaration of the director of the Japanese Institute of Forensic Medicine and Science, Dr Tatsuo Nagai, who accused the Russian government of concealing the fact that the bones reburied in Saint Petersburg in the summer of 1998 were not the remains of Nicholas II's family. His assurance was based on analysis of Nicholas II's sweat particles from the lining of one of his vests, very well preserved.

Doctor Tatsuo Nagai had been doing research since 1986, first in Tokyo University and then in Osaka. He specialized in studying viruses causing human immune deficiency and is very well known for his publications on forensic science. He is a member of the Japan Centre of Research and Identification. Though now retired from the university, he now investigates the Hepatitis C virus with the institute bearing his name. According to Nagai, DNA results from the sample of Nicholas II's vest matched the DNA samples taken from the hair and nails of his brother, Georgi Romanov, but had nothing in common with the remains of the alleged Romanovs buried in 1998. Therefore, Dr Nagai came to the conclusion that those buried at the Peter and Paul Fortress are not members of the Romanov family. He participated in a conference in Russia where he presented his conclusions and gave a private lecture to a group of Orthodox priests headed by Patriarch Alexei II. They gave him an icon and a document attesting to the value of his study and presentation.

Vadim Viner, professor of the Russian Academy of History and Palaeontology and president of the Ural Centre for Investigation of the Tsar's Family Murder, answers the question of who was actually buried. According to him, the grave at Ekaterinburg, from which the Romanovs' remains were taken in 1991, was created on Stalin's orders back in 1946. At that time there was a search in the USSR for the hidden gold that had belonged to the Tsar, so there were a lot of pretenders claiming to have survived the execution. The government needed proof of death of all Romanovs, which is why Stalin ordered the creation a false grave. The files containing the pertinent documents are still rated top secret in the FSB archives, Viner stated, with reference to his personal sources.

More recently, in 2008, the laboratory of the Armed Forces of the United States performed a series of tests on some bones provided by Dr Ivanov, not just from the first group of bones of 1991, but also from several bone fragments and teeth found in 2007 supposedly belonging to the two skeletons (Alexei and Maria, according to the Russians) missing in the first grave.

These American scientists, led by Dr Coble, supported the results given by Dr Gill and Dr Ivanov. Did the Americans just receive the bones handed to them, with the unquestioned conviction that they belonged to the Imperial family? Did they ever hear about all the controversies, theories of survival and testimonies of many people assuring that the Romanovs had escaped alive from Russia? Did they ever learn about the scandal in Italy and other countries in Europe after the death of Mother Pascalina Lenhert, governess of Pope Pius XII in November 1983, because of her statements related to the Vatican and the survival of some members of the Romanov family? Probably not. We want to make clear that we do not believe they were involved in any wrongdoing, nor that they were part of any cover-up. We just think that unfortunately, they seemed not to have given proper attention to this whole ocean of other information that was available.

Speaking of DNA, in 2009 Dr Dan Frumkin of Nucleix, a company based in Tel Aviv, Israel, and his group of scientists showed how DNA can be fabricated and used to contaminate samples found in crime scenes. He even fabricated DNA, as was reported in several international newspapers, including the New York Times.[3]

All of the above makes us believe that the Russian Orthodox Church and the RECA (Russian Commission of Experts Abroad) are right when they claim those bones do not belong to the Imperial family. Then what was their fate after that infamous night?

We believe that Anna Anderson was without any doubt the Grand Duchess Anastasia of Russia. It is impossible to accept a tainted DNA conclusion to the contrary. To accept what recent publications present to the public, that Anastasia Manahan was a Polish peasant, is ludicrous.

---

[3] Andrew Pollack "DNA Evidence Can Be Fabricated, Scientists Show," *The New York Times,* 17th August 2009.

The mitigating evidence in her favour, as we just pointed out, was overwhelming. It is absolutely impossible for an impostor to be so lucky as to have all her traits. With respect to the other members of the family, we believe that further investigation should be made.

Grand Duke Andrei Vladimirovich of Russia said before his death in 1956 that until the Danish, British, Soviet and German archives on the matter are made public, we won't know for certain the real fate of the Imperial family. To those archives we add the Chivers papers contained in "the Romanov File" in the US, and the Vatican's secret files on the Romanovs.

The allegations of Marga Boodts, the woman who briefly claimed between 1956 and 1960 to be Olga Nikolaevna, and lived in Italy from 1939 until 1976, deserve closer examination because her story is also fascinating. After she died in Italy, she left behind her autobiography entitled *Io Vivo* ("I Am Alive"), recently published in Spain for the first time,[4] after fifty-six years of obscurity. Her archives comprised thousands of documents, letters, pictures and Romanov memorabilia that are now in the hands of dedicated researchers and historians, and it is possible that the sume of evidence could demonstrate that she was indeed Grand Duchess Olga Nikolaevna of Russia.

We also have the story of Prince Alexis D'Anjou Durassow, who claimed to be the grandson of Grand Duchess Maria Nikolaevna. According to his books, published in France in 1981, in Spain in 1982 and later in Italy in 1989, after Maria's evacuation from Perm, where she was held with her mother and sisters, she was taken to Moscow, then to Kiev, and later to Bucharest under the protection of Queen Marie of Romania, where she married Prince Nicholas Dolgoruky, the son of General Alexander Dolgoruky. Later they were provided with Italian passports, issued by the Italian Ministry of Foreign Affairs under the names Count and Countess Di Fonso. With these false identities they were able to live all over Europe and Africa. They had two daughters, Olga Beatrice and Julia Yolanda. The Grand Duchess Maria died in Rome on 1st December 1970. She left a civil testament as well as a personal testament to the truth of her escape and life undercover. Prince Alexis D'Anjou sent copies of hundreds of relevant documents to Patriarch Alexei II in Moscow. He personally gave seven files to the Russian Ambassador in

---

[4] Olga Nicolaievna. *Estoy Viva: Memorias inéditas de la última Romanov*. Martínez Roca Editores, Madrid, España.

Madrid in November of 1993, and to the American Consul in that same city, in support of his claim. Scientists and some monarchists in Russia supported him. Prince Alexis died under suspicious circumstances in January of 1995, but he had provided samples from his grandmother, mother and himself for DNA testing in 1994. Hopefully the results of those tests will be known in the near future. Dr Pavel Ivanov was wholly aware of his claim and of the samples he voluntarily submitted in 1994. Written correspondence shows this – but Dr Ivanov never mentioned any of this to the media.

There is also the very interesting account written and published in 1998 by Michael Gray, titled *Blood Relative*. Gray believes himself to be the legitimate son of Tsarevitch Alexis and Princess Marina of Greece (widow of the Duke of Kent). Michael Gray, whose real name is William Lloyd Lavery, lives in Northern Ireland.

Another interesting claimant who deserves further examination was Heino Tammet-Romanov of Vancouver, Canada, who suffered the same blood disease and had the same physical characteristics as the historical Alexei. According to his widow, Mrs Sandra Romanov, who is still living, he told her many stories of the Imperial family, including his escape and secret life under an assumed identity. His case has been presented on the internet by journalist John Kendrick, and Mrs Romanov has written a book (still unpublished) with all his memories. She gave two of Mr Tammet-Romanov's teeth to Dr Ivanov for DNA testing, but never received the results. Heino Tammet had two children.

And last but not least are the revelations made by Alexandre Eleazar in his book *Operation Aliss*,[5] published in France in 1990. He claimed to be the son of Grand Duchess Tatiana and King Faisal bin Hussein bin Ali al-Hashemi of Iraq. According to him, the Grand Duchess disappeared in the late thirties. He believes that she was involved with White monarchists in Paris and was eventually captured by Stalin's secret agents. Alexandre passed away, but had a son, who lives in Spain.

Other accounts related to the fate of Tatiana mention not only her survival, but also her frequent travels between Europe and the US, protected by MI6, and her involvement in smuggling into the US expensive pieces of art that had belonged to the Imperial family. Rumours circulated in Poland that sometime during the late thirties Tatiana travelled to America to retrieve some money deposited by the

---

[5] Operation Alice (Alix).

Tsar in a bank in Detroit, and never returned to Europe. Whether she was captured by Stalin's spies (like many other White generals and monarchists) or died under other circumstances while in the US is another mystery. A man still living in the US claims that his mother was paid during the early thirties by Lord Louis Mounbatten of Burma to act as a double for Tatiana.

It is clear enough that despite the official Russian stand and the acceptance of it by the world at large, the case is by no means closed. Even where scientific process is concerned, it is quite possible that particular national agendas are served.

The lost icon that had been cherished by Anastasia Manahan and stolen from her home in Charlottesville is undoubtedly now in someone's private collection. It might yet be possible that it also contains her confession or some other hidden secret. Why not? Stolen art ends up in the possession of unscrupulous collectors. We would encourage all our readers to start a quest to find the icon and return it to the rightful owner: Prince Michael Benedict of Saxe-Weimar-Eisenach. That would be the best tribute we could give to Grand Duchess Anastasia Nikolaevna of Russia. The best tribute to the memory of an extraordinary woman whose name is still synonymous with enigma.

# ACKNOWLEDGMENTS

**Carlos Mundy's acknowledgments:**

This book is dedicated to Their Royal Highnesses the Prince and Princess of Tirnovo, Their Serene Highnesses Prince and Princess Andreas von und zu Liechtenstein, Karolina Kurkova, Marisa Berenson, the Countess of Baccoli, the Duchess of Fernandina, Cristina Macaya, the Count of Guaqui, Count Geoff von Weiss, Irma Rolon, Karen Bonadio, Dominique Mirambeau, my god-daughter Princess Sandra Nazarewicz, Rita and Fernando de Orbaneja, H.R.H. Princess Padmaja Kumari Mewar of Udaipur, H.R.H. Princess Beatrice of Orleans, Dr Andrux Mejias, Frances Aldrich de Llopis, the Duke and Duchess of Alburquerque, Count and Countess Karl von Walburg, Lola Alcaraz, Ioanna Caparros, Elga Wimmer, H.R.H. Prince Hatem Bey of Tunisia, Emilio Lamarca, Bennu Gerede, Dr Enrique Monereo, Prince and Princess Ivan Nazarewicz, Prince and Princess Phillipe Nazarewicz, Prince and Princess Christian Nazarewicz, Izaro Eguia, Victoria Florez-Estrada, Dr Manuel de la Pena, Lord Nicholas Smith, Marieli Revuelta del Peral, Lady Karen Hardwick, Cristina Barrios, Melissa Rossi, Dr Victor Zambrano, Ignacio Fagalde, Nabil and Nabila Baraka, Natalia Escalada, Manuela Vilches, Nuria Monino, Patricia Pacual-Zamora, Baroness Prisca Bertin de la Raymondie, Richard Hudson, Vaitiare Hirshon, Alfredo Fernandez-Duran, Donna d'Cruz, Santiago Bandres, Angel Fernandez, Josie Kayser, Diego Orlando Manchimbarrena and all the wonderful friends around the world as they have always been through the years so supportive of all my projects – however crazy!

To my brothers and sisters: Simon, Ivan, Charis and Sandra, and to Rosa Mundy for always being there for me. To my nephews and nieces: Carla Mundy Noboa, Jetsun and Harrison Mundy, Carola and Dylan Leoz, as well as to H.R.H. the Princess of Panagyurishte and Jaime, Guillermina and Vega Royo-Villanova.

My gratitude to our agent Alicia Gonzalez-Sterling and to our publisher Kamaljit Sood.

Thank you all from the bottom of my heart.

## Marie Stravlo's acknowledgments:

I want to express my sincere thanks to my family and friends for their support during the years that my investigation has taken me away from home many times, and for the countless hours spent with me while I was devouring books related to this case, or carefully examining and translating thousands of documents found in archives spread out in many countries.

To Professor April Davis for helping me with the translation of innumerable documents from German.

To my special consultants: Andrew Hartsook and Robert Crouch. Without them the story of the icon wouldn't have come to light.

To Baroness Marion von Gienanth, Cruz Sanchez Countess of Baccoli, historian and archivist Lupold von Leshten, Debbie Simonson, Lydia Prous Rossel, historian and author Michel Wartelle, Grazia Vannini and her family, Mons. Fernando Lamas, historian and author Ricardo Mateos y Sainz de Medrano, Ecumenical Knights of Malta, O.S.J., Jose Carmona Chavez, Baron Emilio Lobera, Renate Schmidt, Friedhelm Kugele, Walter and Rachel Kugele, Mr and Mrs Peter Prömm, Ms Sandra Romanov, Tereshinha Flores-Fernandez, Rosa Llanos Montes, Yorlene Gomez-Clapper, Hilda López, REDCULTURA, Sir John Walsh of Brannagh, Pauline Butler, Admiral Ralph Wollmer and other loyal supporters of Anastasia, which for special reasons wish to remain anonymous.

To my dear friends in all corners of the world, who have waited anxiously for this publication.

A sincere gratitude to Carlos Mundy for his friendship and the opportunity to write this historical novel together. To Alicia Gonzalez-Sterling, our literary agent, and to our publisher in London, Kamaljit S. Sood, for believing in our projects and encouraging us to present them to the public. God bless you all.

# BIBLIOGRAPHY AND
# FURTHER READING

*Anastasia, The Riddle of Anna Anderson* by Peter Kurth, Little Brown and Co.,1983.

*Anastasia, The Lost Princess* by James Blair Lovell, Regnery Gateway, 1991.

*Estoy Viva: Memorias Inéditas de la última Romanov* by Olga Nikolaevna. Martínez Roca Ediciones, Madrid, España, 2012.

*The File on the Tsar* by Anthony Summers and Tom Mangold, Victor Godlance Ltd,1976.

*El Expediente sobre el Zar*, by Anthony Summers and Tom Mangold, Plaza y Janes, 1978. (It has an extra chapter about King Alfonso XIII and the Romanovs.)

*The Sokolov Investigation* by Nicholas Sokolov. Translated from the French by John O'Conor. Robert Speller & Sons, 1971.

*Yo, Alexis, bisnieto del Zar* by Prince Alexis D'Anjou, Plaza y Janes S.A, 1982.

*The Hunt for the Tsar* by Guy Richards, Fletcher and Son Ltd, 1971.

*The Rescue of the Romanovs* by Guy Richards, The Devin Adair Company, 1975.

*The Romanovs: The Final Chapter* by Robert K. Massie, Jonathan Cape, 1995.

*Rescuing the Tsar* by James P. Smythe, Biblio Bazaar, 1920.

*The Real Romanovs* by Gleb Botkin, Fleming H. Revell Company, 1931.

*The Secret Plot to Save the Tsar: The Truth Behind the Romanov Mystery* by Shay McNeal, Century, 2001.

*I, Anastasia* by Grand Duchess Anastasia Nikolaevna with notes by Roland Krug von Nidda, Penguin Books, 1961.

*The Last Grand Duchess* by Ian Vorres, Charles Scribner's and Sons,1964.

*Nicholas II* by Marc Ferro, Editions Payot & Rivages, 2011.

*Nicholas II, Emperor of all the Russias* by Dominic Lieven, John Murray, 1993.

*The Last Tsar* by Edvard Radzinsky, Arrow, 1992.

*The Many Deaths of Tsar Nicholas II* by Wendy Slater, J. Routledge, 2007.

*L'affaire Romanov, ou, Le mystère de la maison Ipatiev* by Michel Wartelle, Corteau 2008.

*A Lifelong Passion: Nicholas and Alexandra: Their Own Story*, by Andrei Maylunas and Sergei Mironenko, DIANE Publishing, 2005.

*The Murder of the Romanovs: The Authentic Account* by Paul Bulygin and Alexander Kerensky, New York: Robert McBride & Co. Inc., 1935.

*Rasputin, The Saint Who Sinned* by Brian Moyhahan, 1 Random House, 1997.

*Queen of Roumania* by Hannah Pakula, Eland, 1985.

*The Lost Fortune of the Tsars* by William Clarke, 1994 Orion Publishing Group, 1994.

*The Quest for Anastasia* by John Klier, Smyth Gryphton Ltd., 1995.

*Michael and Natasha* by Rosemary and Donald Crawford, Weidenfield & Nicholson, 1997.

*A Fatal Passion* by Michael John Sullivan, Random House, 1997.

*The Murder of Rasputin* by Greg King, Century, 1996.

*The Fate of the Romanovs* by Greg King and Penny Wilson, John Wiley and Sons Inc., 2003

*Ekaterinburg: The Last Days of the Romanovs* by Helen Rappaport, Windmill Books, 2009.

*The Romanovs* by John Van der Kiste, Sutton Publishing, 1998.

*Estoy Viva* by H.I.H. Grand Duchess Olga Nikolaevna, Martinez Roca, Spain, 2012.

*The Secret Archives of the Vatican* by Maria Luisa Ambrosini, Little Brown, 1996.

*The Entity* by Eric Frattini, JR Books, 2009.

*Viñetas Historicas* by Carlos Seco-Serrano, Espasa Calpe, 1983.

*Operation Aliss* by Alexandre Eleazar, 1999.

*The Romanov Mystery and the lives of Sigismund and Charlotte* by Marie Stravlo. (Unpublished)

*The Escape of Alexei* by Vadim Petrov, Igor Lyshenko and Gregory Egordy, Harry N. Abrams Inc., 1998.

*Blood Relative* by Michael Gray, Victor Gollanz, 1998.

*The Conspirator who saved the Romanovs* by Gary Null, Pinnacle Books Inc., 1971.

CPSIA information can be obtained at www.ICGtesting.com
Printed in the USA
LVOW131426141112

307321LV00004B/30/P